THE WHITE BILLIONAIRE: COMPLETE SERIES

BOOKS 1-4

An Interracial BWWM Romance By..

LENA SKYE

D1359067

Summary

Money, lies, betrayal, misunderstandings and much more. Dating a billionaire is never easy.

Camille is a young, ambitious African American woman who lands herself a new job as personal assistant to young Billionaire, Kyle Kane. Kyle is the sexiest white guy that Camille has ever seen and concentrating at work is not going to be easy with such a dreamboat around.

However, things get very interesting when Kyle suggests that her job as personal assistant is set to be much more "PERSONAL" then she first imagined....

Copyright Notice

Contents

#1 Dating The White Billionaire
#2 The Secret Of The White Billionaire
#3 Submitting To The White Billionaire
#4 The White Billionaire's Baby

Special Thanks To Those Who Supported:

Karen T Foster, Lucy Dean Cain, Debra Carr, Lashun, Sunshine, L, Diane, Steph T, Pesk4, Michelle Briggs, Nana 51, Myisha Davis, CAC, Roxie, K Singh and anyone else who left a good review on the Amazon store!

Other Popular Lena Skye Series

<u>Pretty Fly For A White Guy</u>

He is cute. He is sexy. He is confident. He is charming. He is Kenneth, a white man and the love of Nicole's life. However, it has been over a year since they were together officially and all signs are suggesting it is over for good between them. The fact he is now dating her ex-best friend is just the tip of the iceberg.

Can she ever get over him and find happiness with someone else? Or should she fight for the man she believes she is meant to be with?

**

#Book1

DATING THE WHITE BILLIONAIRE

#Chapter1

"I'm classy, sexy, street smart, and I'm definitely not to be fucked with." -
Camille

**

"Facebook is the devil!"

I tell myself over and over again to log off but I never comply. I keep torturing myself with looking at photos of my friends. They seem so damned happy, disgustingly so. I mean seriously, I get that you're in a relationship but why do you have the need to plaster pictures of you and your boyfriend kissing all over the internet? A part of me knows that I'm being a jealous bitch but I really don't care. I'm so damned annoyed with my life right now.

Deciding to stop feeling sorry for myself I head to the bathroom to begin primping for my night out with my friends. My apartment feels so empty without Marcus here to share it with me. I know that I should be happy that he's gone but we've been together on and off since I was 12. Now that I'm 24, I just feel so damned lost. I didn't finish school, I have a crappy job, and a bunch of loser ex-boyfriends along with it. I guess I'm just lucky that I didn't turn out like my sister, because I would have 3 kids joining me in my personal misery.

Marcus wasn't much of a man but he has always been comfortable. Even though we dated other people from time to time, I always knew that I could count on him. So imagine my surprise when he said that he was done with me for good. He got that skank Charity pregnant and now they want to play house with each other. It still hurts that he could do that to me especially as we were supposed to have been together during that time which means he cheated. I always thought that he was better than that, now I know different.

I still can't believe that he did that to me, after all that I've done for him.

Marcus is no angel, not by a long shot and I'm not either. We both grew up on the west side of Chicago and it was no picnic. He was a foster child and I always kind of wished that I was one. It's a terrible thing to say but my mom sucks, and I feel like I may have been better off not knowing her at all. That way I could make up stories about how great she was in my head and how she was a young mother that couldn't take care of me. I spent the majority of my childhood taking care of that woman and now I just refuse to do it anymore. I stopped calling her mom when I was 9, she is simply Lauren to me.
Because I have a mother that's incapable of thinking of anyone but herself, I resorted to holding drugs for Marcus and in return he would share his funds. I've gotten him connections that he could only dream of, I've charmed some of the biggest drug pushers in Chicago, and it was all for him. Everyone who is anyone in the drug game knows who "Camille" is. I'm classy, sexy, street smart, and I'm definitely not to be fucked with.
You wouldn't see any evidence of that if you looked at me today, because at this moment, I look an absolute hot mess. My weave is completely out of order and that's only because I haven't combed

it in days. It's a shame that I've spend so much money to look fabulous, only to sit around and feel sorry for myself. Luckily I've purchased great hair and so it won't take long to get the snags out of my 18" inch tresses.

An hour later the buzzer to my apartment rings and I know that it's Sandy and Cynthia. I buzz them in and they storm inside of my apartment.

"Girl! You aren't ready yet? You were supposed to start hours ago," Sandy said dramatically.

I smacked my lips "Whatever, I told you that I would meet you there. You decided that you wanted to come pick me up and –"

"Well that's because you were going to flake on us, just like you have for the last 2 months." Cynthia interjected.

I give both of them the stink eye and walk back to the bathroom to finish my makeup. Sandy and Cynthia help themselves to the contents in my refrigerator. I sigh as I look into the mirror, I'm determined to have a good time and to not ruin our girl's night. I apply lipstick to my full lips, mascara to my almond shaped eyes, and give myself a last look over. My high cheek bones, covered in my flawless milk chocolate complexion look great. I smile in the mirror because I'm back to my old self.

"Put on your clothes! It's time for us to go," Sandy said as she shoved my spandex black dress into my hands. "And what are you gonna do about a job? Kiesha had to hire someone else because you've been a no call no show for 3 days."

I give a nonchalant shrug, even though my stomach drops. I don't know why I decided not to call the restaurant to give a crappy excuse. But the truth is that I just couldn't pull myself out of the bed and I didn't want to talk to anyone. I hated being a waitress but I needed that job. I know that I can call and try to weasel my way back in but I just don't want to. I stand up straight and fake the confidence that I wish I had.

"Well, I'm going job hunting on Monday, and I'm sure that I'll find something. I mean, who can resist hiring all of this," I grin and spin around.

"Alright, I sure hope so because I would hate for you to lose your new apartment. This place is nice, you're making me want to move to the south suburbs too."

"I won't let that happen." I say, "Now let me get dressed so that I can find me a new man!"

***

Sleep is evading me, it's 4 in the morning and my friends are sleeping, Sandy and Cynthia are on my sectional couch passed out. Even though they're here with me, I feel so damn lonely…and horny.

Alcohol and dancing always gets me revved up, I'm not sure if tonight was such a good idea. Don't get me wrong, it was great spending time with my girls but now I feel like I'm plummeting from my high.

I miss Marcus so much.

He knows my body inside and out, that man can effortlessly send my body into multiple orgasms. He has a huge dick and a hurricane tongue. I feel my pussy begin to throb as I imagine my ex's tongue lapping at my damp folds. He always pays special attention to the lips and completely ignores my clitoris in the beginning. A few minutes in and I'm writhing against his face, trying to push him further in but he has a lot of self control. Then he darts his tongue and probes inside.

I open my legs and begin to massage my warm mound with the palm of my hand through my panties. I raise my hips and take myself to ecstasy as I envision him in between my thighs. As I recover from my orgasm, my mind drifts to why I need to forget Marcus.

I've been trying to change my life but I've been a mess without him. It seems like all I date is losers, and that is why I'm by myself now. I would rather be alone than allow myself to get caught up in a life of scheming, drugs, and death. I've seen enough horror to last me a lifetime and that kind of lifestyle doesn't have a happy ending. That's probably why he left me; he says he was tired of me "acting brand new". I wouldn't allow him to keep his drugs at my new apartment or to bring guns here and he would get pretty upset.

I would love to find someone else but few men exude the raw power that Marcus had. Maybe I just need to find a regular guy that I can settle down with. But that just seems so boring; I like a man with spunk.

On Monday morning I'm going to get online and start job hunting. I can't sit around feeling sorry for myself because I'll end up homeless. The shelter life is not for me; God knows I've lived in enough of them with my mom. There are just certain places that I will never allow myself to be in again. I'm grateful that I was taken care of but I hate that part of my life.

I finally drift back to sleep with thoughts of the past firmly at the forefront.

#Chapter2

"Stay Put?!? Dogs Stay Put!" - Camille

**

I've come to the realization that my resume sucks!

I don't have any real job skills because I've spent most of my time hustling, making, and creating connections for Marcus. I only worked my job as a waitress for about 6 months and I can only hope that any job that's interested in me doesn't call my previous employer. I don't even know why I'm bothering, I should just call my old job back and grovel to Keisha. I bet that bitch would love to hear me beg and I refuse to give her the satisfaction.

I search on Craigslist and take a look at the administrative section. One post immediately stands out to me which is looking for a personal assistant. That's a job that I can do easily, anyone would be lucky to have me on their team. I'm going to make sure I write a killer cover letter because ultimately that is what's going to get me through the door. What I lack in credentials, I make up in skill. If I could charm Diesel the biggest drug distributor on the West side then the people in corporate America are nothing. I find about 10 other jobs to apply to and call it day.

I contemplate watching some television but I think that I've watched enough of it to last me all year. I've been mindlessly staring at my flat screen for weeks and eating. I've been eating a lot, and I've gained a few pounds. I have had enough Oreo cookies to last me a lifetime.

Luckily for me, my weight goes straight to my ass, and my thighs, so men never complain. I plan on losing these extra pounds that I've gained because I love being a perfect 150 pounds because it looks great on my 5'7 curvy frame.

I get prepared to hit the gym so that I can work on whipping my body into shape and I notice that I have an email. My heart starts racing when I see that it's a reply from the personal assisting job.

Damn, that was really quick.

I open it and its short and to the point, they want me to come in and interview tomorrow. I can't help but think about how odd it is that everything is moving so quickly. This means that I won't have much time to prepare for my interview. I respond quickly, my heart still racing, and let them know that I can come in for the interview at 11 a.m.

Okay, now I definitely have to go to the gym to run some of this nervous energy off!

I arrive at the gym about an hour later and I spend most of my time on the treadmill. I used to run track in high school, I ran the 400 meter and I loved it. Running requires strategy, stamina, cursing power, and a quick burst of closing kick energy. It always got my blood pumping and I was always nervous before I started but once I hear the starting pistol, I'm like a horse let out of the starting gate. The adrenaline rush that I got from running competitively is unparalleled. It kept me from getting in a lot of trouble, I got to stay away from my mom longer, and I got to keep my body in shape. I didn't need to be a cheerleader in high school to get attention because my personality and my killer body were all the credentials I needed.

As I headed to the locker room to clean up I see Rodney. Rodney is your typical muscle head but he's always so sweet to me, and I know that's because he wants to fuck me. I refuse to fuck a man from my gym because if our relationship goes sour I don't want to want to see his face or run into him every day. I tire of men pretty easily and so that's a highly likely scenario.

"Hey Camille, how are you doing," he says as he flashes his pearly whites.

I mirror his smile, "Hey sexy, how are you doing today?"

"I'm doing alright, I would be even better if you would let me take you out"

I roll my eyes, "Now you already know, I don't mix pleasure with my workouts."

"I know, I know. But you can't blame a brotha for trying," he says as he looks me up and down and licks his lips.

Normally, this kind of behavior would repulse me because I've always found that look to be creepy. That's the same way my mom's boyfriends would look at me and the only person that would keep me safe was Marcus.

But today, I find it to be pretty sexy.

I imagine riding Rodney while he's lying down on the bench press machine. Now that would be a lot of fun, I wonder how big his dick is. I've never gotten the opportunity to see a print in his pants; he's not a show off like the other men in the gym. I can't even begin to count the amount of men who parade around the gym in basketball shorts with their hard dicks bulging from the fabric. Maybe they are doing that for each other because I think it's disgusting. I don't want to have sex with a man and every woman knows what he's working with.

"Camille, what's up? You're looking at me like you want to eat me up or something. Not that I'm opposed to –."

I smack my lips "Boy please, if I wanted to do all of that to you, you would know and you would enjoy it, thoroughly."

"Oh well excuse me. Just know that my offer still stands. I wouldn't be the only person enjoying myself, I know that you would have a really good time too."

"Well, the world may never know. Thank you for asking though," I say as I walk away. I can feel his eyes on my tight round ass.

I love to flirt; it's one of my favorite things to do.

Being hard to get, but seemingly available is what I do best. Men love to have their egos stroked and they love banter even more. No one wants an easy girl with no brain. I'm from the ghetto but I'm smart and that's what got me as far as it did. While everyone else was drinking beer and hard liquor, I preferred a great bottle of wine. Other girls my age were listening to Rap and I enjoyed country, pop, and jazz. I still love my people, our music, and culture but I've always known that there was more to life.

I want more for myself but sometimes I have no idea about how to go about getting it. Sure, I can go to school but I feel like that's not going to do anything but leave me with a bunch of loans. It will also take me forever to get a degree going to school part time. I feel pretty old even though I'm only 24, I don't know if I'm ready to sit in a classroom with a bunch of 18 year olds.

As I'm walking to my car I feel my phone buzzing and I see that it's my mom. I really don't feel like talking to her and that's evident because I've been dodging her phone calls for the last month. She never calls to just say hello, she always has an ulterior motive. I decide to pick up the phone.

"Yes mom?"

"Hey Cam, where are you right now?"

"Why? What do you want," I say in an annoyed tone.

"No need to get an attitude. I just wanted to know. I've been calling you for over a month."

"I've been busy with my own life."

"Wow, so it's like that? This is how you speak to your mother?" She can be so damned manipulative. But nevertheless she is my mom and so I soften my tone.

"Okay mom, what's up?"

She sighs and says, "They're going to turn off my lights if I don't come up with the money in two weeks. I just got the shut off notice. I was trying to reach you before it got to this point."

"How much is it?"

"I need $650"

"Damn! When was the last time you paid your light bill?"

"Things have been tough for me Cam, you haven't been giving me the money that I need any more for a while and the only reason I moved in this big apartment was because I thought you had my back," my mom says in obvious distress.

"Well, I never promised to support you, that is not my job," I counter. "I never told you to move into a 3 bedroom apartment. That's absolutely ridiculous, you don't need that much room, and I don't have that kind of money to give to you. What's the point? I know you, your gas is probably about to get cut off too."

I don't hear anything but her breathing on the other end of the line. I can almost hear her brain working overtime to come up with an excuse. We sit in silence over the phone for almost 30 seconds and then she finally speaks.

"Can't you just ask Marcus for the money?"

"This is why I don't answer your calls mom. I'm not asking Marcus for anything, this isn't his problem either. I'm sorry but I can't help you. I'm about to start driving and so I will call you later."

I don't wait for her to respond and I press the end button on my phone. I fight the urge to throw my phone against the concrete and stomp it. I don't know why I let her to get to me the way that I do, she's been like this every since I can remember. I doubt if she will ever change. It looks like she is just going to have to move back in with her sister because she is not welcomed at my house.

I get into my car and take a few deep breaths and head home.

I really do wish that I could call Marcus to vent but I no longer have that luxury. I'm sure that if I called he would answer and talk to me but he made himself pretty clear the last time we talked. He has moved on to be with Charity and they are going to be a family. I won't be a third wheel to their relationship and so he can no longer be my friend anymore even though he offered. I wanted to hit him in the face with my stiletto when he asked 'Can we just go back to being friends?' I still shake my head at the level of nerve that must have taken.

Now I'm just ready to take my aching body home, get in the shower, take a nap, maybe read a Lena Skye novel on my Kindle and then prepare for my interview in the morning. I'm ready to knock it out of the ball park because I need a real change in my life.

***

I woke up at 5 in the morning because I was so excited for my interview.

I couldn't get to sleep until midnight; I was up all night researching the job of personal assistants, and the salary. Some get paid a lot of money and I hope that this job offers a decent salary like the ones that I researched. Most importantly, I researched the company. Kane Global Investment Management is one of the top 5 investment companies in Chicago and ranks in the top 20 in the nation. It was created in 1986 by Kyle Kane Senior and they specialize in health care services, information technology services, and consumer industrial businesses. I felt in over my head and decided to just go to bed before I freaked myself out.

I decided to skip my usual morning coffee to avoid the jitters. I drove to the Metro station and took the train because parking downtown is absolutely crazy and I didn't want to run the risk of being unable to find a parking spot. Looking for a parking space in downtown Chicago is an extremely frustrating experience. I'm definitely not in the mood to be annoyed today of all days.

The office is the Magnificent Mile and it's inside of a huge glass building. The lobby is massive and filled with people that are coming and going. I walk to the big half circle desk and let the attendant know that I'm there to see Kyle from Kane Enterprises. The attendant raises his eyebrow and tells me to hold one moment and that someone will be right with me. I take a seat in the lobby area and try to stop clicking my black 4 inch Nine West heel against the floor.
A beautiful petite blonde approaches me.
"Camille?"
"Yes," I say as I stand to meet her handshake. "It's nice to meet you—?"
"Amanda," she says in a pleasant but detached tone. "It's nice that you could come on such short notice, we're looking to hire for this position pretty quickly."
"It was a relief to be contacted so soon, although I do admit that it was a surprise," I say honestly.
Ignoring my comment she says, "Follow me, Kyle is finishing up a meeting and so you will have to stay put in the waiting area until he's ready for you."

Stay put? Dogs stay put, children stay put, and I'm neither.

But I don't acknowledge her slight and follow her onto the elevator and to the 30th floor. We walk through huge double glass doors and she points to the plush waiting area and walks away without another glance in my direction.

I sit in one of the black leather contemporary couches. The lobby has a very modern and sleek feel. Black leather couches, light hardwood floors, warm lighting, with a big glass desk in the front. The woman sitting behind the desk is a gorgeous brunette that looks like she stepped off a runway. As I look around I notice that most of the women in the office are beautiful and white. I look at my phone and notice that my interview was supposed to start 5 minutes ago.

Soon a cute blonde is escorted through the double doors by Amanda and motioned towards the couch. Amanda is a lot sweeter to this girl than she was to me. I then hear Amanda tell her 'Kyle is running behind schedule and we have an interview before you, so just sit tight and he'll be with you as soon he as can.' She then gives her a huge smile and asks her if she wants anything before she walks off.

I can't help but wonder if my color is the reason that I got such poor treatment. Maybe it's my clothes because everyone here is dressed immaculately. I have on a black suit from New York and Company and I thought that I was pretty cute this morning but now I feel severely under dressed and cheap. Nine West shoes aren't impressive when the women here are wearing Jimmy Choos!

I take a look at the girl sitting next to me. She has on an expensive tan suit that was tailored to fit her slender frame. Her shoes look out of my league and so there is really no use in asking her where she got them from. Her manicured nails are holding on to her leather briefcase and she makes my binder look downright juvenile. I want to go home. I can't believe that I have wasted my time coming down here. I no longer feel like the confident girl from yesterday morning.

"Camille, follow me," Amanda says to me and immediately starts walking to the back.

I follow her along the hallways and she walks inside of a big office that mirrors the lobby in décor but ups the ante with the plush white carpet and crystal everywhere. I have to make sure I don't knock anything over because I can't afford to buy it if I break it. Although everything is glass, his desk is cherry wood and it's beautiful but it looks out of place. On the desk I see the name plaque 'Kyle Kane, CEO'. Whoa, I'm interviewing with the CEO? I am so not ready for this.

"Hello Camille," I hear a smooth voice say from behind me. I jump slightly and turn around.

"Mr. Kane, this is Camille Wood. Camille this is Kyle Kane, the CEO," Amanda says before makes a graceful exit.

"Please, have a seat," Mr. Kane says as he makes a gesture towards the chair sitting directly across from him. A glass coffee table separates us.

"It's nice to meet you Mr. Kane," I say as I take my seat.

"Please call me Kyle, Mr. Kane is my father," he says with a sly and sexy grin.

Oh yes, I said sexy. This man is off of the charts when it comes to sexy and I don't even like white boys. Well at least I thought I didn't. I'm willing to ignore his corny line because who cares what he says when he's so damned hot?

He looks to be in his early 30's. He has thick tousled black hair, beautiful green eyes, and a clean shaven face that shows off his square jaw line, and I can tell that he works out. His suit jacket is neatly laid across the back of the chair in the middle of us and so his muscles are straining against the white business shirt that he's wearing so well. How would any woman be able to keep her hands off of him? I wonder if he likes black girls.

"Okay Kyle," I say. "Thank you so much for having me."

He smiles as he says "Well, you had a cover letter that we just couldn't ignore. You're a little arrogant for a person with so little experience and I must admit that I was intrigued."

I blush and tell myself to stop acting like a little school girl. This is an interview and not a date.

"I'm not arrogant, I'm self confident. I know my worth and my value. I'm an asset to whoever I work for and you'll never find another candidate that can do things as efficiently as me, or that has the drive that I do."

He raised an eyebrow at me and begins to ask me a series of questions. I feel like I'm on auto pilot because in my head I'm somewhere else. In my head I'm laid on my back naked on top of his cherry wood desk and he's on top of me impaling me with his big cock. Do white men even have big dicks? Maybe one day he'll show me. I would love to know what he feels like sliding in and out of me as he looks at me with those green eyes.

"Camille?" he says, snapping me out of my trance.

I lick my lips suggestively out of habit and I see him adjust in seat. Hmmm, so he does like me. I can't believe I'm flirting with a white man and on a job interview, this can't be professional. I try to shake it and continue on with the interview. I'm clearly lusting after him because of my lack of sex. I should have rocked Rodney's world yesterday when I had the opportunity because my hormones may lose me this job.

"Yes?" I ask.

"Why should I hire you? Especially with your lack of real experience?" he asks sternly.

"My experience is very real," I clarify. "I may not have standard corporate experience but my real life experience gives me the edge that you truly need. You can trust me to not just get your coffee but to handle your clientele with ease and secure new ones. I'm extremely attentive and you'll only need to tell me things once. I exist to make your life easier and I take pride in that."

He gives a slight smile, "You're talking as if you have the position."

"In my personal experience, that's the only way that you really get what you want. I know that I'm the best, and I know that you want the best and so we're a perfect match."

"That's all that I need to hear today. Please take my card, and feel free to call Amanda if you have any questions. She's my personal assistant. You'll be hearing from her within the week to hear the news," he says as he stands.

I stand and see that he's tall and looks to be about 6'2". I usually tower over men when I'm in my heels but he still has me by about 3 inches and that makes me feel...aroused. I get closer to him and inhale his clean scent as I shake his hand. His hand is huge and it completely swallows mines. He rubs his thumb over the flesh in between my pointer finger and thumb and the sensation goes straight to my panties.

"Thank you sir," I say "I look forward to hearing from you," and I turn and walk out of his office.

Sir? Did I really just call this man sir? He is not my father and I don't call me sir unless they're over the age of 60. But it just seemed to fit the moment and he is obviously accustomed to being called sir. Why wouldn't he be? He's a powerful man.

Now I just have to sit back and wait to see if I got the job. I walk out into the lobby and see the confident blonde sitting there. I try not to think self defeating thoughts because she looks perfect in this environment and I'm obviously out of place. I'm ready for something good to happen to me in my life. My life needs to change and I know that this job can change my life.

So screw Becky (that's what I guess her name is), I need this job way more than she does.

I walk through the double doors with my head held high but I'm faking the funk. I don't think I got the job.

#Chapter3

"I wonder how she'll look with a collar around her neck" Kyle

**

I need a breather after Camille left my office.

I've always thought that black women were sexy but there aren't many of them in my circle. The ones that I know are usually already married or they don't date white men. I could go and actively seek them out but that's always seemed to be really classless. But today, she sashayed into my office, and she has a body that's meant for sin and the face of an angel.

I brought her in for an interview out of sheer curiosity because her resume was so bare but her cover letter spoke as if she had a ton of experience. I figured she would come in and sell me a bunch of bullshit but I was willing to take that chance. I'm looking for an additional personal assistant that can help me woo clientele and that can think quickly on her feet. I don't need a drone; I need a sharp person that thinks for herself. Camille obviously fits the bill and I believe that she can back up every word that she said. My intuitions are hardly ever wrong.

It was an interesting interview. I had a bit of a tough time because her full lips were mesmerizing. I kept imagining my cock on the edge of her soft lips. When she licked her lips I almost lost it. I'm still hard just thinking about it. I want her, and there's no denying that. I'm used to getting what I want and putting her over my knee so that I can spank that plump ass is exactly what I want. She has a sassy little mouth and so I'm sure she'll deserve it.
Her clothes and shoes did her no justice. She's a woman that belongs in the best and it's obvious that she believes that too. Even though her clothes weren't expensive she takes really good care of herself. Her hair was flawless, her nails were professional, and her makeup was very becoming. If I hire her I will have to give her the company card so that she can go shopping.

Who am I kidding? I'm going to hire her and hopefully I'll have her in my bed soon. She should belong to me. I wonder how she'll look with a collar around her neck, and tied to my bed. The thought gets me hard again and I realize that I'm going to have to do the next interview while sending behind my desk. I press the intercom button.

"Amanda, send the next one in."

***

It's been an incredibly long day and the interviews were the most draining. Sitting through the last 3 of the day, when I already knew that I wanted Camille was boring. I tried to not be short or rude with them. Their qualifications are impressive but they don't have the bite or edge that I need. Looking great on paper is one thing but the intelligence to naturally navigate a conversation, to manipulate, and to get what you want is another.
It's not that Camille seems like she lacks morals, but I can tell that she is woman who is accustomed to getting what she wants. She doesn't take no for an answer and even when she's outclassed, she doesn't let it stop her.

That's what I need.

A lot of the women that I've hired in the past are all the same. Beautiful, educated, and talented but they lack the fire that can only be ignited by pressure and life experience.
She will have all of my clients wrapped around her perfectly manicured finger.

Hopefully that won't extend to me but I have to admit that if she asks for something, I'll do my best to get it for her. Some women just have that effect on a man and usually I'm immune. I mean I've seen it; my mom has that kind of influence on my dad. One smile and he is putty in her hands. I've always thought that it was cute but it's not something that I've desired for myself; at least not yet.

Getting my dad to hand over the company to me last year was no easy feat. His objections usually revolved around how young I am. He wasn't sure if I could handle the position at only 32 years old. Now it's a year later, and our offices are still expanding and thriving. I've been working my butt off since I was 15 to learn the ins and outs of the investment business. My father had a series of minor heart attacks when I was 30 and gave the entire family a scare, so my mom put her foot down and he handed the company over to me.

I can see how this business would cause a man to have a heart attack. The only thing that keeps me sane is scotch and women. I tend to keep the both of them separate because when I'm enjoying a woman, I need to be in full control. When you're flogging a woman you have to be in control of your faculties. I never want to make a mistake and injure her, beyond her personal limits.

As I straighten things up on my desk for the evening, Amanda walks into my office. She usually stays longer than she has to and I practically have to push her out the door. I would say that it's because she loves her job but I know different. She's interested in me, but she missed her chance. It's the same chance that I plan on extending to Camille. I give my personal assistants the opportunity to not only work for me but to belong to me as well.

Mixing business with pleasure is something that I've done for quite some time and makes my life a lot more enjoyable. After all, business is often a pleasure to me as it is.

Having my submissive close to me at all times is something that's important to me. Best stress relief ever. After a difficult meeting I can close my office door and bury myself deep into her pussy, or tie her to the chair and sensually torture her until she's begging for release.

"Well, good evening Mr. Kane," Amanda says coyly.
"Good evening Amanda, when do you plan on getting out of here. You know that I don't pay overtime," I say with a chuckle.

She grins, "I'm well aware of that, but you pay damn well. I just wanted to stick around and see if you've made a decision about who to hire. You're the kind of man that instantly knows what he wants."

"I plan on hiring Camille," I say in a matter of fact tone.

She narrows her eyes at me, "Camille, that girl with the cheap shoes? I don't think that she will fit in here. What qualifications does she even have to achieve such a position?"
Amanda is such a little snob but she is good at what she does. Anticipating my needs is something that she's great at and she has a memory that will rival an elephant. So she fits in great at this office. She looks just like most of the other administrative and personal assistants on the floor. She is white, pretty, and dressed impeccably. I would be lying if I said that her little skirts didn't make me hard. Some days I've wanted to have my way with her but I don't date a woman after she tells me no. She wanted to sign on as just a personal assistant and I granted her that.
"She's qualified because I say that she is, I have a feeling that she can hold her own, and I don't owe you an explanation."
She looks at me with a stunned expression but quickly recovers.
"I apologize, I didn't mean to pry. I was just anxious to figure out who my new colleague would be," she says demurely.
Her fake meekness makes me chuckle, "If I didn't know any better, I would think that you are jealous."
"I have absolutely no reason to be jealous of that girl. I'm the one that decided to keep our relationship limited to personal assisting."
"That's true, but I know that you regret that decision."
She scoffs, "Hardly. I enjoy my freedom, and vanilla is my favorite flavor."
"Hopefully Camille's is chocolate and vanilla swirl," I say as I wiggle my eyebrows.
"You're such a freak, but she doesn't strike me as the kind of girl to cross the racial lines. She seems very ummmmm…urban."
"She's definitely from the urban area but she carries herself with class and dignity. I think that her mannerisms are a part of her charm. Anyway Amanda, it's getting late. I'm going to the

restroom, file those resumes away, and let's get out of here." I say, effectively ending the conversation.

On the drive home, I have *Charlotte* on my mind.

She was my last submissive and personal assistant. She quit two weeks ago and walked out of my life forever. She wanted more from me that I could provide her with. She wanted our relationship to go public and she was tired of 'being my secret'. I really enjoyed Charlotte's company; she was really sweet, funny, and obedient. But a woman can only take so much before they break. I should have seen the signs earlier. She was becoming increasingly moody over everything, and she needed constant validation. To be quite honest, she was starting to get on my nerves, and she just wasn't fun anymore. I was surprised when she quit, but I can't say that I was upset. Relief flooded my body when I read the "I can't do this anymore" note that she left on my desk. I made sure to give her an excellent bonus and I paid off her car as a parting gift.

The drive home for me is short. I could take a cab because I live in a penthouse loft in the west loop, but I can't resist driving my new Maybach 57. I debate calling my younger sister, because she called me yesterday. As the oldest and the only boy, my twin sisters are a thorn in my flesh. I love them but they are a handful. I'm 12 years their senior and their 21st birthday is right around the corner. I don't know whether to be happy for them or to call in the cavalry. Chloe and Claire are real beauties, every woman and man knows it, and it drives me crazy.

When I'm finally relaxed with glass of scotch I call my sister Chloe.

"Hey Kyle," she says in a tone that I know is reserved for begging, snooping, or both.

"Wassup Chloe? I saw that I missed your call and I just wanted to make sure that you're okay."

"Everything is fine; Claire and I just wanted to make sure that you still plan on coming to our 21st birthday party."

I smile and say, "You both know that I wouldn't miss that for the world. Now tell me what you two really want."

I hear Claire in the background urging Chloe to just come out with it. They bicker for a few more seconds, have a vocal struggle over the phone, and Claire won the battle.

"Hey Kyle, what Chloe was struggling to ask you is, can we please use your condo in Vegas for a week next month? Pleeeeeeaaasssse, we promise not to trash it," Claire begged.

My first instinct is to say hell no. I remember all the debauchery that I indulged in when I was in my 20's and in Vegas.

Hell, I remember what I did just last year.

I'm not sure if I want the two of you running around in Vegas for a week," I groan. "But I know that I can't stop you. So yes, you may use it but don't be surprised if I send someone to check in on the both of you."

I had to move the phone away from my face because the two of them squealed so loudly.

"Thank you, thank you, thank you," they repeated over and over into the phone.

"Sooooo," Chloe said, "Are you bringing a date to our party in two weeks?"

See, here comes the snooping part. Chloe and Claire have always hounded me about women. They've most likely picked up this habit from our mother. All of them want to see me settle down with someone and provide them with grandchildren, nieces, and nephews. However, I'm just not prepared to take that step with anyone yet. It's my life and so I'll live it however I see fit. Even though I date a lot of women, I don't bring them around my family because I don't want either party getting too attached.

"Do I ever bring a date?"

"Well, we were hoping that you would surprise us this year," Chloe pouted.

"Sorry to disappoint you sis, you enjoy your night. I'm about to unwind."

"Good night," they both yell through the phone.

I'm not going to upset myself tonight by thinking of the sin that they have cooked up for Las Vegas. I'm just going to sip my scotch and think about what I'm going to say to Camille when I call her in three days. I'm excited about having her on my staff, but

I'm really hoping that she wants to be more than my personal assistant.

#Chapter4

"How is a woman supposed to think straight with an American Express card in her hand?" Camille

**

Sending in my resume to different places is a little disheartening even though I'm trying to stay positive. The qualifications that they want you to have for the simplest of jobs is absolutely crazy. My stomach has been in knots because every time my phone rings I'm hoping that it's Kyle calling to offer me the job, hell I don't even mind if Amanda calls. Just thinking about working in that huge building for that sexy ass white man makes my heart flutter. I'll come to work early and leave extra late every day just to hang around him. Maybe he'll fuck me on his desk like I imagined, I bet he's never had a girl like me.

My mind has been going along this stream of thought for three days, and I've been jumpy and moody. I'm worried about my finances and I'm horny so that job would work out for me in so many ways. I better not get to excited because he's probably already screwing Amanda. I couldn't blame either of them if they were having sex. He's hot and she's gorgeous, pair that up with some sexual tension, and things are bound to explode. That would make him off limits to me because I don't deal with sloppy seconds and that would make for one awkward situation.

I'm not joining anyone's harem, especially not his.

The only thing that's been helping me unwind is the gym so I pack my bag and get ready to head out of the door. My body collides into another that's directly in front of my door way. I take a step back in surprise and see that it's Marcus. What the hell is he doing here? I want to push him out the way and just go to the gym. I'm not ready for a complete show down with him and I kind of want to use my boxing lessons on him too. But I decide to play the cordial role.

"What are you doing here?" I say quickly

That's about as cordial as I can get right about now, and I want to slap grin off of his face.

"Hey Camille, can I come in?"

I sigh dramatically as I think about it. Now do I really want to let his ass into my apartment? My curiosity gets the better of me and I stand to the side and tell him to come in.

"Okay, you're in. Now what do you want?"

"Damn girl, you don't have to be like that. I thought that we were better than that," he responds in his baritone voice.

His voice has always been my weakness. When he hit 13 it began to change and I was putty in his hands after that. His deep voice travels from your ear canal and straight to your pleasure center. But I'm not falling for it anymore, especially since he told me in that very voice that he was done with me.

"Well, I thought that we were better than that too Marcus, but you showed me differently."

"Okay," he says holding his hands up in mock surrender. "I'm just coming by to see if you need anything. I spoke to your mom and she told me that you didn't have any money. I wanted you to know that I paid her bill for her too. We may not be together but I'm always going to take care of you."

"It wasn't her place to tell you anything about me or my finances. You shouldn't have paid her bill either. I wouldn't have paid it even if I did have the money. We can't take care of her anymore," I tell him. "I don't want any of your money because we both know where it comes from. I want my hands clean of all it. I can't afford to have everything taken away from me because I'm dealing with you."

I can tell that my comment hurt him but he tries to save face by laughing.

"I remember a time when you loved spending my money. Now all of a sudden you're too good for it. You move all the way out here in the burbs away from all of us ghetto folks. This is exactly why I moved on, because I can't deal with this shit."

His comment feels like its hit me in gut.

"Don't get upset with me because I want a better life for myself," I yell. "The reason you moved on was because you wanted something easy, and Charity is exactly that. You didn't want to have to change your life. We both agreed when we were young that living that life was temporary for us, a means to an end. You want it to be your life and I don't want to end up dead or in jail, so you can go fuck yourself."

Watching his jaw tighten gives me a level of satisfaction.

"Look, I didn't come here to argue with you. I just came to let you know that I'll hold you down."

"Thank you, but I don't need you to take care of me. I still have enough money to hold me over until I can find a job. I understand that you drove out here to check on me but I think it's time for you to leave. Please don't come again without calling and asking me first."

He stares at me in silence for a while, and walks past me, and out of the door. I feel stunned because I wasn't expecting to see him again anytime soon. I always hate fighting with him because I still care for him so deeply. I don't know if I made the right decision by refusing his money. I would hate to have to call him and ask for help in a few months. I have to keep looking for jobs so that I can continue to take care of myself.

I pick my bag back up and head for my door again. My phone buzzes and I curse loudly because I just know it's Marcus calling to say something ridiculous. I look at the number and I don't recognize it but I know it's from downtown because of the area code. My hands shake as I try to steady my breathing and answer the phone.

"Hello?"

"Hello, is Camille Woods available?"

"This is she."

"Great, this is Kyle Kane and I'm calling to discuss the position that you interviewed for on Monday. Is now a good time for you to talk?"

I drop my bag again and head for my couch.

"Yes, I can speak freely."

"I was extremely impressed with you during your interview. You have the gift of gab and that's very important in the position that I'm offering. So I will like to offer you the position of being my personal assistant. This is a contract position that lasts for 1 year with the option to renew for a longer period of time if we are a good fit," he says casually.

My heart feels like it's' going to pound out of my chest as I hear his silky smooth voice through my phone. I go to my desk and prepare myself to ask questions.

"Wow, I'm very happy to hear that I've been chosen for the position. Salary wasn't something that was discussed during the interview. May I ask how much you're offering for this position?" I ask in a voice that's cooler than how I actually feel.

"Of course, the base salary for this position is $69,000 a year, full health care, medical, dental, and vision. Of course there are quite a few perks as well."

I sit on the end of the phone in complete silence. Is this really happening to me? Am I being punked? There is no way that I just landed a job this amazing.

"Hello? Are you there?" he asks.

I clear my throat.

"Yes, I'm here. I welcome the opportunity to be able to work with you Mr. Ka—, I mean Kyle. What is the process?"

"I need you to come in to complete some paperwork, I'll have Amanda email you over some documents that you need to take a look at. Can you come in tomorrow?" he asks.

Is that relief that I hear in his voice? He almost sounds as if he thought I was going to turn down the position. There is no way I'm turning that down even if he's the boss from hell, I will learn how to cope.

"Yes, I can come in tomorrow. What time should I arrive?"

"9 a.m. will be best and I also want to speak with you about another opportunity on the table. You have the right to refuse and there will be no pressure. I must warn you and say that it's a proposition. If you know off the bat that you won't want to discuss it, feel free to tell me and I will drop the issue, no questions asked."

What the hell is he talking about? I don't want to jump to conclusions so I ask for him to clarify.

"What kind of proposition?" I ask.

"I'm interested in you Camille and I would like the opportunity to get to know you better, but on my terms. I want to reiterate that you have every right to refuse me, and it will have no effect on your personal assisting position," he says.

"Ummm okay, I'm interested in hearing what you have in mind," I say cautiously.

"I'm glad to hear it, I will see you tomorrow and if you have any questions, call me personally, this is my line."

We both say our goodbyes and then hang up. What in the hell have I walked into? Does he expect me to be his personal whore? I have to admit that the idea intrigues me in theory but I've never been one to sell sex. How am I supposed to walk into that office tomorrow and look him in the eyes? I was so much more confident when his attraction towards me was unspoken. I've always known how to use a man's attraction towards me to my advantage. I don't sell sex but I never let them know the possibility is off of the table. Most men don't respect women that they consider to be sluts and they find virgins to be annoying. I'm somewhere right in the middle, because I don't have a reputation for sleeping around but my sex appeal is off the charts and I love to flirt. I have to admit that I love being the woman that men desire but that they can never have. Because of this, there isn't much that they won't provide, all in the hopes of getting into my panties. This is how I got so much information for Marcus.

Men have spilled all of their secrets and connections while in a simple conversation with me. I know who sells to who, where they get their supply from, who killed who, and much more. That's a huge reason as to why I wanted to get away from that lifestyle. No one is looking for me because Marcus has always kept me safe but I don't want anyone to get the idea to either. Knowledge is power and I have a lot of it, and I don't even want it anymore.

I finally stand back up, grab my gym bag and head out of the door.

***

Sitting in Kyle's office again is a surreal experience. I've completed all of my paperwork and now I'm officially his new personal assistant. It was a hard pill to swallow when I found out that Amanda really is his personal assistant as well. She's pretty but she's such a bitch, and she clearly doesn't care for me. Now, I'm waiting for Kyle to come into the office so that we can talk. My palms are all clammy and my breathing is shallow. He makes me nervous but in a really good way.

He finally enters the office and closes the door behind him. He looks absolutely amazing, and I take all of him in. He's wearing an impeccably tailored ensemble. Black slacks, white shirt, grey vest, and camel blazer. Who dresses this man? Because few men would know that an outfit like that could work and I am impressed.

"Good morning, and welcome to the team," he says breaking me out of my trance as he closes the massive cherry wood door behind him.

"Good morning Kyle, and thank you for having me," I say as I stand to greet him. He gives my clammy hand a shake and kisses me on the cheek.

"You will have to excuse me, I can be pretty informal. If it ever bothers you please let me know and I will back off."

"It's okay I'm used to it and kisses on the cheek don't creep me out, I've had to deal with worse," I say honestly.

He raises his eyebrow at my comment but continues.

"I'm going to conduct this meeting in a pretty formal fashion because I would like for you to be comfortable and for there to be some space between us. I'll sit behind the desk and you will remain there. I want to let you know now that, if you accept my offer, there won't be much space between the both of us again."

Oh shit, he's serious. I watch him intently as he walks behind his desk and sits in his imposing leather chair. I don't know if this is making me more comfortable or more nervous.

"I understand, and I'm interested in hearing about what you have in mind."

"There are a couple of things that I want to know first. Are you sexually attracted to me, and are you in a relationship with someone?"

I open my mouth to answer and then promptly close it. He's pretty forward and I honestly didn't expect to be put on the spot this way. However, none of what I've expected has actually been happening lately.

I finally answer, "Much to my surprise, I am attracted to you…sexually, and no I'm not involved with anyone. I'm assuming that you're in the same boat?"

He nods, "Yes I'm in the same boat. Obviously I find you attractive and no I'm not currently involved with anyone."

"So you and Amanda..?" I ask.

"No, we're strictly professional."

That's interesting because she sure struts around the office as if she's fucking the boss.

I make an audible sigh, and say "That's good to know. I don't mean to be rude but can you please put me out of my misery, and tell me what's going on?"

He laughs and then smiles at me. His smile makes him look like a sexy carnivorous predator. He has beautiful teeth with slightly elongated canines. I've never been into the whole vampire thing, but he can bite me anytime.

"Well I prefer my relationships the same way that I like my life, with structure. Furthermore, I'm into bondage, dominance, and submission. What I'm asking from you, is for you to become my submissive. In return –"

"Wait, what? You want to own me? You think I would want to be your property? So you're Thomas Jefferson and I'm Sally Hemmings? That's wrong on so many levels dude," I laugh incredulously.

He is taken aback by my response and looks as if I slapped him across the face.

"N-no that's not what I meant at all. Yes I want to possess you but I don't want to own you. I want to get to know you, enjoy you, and ..ah shit. I'm such a dumbass for bringing this up. I can't believe that I didn't think of it that way," he stammers as his face reddens. I was upset but seeing his embarrassment calms my seething anger down. I guess he didn't mean it in that way. It's just hard to know how to react when a white man says that he wants to own you. Ummm hello, has he studied his history?

"Then please, tell me exactly what you mean."

"Camille, I'm so sorry for making you uncomfortable, please forget that I ever brought it up," he says.

"I have a pretty good idea of what you want Kyle, and unfortunately I can't offer you that. I'm not walking around with your collar around my neck as if I'm your house slave. However, if you want to date, add some kink, and go from there, then I'm game," I offer.

A look of relief floods his face and I almost burst out laughing. I've never dated a white man before and I've definitely never slept with one. I've found them attractive especially actors like Brad

Pitt, George Clooney, and Ryan Gosling. I'm unattached and I have a chance to throw caution to the wind.

"Okay, so how about you let me take you to dinner tomorrow night and we can get to know each other better?"

"That sounds wonderful," I say.

"Camille, there are perks to being with me," he says as he reaches inside of his drawer and pulls out a credit card. "This is one of one them," he says when he hands me an American Express card with my name on it.

"Today you'll go shopping; I will have my driver outside waiting for you in about 20 minutes. Please feel free to get anything you want, no limits. Go on Michigan and shop until your heart is content," he grins.

Well he sure knows the way to woman's heart. I hold on to the card and I'm not sure if I want to actually use it or not. I just got out of a relationship where a man held his money over my head. Am I ready to enter another? Granted this level of money is much higher and he's so rich that he'll never miss it. How is a woman supposed to think straight with an American Express card in her hand?

He stands up, walks around to my chair, and I instinctively rise to meet him. He cautiously invades my personal space checking for my reaction. I inhale his scent and he smells…fresh. I would expect for a man like him to smell of expensive cologne and aftershave but he smells like Zest. The heat radiating from his body is intoxicating and I lean in, our faces only inches away from each other. My eyes gravitate towards his lips and my heart begins to pulsate. Should I kiss him? I sure want to but damn, this is really soon.

His arms encircle my waist doing away with any space that we had between our bodies. My voluptuous firm frame fully presses against him and I feel his bulge against the lower portion of my stomach. Alarms go off in my head because he is packing some serious heat downstairs. I tilt my chin and lightly brush my lips against his. A slight groan escaped his lips and I feel my body slowly lighting up. I pull back slightly and I look into his eyes, he shakes his head, as one of his hands slowly lowers over my ass.

"Your body is amazing. I want my hands everywhere," he says in a whisper.

I smile and kiss him deeply, catching him off guard. I bring one of my hands up to the nape of his neck so that I can kiss him thoroughly. I trace his lips with the tip of my tongue before both of our tongues meet in a passionate embrace. His teeth nip at my lower lip before he pulls away.

"If we keep this up Camille, I'm going to fuck you right on my desk," he says.

"Well, I don't mind that. Actually I would like that a lot, but you're right. We should wait, at least until after our first date," I sigh.

I take a few steps back from him and straighten my clothes. The desire in his eyes is enough to make me want to jump his bones. I breathe deeply and tell myself to calm down. I'm thinking like a sexed crazed freak, and that's probably because I haven't had any in way too long. That's probably what is driving my decision making, I'm horny and now I'm about to fuck this white boy.

Hormones can make you do crazy things.

#Chapter5

"I'm not giving you the pleasure until you beg for it.." Kyle

**

Driving to pick up Camille is a nerve wrecking experience. I'm doing my best to stay calm under pressure but that verbal ass whipping that she gave me yesterday is stuck in my head. How could she think that I would want her in that way? I'm not that kind of person but she had a valid point about the historical implications of what I was asking. I've never had to tread on that kind of territory with the other women that have 'belonged to me' because race wasn't a factor.

I finally pull up in front of her building and I would call but I want to surprise her. I love a woman that's prompt and so this is a test of sorts. She lives in a nice and quiet neighborhood, I wasn't sure what to expect. I walk up to the door and look for her name on the buzzer, but she's beaten me to the punch. I see her walking down the hallway through the glass door. She looks breath taking, I knew that she was beautiful but she's turned it up a couple of thousand notches.

She reaches the door and timidly smiles. Her dress is a form fitting leopard animal print dress that stops directly above the knee, and it has strategically placed black lace appliqués that accentuate her figure. I don't know what it is about black women but they hold weight well. White women her size would be considered a tad bit over weight, but she is perfect. Her hourglass frame, shapely exposed legs, and black heels are making me harden.

"You look amazing," I blurt out.
She blushes as she takes my hand and I walk her to the car.
"Thank you, so do you. I purchased this dress and the shoes yesterday, so thank you again."
"No need to thank me for that, it's truly my pleasure. I see that you have exquisite taste."
"Well, I have to admit that it's hard to go wrong when your funds are unlimited," she grins.

"You would be surprised, some of my exes still managed to find a way to look unkempt. They would spend a lot of money on the most horrible things, I've ever seen."

Her grin fades a bit and I realize that I probably shouldn't have mentioned my exes on my first date. I open the door for her and we head to the restaurant.

About a half hour later we reach one of my favorite places, the Signature Room. The restaurant is located atop the John Hancock building along the magnificent mile in downtown Chicago. I want to really impress her and nothing beats the view. We're escorted to our seats and Camille looks as if she wants to say something.

"Have something on your mind?" I ask.

She looks embarrassed but speaks anyway, "Yes, your car is absolutely amazing. I would probably live in that thing if I could. How do you stay out of it?"

I can't help but laugh, "Believe me, I know what you mean. I drive to work every day just so that I can get in my car. I have others but that one is my girl."

"Oh, and here I was thinking that I was on my way to becoming your girl. Please don't tell me that I have to compete with her," she says coyly.

"There's no competition there really. I'd choose you any day but I'm hoping that we three can co-exist."

"I think I can deal with that, but only if you let me drive her at least once."

"I think that can be arranged," I grin.

Looking at her is keeping me at a high level of excitement and I wish that I'd worn different pants. Her beauty coupled with her sense of humor and intelligence makes her phenomenal. I already know that our night just can't end at dinner. I want to be around her more, she's easy going and laid back. Our conversation doesn't feel forced and I can tell that she's being herself even though she's nervous. I can't help but to touch her continuously.

I reach across the table and grab her hand after we've ordered our drinks and appetizer.

"I'm so happy that you're here with me tonight," I say as I look into her chocolate brown eyes. "I hope that you're having just as good of a time as I am."

"Honestly, this is turning out to be one of the best first dates that I've ever been on. I wasn't sure what to expect but I'm happy." We continue to speak about our family and relationships. Her experiences with her mom explain a lot about her maturity and growth at such an early age. I can't really say that I blame her for her past because if I had been dealt the cards that she had, I probably wouldn't have done as well. The candid way that she speaks about her life makes me like her even more. She's a straight shooter that doesn't pull any punches. She didn't tell me her life as if it's a sob story, but she told them in a way that made me appreciate her. I tell her about my sisters and she thinks it's funny that they have me wrapped around their finger.

"Just wait until you meet them," I say.

"I would love to," she responds.

Okay what in the hell just happened there? I never invite women to meet my family; maybe I can introduce her as my personal assistant. I quickly change the subject.

"I'm looking forward to exploring with you. I would like to keep our relationship as professional as possible in front of others but behind closed doors, I would like the freedom to do as I please." She coughs as she eats her entrée.

"And what is it that you would like to do?" she asks.

"I have to show you what I have in mind. Would you be willing to come back to my place for a preview?"

She tilts her head to the side as she slides her leg in between mines. I can tell that she's considering my offer.

"Sure, but know that I'm not sleeping with you tonight. Can you handle that?"

"That won't be much of a problem. I'm not giving you the pleasure until you beg for it anyway."

The drive back to my place seemed so long even though it's a short distance from my home. The idea of getting to play with Camille has kept me on edge since she agreed to let me give her a preview of what I have in store for her. I know that she's going to let me go further than she intends but I'm going to make sure that she tells me emphatically that it is what she wants. She's so sure that we won't be sleeping together tonight but I know different.

Tonight I'm going to tease her until it takes her over the edge and she's quivering with need. I can't wait to see that coy smile wiped from her face and replaced with raw need with no traces of pride. I enjoy her strong will but that's partially because I want to completely break it...sexually. It's no challenge to get a naturally submissive woman to do as I please but Camille is a real challenge and I'm going to enjoy stalking my prey.

As we get off of the elevator and walk into my penthouse, I see Camille's eyes light up and it's a sight to behold. She bites her ample bottom lip in an effort to keep her obvious excitement silent. I fight the urge to mimic her behavior for the time being, I want to suck the luscious flesh into my mouth but that will come later.

"Would you like a tour?" I offer.

"Yes, that would be wonderful," she smiles timidly.
Is she nervous? It's nice to know that I have the same effect on her that she's been having on me. I've been unable to get her out of my head since I've felt her soft firm body against my own. She's a conundrum to my senses, she has so many qualities that seem to be in direct opposition to the other. She's bold and shy, soft and firm, poised and raw, and a demure vixen. She sure knows how to keep a man rock hard and on his toes.

However, tonight I will be running the show.

"Alright, follow me," I say as I grab her hand.
We exit the foyer, and head into the grand living room. I must admit that I love my home. It's a really good representation of myself and women's panties seem to become instantly wet when they look around it. It does all of my sweet talking for me, women love 'stuff', especially expensive stuff.

I give her the tour of my grand living room, filled with the traditional bachelor black leather sofa, love seat, white carpet, huge projection tv, and electric fireplace. We enter the kitchen that's filled with black and stainless steel appliances, dark cherry wood cabinets, and black granite countertops accompanied by this island in the middle.

"Oh my goodness, I would love to cook in here. Well, I would love to learn how to cook in here," she giggles.

"Just say the word and I'll have my chef, show you how to cook a gourmet meal in less than 30 minutes," I grin.

"You have a chef?" she asks, "Of course you have a chef, what don't you have?"

"Do you really want me to answer that question honestly?," I tease. "Because, I can think of a certain person that I don't have fully within my grasp," I whisper into her ear.

I can feel her body shiver and she slowly steps away but I grip tighter onto her hand.

"Come on Kyle, show the rest."

I hastily show her the rest of my home, the dining area, my master bedroom, master bathroom, spare bedroom, and more. I then take her upstairs to my favorite portion of my home. The black steal winding staircase leads to a lofted area full of comfort. There are no couches or real chairs upstairs. There are just a lot of oversized pillows and a coffee table. I love to sit upstairs and think here because it leads to my outside private deck that's beautiful in the summer and breathtaking in the winter.

"Oh wow," Camille exclaimed as she plopped down onto a plush white pillow that's almost the size of a loveseat. "This is divine; I don't think I'll ever get up."

"Unfortunately, you're going to have to. Follow me," I say as I grab both of her hands and help her to her feet.

I decide that it's time to turn up the heat, it's a beautiful spring night, and it's time for me to get to know Camille better.

We head outside and the warm air breeze hits us as we look out at the glistening Chicago skyline. I hear her sigh and I can tell that she's restless and nervous. It's time for me to take control of the situation. I don't want to push her too fast, especially considering that she chewed me out when I brought up the subject. However, she did say that kink wasn't off limits.

I take a seat in one of the padded chairs and she starts towards the one that's next to me.

"No," I say causing her to halt. "Come stand in front of me"

I see a myriad amount of expressions cross her face in a matter of seconds.

"Come now," I say again more forcefully.

She narrows her eyes at me and I give her a toothy grin. This causes the tension to leave her body and she comes to meet my request.

"What now, sir?" she says in a low tone as her breathing becomes more shallow.

I watch her breast rise and fall in the dress that hugs her curves, and I see the top of her lacy bra showing though. My dick hardens in response.

"Have you ever been tied up before?"

"N-no, I can't say that I have. I've been blindfolded but only for surprises, never during sex," she says.

"That's something that's going to change very soon," I say. "As much as I love that dress, I'm requesting that you take it off for me."

"Here? Outside?" she asks nervously.

"Yes. Are you afraid that someone will see you? I didn't take you for a shy woman. You said that we could add a little kink, and that requires you to follow my orders.

I watch as she bites her lip again and I growl, "Keep biting your lip like that and I may have to take things a bit faster."

She turns around so that her ample ass is facing me and backs up so that her legs brush against my knees. She brushes her hair over one shoulder and exposes her long graceful neck.

"Are you just going to sit there and stare, or are you going to unzip me?"

"Being a tease are we?" I ask as I reach up and unzip the dress that's perfectly molded to her frame. Exposing her creamy chocolate flesh and the curve of her ass is just too hard to ignore. I lean in and kiss the dip of her back. I hear her quick intake of breath and I have a deep sense of satisfaction. I'm having the same effect on her that she's having on me.

She takes two steps forward away from my grasp and turns towards me.

"I think you're bringing the tease out in me," she says as she slides the dress from her shoulders, shimmies out of it, and throws it at me.

In this very moment, I know that she's going to be around for a long time if I can have my way. Her body is immaculate and I've been missing out for a long time. Her black and tan lace bra with the matching panties is a sight to behold. My entire body responds as I look at her standing in her undergarments and heels. I know that I have to snap out of it and show some self restraint if we are going to get through this evening without me misfiring.

"Since you've never really done anything like before, I want to take things a little slowly. If at any point you want to put an end to what we're doing, just say stop. Do you understand?"

"Yep, even though that word kind of sucks as a safe word," she grins.

"Well, I like to be as straightforward as possible and there is no confusing that word."

I rise and walk to the ottoman that doubles as a storage device. I lift it up and pull out a bundle of rope, and a silk scarf. I leave it open because I know that I'll be using more of the contents shortly. I stand in front of her and place my hand on the back of her neck and pull her towards my mouth.

"I've wanted to do this all damned night," I say before I kiss her pliant lips.

Her lips part slightly and I probe her mouth with my tongue, pulling her in so that I can deepen my kiss. My free hand trails down her back to palm her thick ass. It feels like all of the blood in my body is racing to my cock. I grind against her as I take advantage of her plush mouth.

Coming up for air, I place my hands on her arms and place some much needed distance between us.

"Okay, we need to get started and you were very clear about what you want, and I don't want to disrespect that".

"You're not disrespecting me at all, I'm enjoying myself."

"That makes me so happy to hear, now close your eyes for me."

She shivers a bit as the cool breeze hits her exposed flesh, and her skin slightly puckers. I can see her dark nipples pebble beneath the lace. Her body is so damned beautiful. I grab the silk scarf and place It around her eyes, securing it firmly in a bow at the back of her head.

"I must really like you, because I don't even want to complain about you messing up my hair."

I give a hearty laugh, "So it's true, black women are really serious about their hair?"

"Hell yes, it takes a lot of work and money to get it to look like this. So if you mess it up, you're paying for it," she says with a laugh.

"That's a price that I will be more than happy to pay," I say as I playfully smack her ass.

She lets out a mild yelp, "So didn't see that coming."

"That's the whole idea," I say. "Now take my hand and walk with me. I love the way that you look in those heels so you're going to keep those on for me."

I lead her to the pillar in the middle of my deck. I grab the rope and secure both of her wrists firmly in front of her, making a small loop in between her wrist. I raise her arms and place the loop inside one of the latch hooks that I've had imbedded into the pillar. Her face rests against the smooth wood. I walk directly behind her and rub my hardness against her ass, as I trail kisses from her ear, down her neck, and to her shoulders.

"I don't think I will ever get enough your skin," I say gruffly.

"Oh my god, I can't believe I'm doing this."

"Do you want to end this?"

"No, it's just…different. So far I'm doing fine."

"Okay, just remember that if you want to stop, I will."

She gives me a silent nod of her head as she impatiently shuffles from one foot to the other.

"Open your legs wide for me, stick your ass out." I command as I slip my hand in between her thighs, pushing them apart. The skin in between her thighs is so supple, and I stroke my thumb against the sensitive flesh of her inner thigh.

I elicit a low moan from her lips and I continue my exploration. I bring my hand higher and graze her warm center before I bring my hand up over her ass and up the center of her back. I can feel her shudder beneath my touch as she relaxes against the beam. I grind against her ass again as my hands sensually assault her breast through her bra. I lightly massage her fleshy mounds and flick my thumbs against her erect nipples. I catch her by surprise and pinch the between my forefinger and thumb.

"Oh fuuuucccckkk," she moans as she arches her back deeper and rocks her ass against me.

"You like that huh?"

"I love it."

I whisper in her ear, "That's a good girl."
Stepping away from her, I go back to the ottoman and grab my suede flogger. I can't wait to use it against her flesh. I want to see the kind of response that her body will give me. Looking at her is almost painful because my throbbing in my pants is so difficult to ignore.
"It's time for your preview, I'm about to flog your plump ass. Take nice even breaths, and enjoy it."
I stand squarely with my feet planted firmly on the ground. I stand up erect and proud so that I can hit the fleshy part of her ass with precision. I raise my arm and hold the handle as if I'm the king of a castle. Holding the tails of the flogger with my other hand, I gather them into my palm and tug gently against my hand that's holding the handle. Gently dropping my arm downwards, I release the flails. It hits exactly where I intended and her gasp is enough to urge me to continue and I repeat the action. Her entire body jumps, she leans down, and once again gives me access to her ass.
I grab the tails again and mimic my actions with more speed. I begin an unrelenting assault on her ass. Her moans grow louder and she begins to squirm.
I put the flogger down and put place my hand on her ass. Her ass is nice and warm; I deliver a smack to her rear end with the flat of my hand before I rubbed it.
"That was amazing," she pants. "I never thought that I would enjoy something like that."
"You would be surprise at things you can find to be enjoyable."
I place my fingers at the clasp of her bra and slowly unhook it, giving her time to refuse me. She remains silent; I remove the straps from the garment, and allowing it to fall to the floor. I reach up and unhook her arms, turn her body around to face me, and secure her hands in place above her again.
Her mouth is open as she pants for air. I respond immediately by taking her breast into my mouth and suckling on it greedily. My earlier need to go slow is completely escaping me. She cries out passionately, as her head thrashes from side to side. I place my hand firmly against the wet mound between her legs and begin to massage her with the palm of my hand through her panties. She's so fucking wet its killing me. I want to bury myself deep inside of her.

She begins to writhe against my hand; I move her panties to the side.

I probe her folds with my middle finger; she's already wet and slick. I dip my finger into her tight wet heat, and her knees buckle. Her pussy is so tight, and it contracts around my finger as I plunge deeper and wiggle it towards her g-spot.

"Yeeeeeessss, don't stop, please don't stop."

I pull my finger from inside of her and put it to her lips. She blindly laps up all of her juices from my finger before sucking it deep into her mouth. My dick twitches in response and I can feel my pre-cum oozing out of the head of my cock. I pull away from her and walk to my seat.

I sit and watch her as her confusion takes over. She doesn't know where I am or what I'm doing. I remain silent.

"Kyle?"

"Yes Camille?"

"Where are you? What are you doing?"

"Our preview is over, did you enjoy yourself?" I ask in a tone that's cooler than what I actually feel.

"I'm so horny; please don't leave me like this. I need to cum."

"I promised you a preview and I told you that I wouldn't take it further than that unless you begged. If you want me, then you know what you have to do."

"Are you serious?" she asks in disbelief.

"As a heart attack," I respond.

She then goes silent. She bites that bottom lip again as she thinks it over. She inhales and begins to speak.

"Can you fuck me please?" she says timidly in a voice so low that I can barely hear her.

"What was that? I can't hear you, you're going to have to speak up."

"Fuck me please, please fuck me," she says again with a little attitude. I can tell that begging isn't something that she usually does. It's something that she will have to get used to because there is a lot of it in her future.

My dick tells me that her pleas are good enough. I feel triumphant because I've conquered a small part of her and she willingly gave herself to me. I walk over to her and unhook her arms. I slowly unravel the rope from around her wrist, and massage her flesh as the blood flow returns to her extremities.

"Follow me," I say as I grab her hand and lead her inside. I tug at her panties and she steps out of them.

"I'm going to help bring you get on your knees".

I support her body as she lowers to her knees. I walk away and go back out to the ottoman to grab a condom. On my way back in I unbuckle my belt, and remove my shoes, pants, and boxers. My 8 inch cock springs up and it's ready for action. My fingers tremble as I open the foil packet and sheath myself.

"I'm sorry, but I don't have it in me to go slow right now, this will probably go pretty quickly so please don't hold back."

I kneel behind her and spread her legs wide as I position myself between them. Placing my head in the middle of her back, I bend her over the large firm pillow. Her ass presses against my erection and I feel like I'm going to erupt already.

"Fuck, you're so damned sexy."

I place the head of my cock against her tight entrance and I plunge deep inside. Her entire body convulses.

"Oh my god!, You're so fucking big," she cries out. Her pussy has my cock in a death grip and I give the both of us time to adjust. My forehead begins to sweat as I take deep breaths and try to focus on lasting.

I grab her ample hips and pull out before thrusting deep into her wet goodness again.

"yessss, again...again," she sobs.

Her cries flip a switch inside of me and I begin to pump my pulsating cock into her furiously. She bucks against me a few times and then her pussy spasms uncontrollably and her floodgates open. Looking down and seeing my dick covered in her juices as I fuck her tight pussy pushes me over the edge. My balls tighten, and I erupt inside of her like a volcano as I plunge deep into her one more time.

I collapse on top of her body. We both lay in silence for what seems like minutes. I turn my head and nuzzle her neck before getting up. I untie the silk scarf from around her eyes and lay on the floor next to her, pulling her down to lay on top of me. Her body molds perfectly to mines.

I honestly can't remember the last time I've wanted someone so badly, or that I came that fast. She has brought something out in me that I never knew existed. I push down my feelings of fear and enjoy the moment.

"We're going to have to do a lot more of that," she says, "But not tonight, because you wore me out. I don't think you know what you've started. I'm going to want to get that treatment all the time."

"There is so much more where that came from. You have no idea."

"I'm looking forward to finding out," she responds as she leans up and kisses me on the lips.

She lays her head on my chest and I stroke her back as we drift off to sleep on my plush floor.

#Chapter6
"Maybe I'm just dick drunk." Camille

**

The last week has been a whirlwind. Is it possible to fall for a man so quickly?

If someone would have told me two weeks ago that this would be my life, I would have slapped them and called them a liar. Well, maybe I wouldn't have slapped them, but you get the idea. Kyle and I have been pretty inseparable since our first night together. It's crazy that we're this comfortable with each other this fast. At least that's the way that it feels. I've been pushing the rational part of myself to the background and just living in the moment. Who knows how long something like this will last.

He seems to love taking me shopping for underwear. We were in La Perla for over an hour and he was very particular about the things that he wanted to see me in. I have to admit that he has amazing taste. I don't know if I've ever felt so sexy, and so expensive. His wallet knows no boundaries. I don't like feeling like I'm being paid for so I make sure to keep my request to minimum. I just genuinely enjoy his company. Me with a rich white man, I feel like the god of romance made an error but I'm not complaining at all. I just feel sorry for the white girl that got the man that I was supposed to have.

Our romance aside, I am doing really well as his personal assistant. I've shocked him by securing two new clients that have been on the fence. I've visited them at their office personally and I always come bearing gifts for them and their assistance. People are a lot more likely to talk to you when you bring a smile, and free stuff. Learning this industry is no different than learning the drug industry. At the end of the day, everyone wants to make money. The key is to reinforce the idea that Kyle's company can bring them profit. In this economy people want to hold their money close to their chests and are a lot less likely to gamble it, and that's pretty much what investing is.

It's always great to see the astonished look on their faces when they meet me face to face. No one expects me to be a black woman. They quickly try to cover up their surprise and I allow them to make a graceful recovery. In a week I've already gotten gifts from companies that are trying to get in front of Kyle. This personal assisting thing isn't bad at all.

On the other hand, Amanda gets more cantankerous every day. I don't really know what her problem is because I've been nothing but nice to her. Maybe she feels as if I've stepped on her territory. I imagine it's hard to watch me working directly with Kyle's clients while she's still serving coffee and picking up dry cleaning. However, that's not my fault. She should take that up with Kyle.

I'm currently sitting in Kyle's office, creating his schedule for the upcoming week. He rarely lets me sit at my own desk. I find that odd, especially since he doesn't want anyone to know about us. I'm sure that most people do know, but they're too afraid to say anything to him about it. He is not the kind of man that you walk up to and ask about his personal business. He can be intimidating, and I've learned to respect him even more this past week. Any man that can make me cum as many times as he can deserves my respect.

My friends have been calling me like crazy because they know that I got a new job, at a 'fancy place' downtown. I try to answer their questions as honestly as I can without telling them all of my business. It seems like every time one of them calls me, I'm out with Kyle. Maybe I'll call them later today and have the long conversation they've been craving.

"Oh, I should have known you were in here," Amanda says snidely as she enters the office.

"Yeah, you would think that you would come to expect it by now," I respond in the same tone.

Hey she started it and I'm not above the occasional cat fight. I'm tired of her snobbish attitude and if I don't deal with it directly, she's only going to get worse.

"I must say Camille, you've been looking pretty good since you've been working here. Your clothes have upgraded tremendously from the time you've interviewed. What's changed between then and now?" she asks with fake interest.

"A huge part of me is wondering why that's any of your business. I also wasn't aware that you watch me so closely. I think you like me."

"You're okay, but I'm sure no one likes you as much as Kyle does. Is he the reason that you've gone from rags to riches within the week."

That bitch! See, if I go west side on her then I'll probably be arrested and that's the only thing that's keeping me from grabbing a handful of her hair and thrashing her head against the desk. I have to just thrash her with my words instead.

"No need in denying it, I know what kind of relationship you have with Kyle and I think it's pathetic," she spat. "That's the only reason he hired you."

"I guess I should aim to be more like you. I hear that you have impeccable coffee making skills. You never mess up his order at the dry cleaners, and his car is always clean. You did a really job of getting it detailed. I hate to fuck in a dirty car, and with you around, I won't ever have to. Screw you, you are just a glorified maid."

Check mate!

The look on her face contorted into one of shock, hurt, and rag. I know that I hit her where it hurts. I usually don't like to hurt people's feelings but that felt damned good.

"I could have had the position being Kyle's personal whore if I wanted to. I chose to decline and make my money the honest way. You're one of many; I'm actually worth his time."

Wait, he offered her the same thing? My face visibly dropped.

"Oh, you didn't know?" Amanda says like a shark that smells blood in the water. "He didn't tell you about Charlotte, Kelsey, or Deborah? Sorry to break it to you honey, but you're nothing special. In the end, they leave, and I'm still here. Just like I'll still be here after you're gone."

I set my face like stone and cover up the fact that she's gotten under my skin.

"I'm not going anywhere, and you obviously know that as well. This is why you've been acting like such a bitch to me. You're trying to push me out, but it won't work. You're nothing to me."

"I'll get you out, just like I got rid of Charlotte. I'm going to give you a chance to walk away with a little bit of dignity, but if you continue to stay around. Things are going to get pretty ugly and fast," she says.

"Bring it on, you don't make me nervous and know that it works both ways.

Amanda turns on her heels and storms out of the office. Who does this girl think that she is? I can't stand bullies and it's insulting that she believes that she can overpower me. She has met her superior this time, and I'm going to see to it that I make her life miserable.

I sit in silence as I feel steam coming out of my ears. I asked him about Amanda and he said that it was strictly professional. What he didn't say was that he wanted it to be more than just that. He didn't lie to me but he didn't offer me the entire truth either. I know that I can't really be upset about his past and I should have known that it's something he's offered others in the past. He did hint at the truth even if he didn't emphatically state it. Now, that I know Amanda wants him and that he wanted her in the past, my stomach is in knots. What's to keep him from sleeping with her? He and I never agreed on being exclusive. Now that I think about it, do we really even have much of a relationship?

I close my eyes and try to slow my heart rate. I've let that that girl get to me, she reminds me so much of the girl that Marcus left me for. She would hang around Marcus all the time while claiming to just be his friend. I told Marcus that she hated me but he always thought that I was just being jealous. Now, he's with her and they're a big happy family. My mind is spinning and I feel like my life is about to repeat itself.

I'm going to have to speak to Kyle openly about this issue so that it doesn't fester. I need to know where we stand so that I don't have to walk on eggshells. If he pushes me away then so be it, at least I can leave before my heart gets too caught up in whatever it is that he and I share. I would hate to give it up, but it's only been a week, so I should get over it fast. Maybe I could just be his personal assistant I wonder. At this point that's probably not an option for me because I can't stand the thought of him sleeping with someone else.

I'm going to wait to bring it up. I'm not ready for reality to come crashing down on my head yet. I want to enjoy Kyle for a little bit longer before I stir things up and risk being hurt again.

***

This week is shaping up to be just as wonderful as the first. I've been making suggestions about little things that need to be done and Kyle has been assigning those tasks to Amanda. I think she hates me a little more every day and that suits me just fine. I've been doing my absolute best to block out thoughts of Kyle being with his previous assistants. He's been making me feel so special and it's hard to imagine him being with anyone else the same way that he's been with me.

I'm not sure if waiting to confront him about the issue was such a good idea because with each passing day, I fall deeper for him. We have breakfast together every morning in his kitchen, and we play and flirt. He's tied me up again on the deck a few more times and he's even tied me to an area in the front room.

Maybe I'm just dick drunk. My friend's call it that, and they would without a doubt accuse me of being addicted to Kyle's big ole' dick. I didn't even know that white men had members that large.

The black community always says that Caucasian men lack in that area. I can't speak for every white man but Kyle is larger then any man that I've ever been with. He's also so much more than his cock. He exudes raw power and he doesn't need a deep voice to stop me in my tracks. When he tells me to do something I listen, simply because I want to make him happy, and he makes me happy in return. That's probably why I'm shifting in my seat now. I have a butt plug in because he's training me to be able to take him inside of me eventually. I've never tried anal sex before but the things that Kyle does with his mouth and fingers are enough to make me want to try.

"Camille," my intercom goes off and I jump. It's Kyle speaking to me from his office.

"Yes, sir?" I hit the button and reply.

"Come here, and lock the door behind you. We have some things to discuss."

Amanda looks over at me with a knowing look that borders on jealousy and disgust. I give her a grin before I sashay into his office.

"I'm hungry," he immediately says.

I wasn't expecting his appetite to be a topic of discussion. Maybe we really did have something to discuss.

"Would you like me to order you some lunch?"

"No, but I want you to take everything off and lay across my desk," he says.

My heart begins to race everything inside of me tightens. I guess I'm on the menu. I slowly undress myself because I love to tease him. I climb on top of his desk that's been completely cleared and lay across the length of it.

"Open your legs wide for me and place them on the edge of desk." I comply with what he says and I feel very exposed but happy to finally be sprawled out on desk naked. I become increasingly aware of the plug in my ass as he sits in front of my open legs and dips his face between my thighs. I whimper in pleasure as he flicks his tongue against my puffy lips and suckles them.

"MMM you taste very good," he says before gently blowing on my taught clit.

"Oh, fuck," are the only words that I can muster as I close my eyes and focus on his mouth.

His tongue probes my center and he runs his tongue from my entrance and up to my clit. His mouth lingers on my clit and his tongue repeatedly laps at my taut button. I feel his finger against my hole and he presses it inside of me. I raise my hips in response, and he wiggles his finger against my g-spot. I cry out as he inserts a second finger, I feel so full he fucks me with his finger and they press against the plug in my ass. His mouth, the plug, and his digits over load my senses.

I completely go still and try to catch the wave of my orgasm when a loud knock occurs at his door.

"Kyyleeeee, open up, it's Chloe!"

"Fuck," Kyle groans.

"It's your sister?" I ask as I hop off of his desk and scramble for my clothes.

"Unfortunately yes," he says s with a look of frustration. "Amanda should have held her off."

"Of course, she should have."

"Kyle, open the door, I know you're in there, Amanda says you're not doing anything important."

"Wait a minute dammit, I'm finishing up a conference call."

Kyle looks over at me to make sure I'm completely dressed. He points to the love seat and I take a seat and try to look as casual as I possibly can. He then opens up the door and Chloe comes bursting through. She enters the office and her eyes go straight towards me.

"Hi, who are you?"

Kyle opens his mouth and answers for me before I ever get the chance.

"This is my new assistant Camille, Camille this is my intrusive sister Chloe."

"Hi, Camille," it's nice to meet you.

"Hello, it's nice to meet you as well," I say as I rise to give her a handshake.

"I'm here to make sure you don't renege on your promise to me and Claire," she says as she turns to Kyle. "We're making plans and we can't afford for you to have a change of heart."

"Don't worry sis, I'm not planning to change my mind. I want you and Claire to have a good time."

"Good!" she says as she lifts up on her tiptoes to kiss his cheek. "Oh! Camille you should come to me and my sister's birthday party. We're turning the big 21 and it's going to be so much fun. Free cocktails all night, a desert bar, and an amazing DJ."

I instinctively look at Kyle and he looks torn at the prospect of me coming to the party.

"Thank you for inviting me, but I'm not sure if I can make it."

"That's crap, you can totally come. I'm sure Kyle will give you the night off to party. You can even bring a date. You'll love it, we're even playing hip-hop."

Kyle's jaw visibly tightens and I can tell that he's tense because of her comment. Don't get me wrong, I love hip hop but I enjoy other music so much more. I can't really get mad at her because she doesn't mean any harm by it.

"Okay, I wouldn't want to miss your party. It sounds like a lot of fun."

"Good! I'm looking forward to seeing you there, I've invited Amanda too."

I should have known that there would be a catch. I should have asked more questions first; maybe I can get out of going. The last thing I want to do is see Amanda outside of work. If I go, I'm definitely bringing back up with me, I'm sure that Sandy will want to come to a fancy birthday party. At the very least, we can see how the other half lives and that will be entertainment enough.

"Well, I'm off to class; it was good meeting you Camille."

I say goodbye to Chloe and watch as Kyle says his goodbyes. The way that he interacts with his sister is really cute. I can tell that even though she gets under his skin, he really loves her. He's spent so much time over the last week and half talking about his twin sisters. He makes me wish that I had siblings; it would have been nice to have someone to share my experiences with. I've only had Marcus and right now he just doesn't seem like enough. He would like to be friends but I know that it's possible for me.

"Sorry about the intrusion, we were getting ready to have so much fun."

I squirm as the plug shifts in my ass. His sister showing up was like someone dousing me with freezing water. The mood had been killed immediately. As much as I would have liked to finish I know that he's due for a meeting in ten minutes. So much for me finally getting the opportunity to be fucked on his desk.

"It's okay; it's not your fault. Your sister is really cute. Do you mind if I come to the party? I'm going to invite my friend Sandy."

"Well, if you don't show up, Chloe will take it personally so I suggest that you show your face," he grins.

"Well, this should be interesting."

#Chapter7

"I'm tripping" Camille

**

"Okay, so run this by me again. You've been fucking the billionaire the whole time?" Sandy asks me disbelief.
I finally told Sandy everything about me and Kyle. I figured that I should let her know because it's been killing me keeping it to myself, and I don't want her to feel awkward when we're at the party together. I'm so happy that she decided to come with me to Chloe's party. We both look great because we purchased the cutest dresses yesterday when I got off of work. It's been nice to spend some time with her and I realize that I've been all about Kyle since he offered me the job. I have to make sure that I continue to spend time with my friends. At the end of the day, they're really all that I have. When Marcus and I blew up, they were around even when I didn't want them to.
"Yes, we've been together for the entire time. I really like him."
"I would like him too if he gave me a credit card, paid my salary, and fucked me regularly."
I laugh, "Shut up! You are crazy. I didn't want to tell you at first because I wasn't sure what you would think of me, and I wasn't sure what I thought of myself."
"So you have to tell me, how big is it? Do you enjoy it? How kinky do the both of you get?"
"All that I'm going to say is that yes I enjoy it a lot, we do things that I've never really imagined doing, and the rumors about white men are not true. He's the biggest I've ever had."
"He's bigger than Marcus?"
"Yes, by at least an inch."
"Oooh, no wonder you're dick drunk. You've been avoiding my phone calls and when I do talk to you it's been pretty short. Now I know what's been going on," she laughs.
"Sorry, girl I've been enjoying myself a whole lot for the last two weeks."

"Believe me, I've noticed. So his little sister is having her party at the Wit and she managed to get the entire roof shut down for her party? They are fuckin' loaded."

"I know, it's absolutely crazy but I'm looking forward it. I'm glad you're coming with me and you get to meet Amanda the bitch."

We park at the Wit and start walking through the hotel towards the roof of the building. I capture a look at the both of us in the mirror and we look really good. If we had Cynthia with us we would look like the black Charlie's Angels. When we step out onto the roof, I'm immediately made aware that we're the only black people in attendance, that aren't working the event. I know that it's something that I'm going to have to get used to but it does bother me. I spot Kyle sitting on one of the white plush lounge chairs and I point him out to Sandy.

"Damn, he's hot. I don't have jungle fever but I would be all over him too," she shouts into my ear over the loud music.

I look at him and smile inwardly. He is pretty hot and not just for a white man either. He's universally hot, and no woman could deny that. I feel pretty lucky and I wish that I could walk over to him and plant a big one on his lips but I know that this isn't the time for place for that. He and I are still keeping our relationship under wraps. I still don't understand that concept, especially since he's the CEO of the company. He shouldn't have to hide what we have from anyone. I can't help but think that it's because he doesn't plan on keeping me around for long. I sincerely hope that's not the case because I'm falling in love with him.

"Camille! You made it, I'm so happy you're here," Chloe shrieks as she approaches me with her twin. They're twins but fraternal, and Chloe is the prettier of the two.

"I'm happy to be here, happy birthday to the both of you," I say to the pair.

"It's great to meet you," Claire says.

"And who is this?" Chloe asks.

I introduce the both of them to Sandy and she says happy birthday. We all do a celebratory shot together. I decide to walk over to go speak to Kyle but I'm stopped in my tracks when I notice Amanda take a seat beside him. She looks good in the white mini dress and Kyle is appreciating the view.

"Aren't they so cute together?" Chloe exclaims interrupting my thoughts.

"Well they both look nice," I respond.

"We've been trying to get the both of them together forever. Amanda is finally deciding to make her move tonight. That's why I invited her; I think that they just fit. Kyle's interested in her but he doesn't know how to deal with a real woman. He's always whoring around. Hopefully they'll settle down," Claire says.

My heart feels like it's about to come out of my chest and my mouth goes dry. I'm a mixture of pissed, hurt, and embarrassed. I've been bragging about Kyle the entire ride over with Sandy and this happens right in front of her. Sandy looks at me with pity written all over her face and it's too much to take. I swallow back the tears prickling at my eyes.

"Excuse me for a moment," I interject before I walk off in the opposite direction.

I have no clue where I'm going and end up going to the rest room. I have to go and get it together. Just because his sisters want him to be with Amanda doesn't mean that it's what he wants. He said that it was just professional between the both of them and I can either choose to believe him or move on. I can't get the idea of the both of them sitting together, and the way that he looked at her. I know that sometimes men can't help it, but he knows that I'm supposed to be here too.

"Camille?" I hear Sandy say as she enters the bathroom. She turns the corner and sees me standing at the sink.

"Sorry for walking off, I just needed some time to breathe. Can you believe that shit?"

"Don't let them get to you, they don't know about your relationship with him. They seem to just want him to be with anybody at this point. It wasn't their intention to hurt you. It's their birthday and they're drunk."

"You're right; I guess I am being super sensitive about this entire situation. I can't believe that I care this much. I'm tripping."

"Like I said, you're dick drunk," she laughed, "Now let's get the hell out of here and start partying. You ready?"

"Yep, let's go."

We exit the bathroom and go back out into the sea of people on the roof. I make a bee line directly to Kyle. When he sees me he smiles brightly and stands to greet me. When his arms encircle my waist I melt into his body and he kisses my cheek. Just as quick as the hug began, it was already over.

"Hey you look great," he winks at me, "Who is your friend?"
I introduce him to Sandy.

Amanda gives me the ultimate stare down and I return it with a polite smile. She leans over and whispers something into Kyle's ear.

"Excuse me ladies, I have something to attend to," he says before he walks away.

What the hell? I'm not a jealous person but I feel slighted. I saw him for all of 1 minute and he's already walking away from me. Unable to stand any more drama, Sandy and I head to the bar. We order drinks and make small talk with other people there. Men are swarming all around us because we're the only black women there and we're hot. Sandy is soaking up all of the attention and I appear to be doing the same. The entire time that I'm talking to the men, I'm thinking about Kyle.

That's right, I'm dick drunk.

I look around the deck for Kyle and I finally see him... kissing Amanda.

My entire body freezes up and I drop my cocktail glass. Everyone surrounding me looks in my direction, and I just stand there. I don't know what to do; the man that I love is kissing Amanda.

"Let's get out of here," I say to Sandy before I head for the door. Without looking back, I start towards the exit.

"Camille!" I hear a voice that sounds like Kyle yell, but I don't let it stop me.

I can't take any more of this, and I don't know what I was thinking. I have no business at a party like this and I have zero business, being involved with someone like Kyle. Other women may be okay with this kind of situation but I can't take it. I don't want to be his secret, while I have to sit back and excuse his behavior. I'm done.

#Chapter8

"If looks could kill, there would have been a massacre" Kyle

**

Have you ever just known that your day was probably going to suck?

That's the way that I felt when I woke up this morning. Today was the first day that family and pleasure collided in my life. I pushed back my fear and moved forward with the day. I was excited to see Camille tonight because she went home yesterday to hang out with her friend, shop, and all of the other things that women do together.

Arriving at my sister's party felt like torture. Watching the both of them drink freely and flirt with men was enough to make me want to punch someone in the face. My solution to this was to subdue my anger with alcohol. I took a seat on the comfortable loungewear and gave myself a view of the entrance. I wanted to make sure that I could see Camille when she finally showed up. It seemed like forever and I almost thought that she wasn't going to show.

I couldn't blame her if she decided not to come. It's not like I decided to invite her as my date. I think that's what she was waiting for but I couldn't bring myself to say it. I don't like to merge those parts of my life, but Chloe had already invited her and I wasn't going to rescind the invitation. Chloe can be so pushy and hell hath no fury like a woman scorned.

Finally, I saw Camille strut out onto the roof and she had my immediate attention. How could anyone not notice her when she walked into the room? She looked just like a sexy ebony goddess and my cock was at full attention. I shifted in my seat uncomfortably and saw my sisters swarm her and her friend. They laughed and chatted for a bit. While I was watching them Amanda came and sat next to me.

"Kyle you're looking especially good tonight," she whispered into my ear.

"Thank you Amanda, you look pretty good yourself," I couldn't help but appreciate the view. She was wearing a hot white little number, with the emphasis on little. All of her best assets were on display. Her fake C cups looked downright delicious. Even though I found her to be attractive, I wasn't interested in taking it beyond that.

"Chloe and Claire told me that you are letting them use your condo in Vegas for a week, you're one trusting man," she says with a sly smile.

I look up from her C cups and look for Camille, and she's nowhere to be found. I wonder where she's gone but I don't think much of it because it's a huge party. Hopefully she's off enjoying herself, but not too much. I laugh and joke with Amanda for a while about my sisters. She knows how much I love them and how much they get under my skin.

I really enjoy Amanda's company. Overall, I think that she's a great person. Everything turned out for the best, and I'm happy that she turned my proposition down. I know that we are better off as friends, she's conniving and I don't like that kind of behavior in a partner. One reason that I keep her around is because she's always been loyal to me. In my business loyalty matters and she's never done anything to my knowledge to hurt or betray my trust.

I look up and Camille is standing in front of me, she looks even better up close. Her curves are to die for and her dress is hugging all of them. I think of her naked spread on my desk as I rise to greet her and her friend. After we all make introductions Amanda leans over to tell me something.

"Gregory is all over your sister," she says.

I look over and I see one of my employees with their hands on Claire's waist. He's damned near 40. I excuse myself to take care of the situation.

"Greg, get your hands off my sister," I say as I stalk towards them.

"Oh please, I'm an adult and I can take care of myself," my sister drunkenly says.

"Okay, I'll just run over to dad and let him know how much of an adult you are," I challenge.

"Whoa, I'm sorry Kyle. You're absolutely right and I won't touch her again," Greg says as he scampers off.

"Wow, you're a real buzz kill, I'm going to the bathroom. You can hold my dress up while I pee if you want," she rolls her eyes.

I don't respond to her comment and I walk to the other side of the deck with Amanda on my heels. I order a drink from one of the servers.

"Don't worry about her, she's drunk and you swooped in to save the day. Believe me; she'll thank you in the morning," Amanda insists."

"I don't care if she thanks me or not, those two are never going to happen if I have anything to do with it."

After a few moments, I look around the deck to see if I can spot Camille, and I see her at the bar. She's surrounded by men making small talk and they have other things on their mind. They are shamelessly flirting with my woman, and she seems to be receptive. My jaw clenches in jealousy and I almost break the glass that I'm holding.

"Don't worry about her," Amanda says, "You have me, and I'm not going anywhere."

She traces the line of my jaw with her hand and lifts up to kiss me on the lips. I instinctively respond before I pull away and grab her hand roughly.

"What are you doing?"

"Something that I've wanted to do for a while now, "she says before stepping in to kiss me again.

I take a step back to get some space between us.

"We are never going to happen; I thought that I was clear about that. You made your choice and now we have to live with it."

"But we have something special and…"

Her words fade out in my brain when I look up and I see Camille high tailing it for the exit. She had to have seen Amanda kiss me. I run after her leaving Amanda standing there while she's still talking.

"Camille!" I yell.

I know that she heard me yell her name because she starts to walk faster; her friend looks back and gives me a cruel stare. If looks could kill, there would have been a massacre. There is nothing like a black woman looking at you evilly, so much is communicated in her eyes and I'm sure she literally wants to rip my head off. I continue behind them and run into the elevator behind them just as the doors are about to close.

"Why are you here?" Camille yells at me.

"I know what you saw but I just wanted to tell you that it wasn't what you think."

"Save it, because I don't want to hear it. You've made your choice and it wasn't me. I refuse to sit around while you publically acknowledge the woman that you really want to be with."

"No, she kissed me, but I didn't return it."

Camille responds with a smack of her lips. My stomach is in knots as I try to think of something to salvage our doomed relationship.

"I only want you Camille," I plead as the elevator reaches the lobby. We walk out in silence.

"Prove it then, take me back upstairs and introduce me to your family as your girlfriend."

She asked for it, the one thing that I cannot give. I'm falling in love with her but what will my family think? What will my clients think and am I really ready for that?

"That's exactly what I thought," she responded to my silence. "You know what; you and that bitch Amanda deserve each other. Tell her that she's won, and she can add me to the list of the women that she's chased away."

"What does Amanda have to do with any of this?" I ask.

"Ask her!" she yells before walking off with her friend.

#Chapter9
"Am I going to go on trial?" Camille

**

It's been a week since that horrible incident at Chloe and Claire's party. I can't believe that I acted out like that in public; I'm usually a lot classier than that. I hate it when I let people bring that out of me. I texted Kyle after the incident and let him know that I needed the week off. He's been calling me like crazy ever since but I don't answer. I'm pretty sure that I'm fired and I don't care.

My pride means a lot more to me than any amount of money. I'll start job hunting tomorrow. Today, I'm on my way to figure out my fate. He's called and requested that I come to his office today. He's still my boss and I don't want to act unprofessionally so I'm showing up. I'm looking forward to seeing him even though I shouldn't. This week has been hell without him. It's funny how a person can become an integral part of your life in such a short period of time.

I walk into the huge office and it seems like all eyes are on me. Everyone couldn't know about the incident could they? As I head towards Kyle's office, Amanda stalks towards me with tears in her eyes.

"I hope you're happy bitch," she says in a low tone and walks out with security behind her.

What the hell is going on? I've worked on keeping myself calm all morning and now all of that has gone out of the window. I walk to Kyle's door and it's closed, I give a hard knock.

"Come in," Kyle's voice says.

I slowly open the door and peek in. I see Chloe, Claire, an older woman, and a man that I recognize as Kyle's father from the party.

"I'm sorry," I exclaim," should I come back at another time?"

"No, we've been waiting for you," Kyle says, "Come in and close the door."

Is all of this really necessary? I can't believe that he invited his whole family here to fire me.

What kind of business is this?

Am I going to go on trial?

"I wanted to introduce my family to the woman that I love," he says quickly.
I stand there frozen and I'm speechless.

There is a brief silence before Chloe's laugh breaks the tension.

"I didn't know that you and Kyle had something going on. You both are down with the swirl and we think it's great."
That comment elicits a laugh from us all.
"It's great to finally meet the woman that has captured my son's heart," his mother says as she rises to give me a hug.
"I'm sorry everyone, but I really don't know what to say."
"Just say that you forgive me, I was an absolute idiot and I should have acknowledged my feelings for you in the beginning."
"Of course I forgive you, and I love you too."
He hugs me in front of his family and they all make soft comments.
"Well everyone, now you've heard it from me. I'm in love with Camille, she's my personal assistant, and I look forward to our life together."
"Well it's about time son," his father says, "We thought that you were going to be single forever. Welcome into the fold Camille."
"Thank you Sir," I say.
"I just want you to know that I took what you said seriously and I fired Amanda today. She's pissed but I can't have someone like that around me. I thought I could trust her but clearly I could not. "

"That's like music to my ears," I laugh, before I kiss him.

Kyle then treats us all to lunch and I sit and listen to his family tell me all sorts of stories about him. They seem to be really happy he has met me and I can tell they really love Kyle.

Well he is quite lovable I guess!

**

5 Months Later...

"Good Morning baby," Kyle says as he kisses me awake. "I've made breakfast for you."
"Coffee too?"
"Yes coffee too, hazelnut," he responds.
"You are the best," I reply as I reach over to the night stand and grab my collar.
Kyle and I have been together for 5 months now and it's been the best five months of my life. I've come to realize that I'm a lot happier under his thumb. He respects me and loves me. I finally took his collar last month and he was surprised when I brought it up. It's still a challenge to sometimes to submit to his leadership, but that's not because of the racial thing, it's because of my stubbornness. Luckily for me, he's a patient man.
I gave up my apartment in the south suburbs and I live with him, and I don't regret my decision for one moment. Kyle is everything to me and I look forward to seeing what the future holds.
I put on my collar, and take a look at my phone. I have 8 missed calls and they're all from Marcus. I haven't spoken to him since the day that I put him out of my apartment. I see that he's texted me and I read it.
I miss you and I love you, can we try again please? I'm done with all of this bullshit. Let's meet for lunch.
Marcus

My stomach drops; I delete the message but I know I will have to respond to it later....

#Book2

THE SECRET OF
THE WHITE BILLIONAIRE

#Prologue

The more things change, the more they stay the same.

I haven't traveled to the west side of Chicago in over 6 months and
I hadn't missed a thing. I know that not much will change in a city
in such a short period of time but unpleasant memories of it all hit
me like a ton of bricks. I never realized how unhappy I was there
until I reached for something for better. Yet, here I was sitting in
front of Marcus' apartment because his calls and texts just
wouldn't stop.

Marcus is my crappy ex boyfriend. He was the love of my life and
we took care of each other as teens and young adults. When I
couldn't depend on my mother to take care of me, I could depend
on him. I will never forget how much he helped me, hell, I
wouldn't live the life I have if it wasn't for him.

He and I made ends meet by getting into the drug industry, the bad
kind. He distributed and I supported and created opportunities and
connections. After seeing one of my friends get killed, I decided
that it wasn't for me any longer. I wasn't in deep and I still had the
opportunity to change my life. We made a pact that the life that we
led wasn't going to be forever. I wanted to change and he wasn't
ready.

I still stuck beside him but it created a rift in our relationship. He
ultimately ended up breaking up with me to be with Charity

because he'd gotten her pregnant. The realization that he'd moved on shattered me. I didn't go to work and so I got fired.

However, that was the best thing that could have ever happened to me. I soon applied for a personal assisting position at a huge company. Much to my surprise, I landed the job... and also landed the CEO.

Kyle is the CEO of Kane Enterprises. Not only is he a billionaire, he's hot, and dominant. What more could a woman ask for from a man? I "belong" to him in the BDSM sense and my life has seemed to be better for it.

So..... why am I sitting outside of my ex's house?

He claims that he's no longer with Charity and that he misses me. His phone calls and texts have been coming in daily and I ignore most of them. A part of me feels like I owe him a chance but now that I'm here, I just want to leave. This isn't the kind of life that I want for myself. I don't want to deal with any baby mama drama. I also don't want to be back in this neighborhood or associated with anyone affiliated with drugs. Not anymore.

I put my keys into my ignition and started it. I'm in a different place and I'm happy. I would be an idiot to go back to the life that I've worked so hard to escape. It's time to move on. I headed to Kyle's house with a smile upon my face, knowing that I made the right decision. I hope I never have to see Marcus again...

#Chapter1

"It's not easy being me, not that I'm complaining"
Camille

"Millie," Kyle said waking me up from my slumber.
"5 more minutes," I begged.
"I gave you 5 more minutes, 5 minutes ago," he laughed as he swatted me on the ass.
"I know, I know, it's time to wake up. You worked me over last night and I'm so tired."
"You're right; I'll have to take it easier on you during the week." Kyle has the sexual libido of a teenager and the sexual intelligence of a 40 year old man, yet his real age is in between. This makes him a dangerous combination. I was tired but I was willing to sacrifice feeling groggy in the morning for the great sex that have.
"No, please," I said, "I like what we do and I don't only want to get it on the weekends."
"Well then show me that you can handle it, I need you operating on all cylinders today."
"When are we going to get another personal assistant? Because this has been so tiring, I love you but I'm only one person," I complained.
I was working overtime since he fired his other personal assistant Amanda. Granted, the bitch needed to go. She was an evil and conniving little thing and she tried to chase me away the same way that she chased away his other assistants. Kyle had no clue, and once he figured it out, he got rid of her. I was happy to be Amanda-free but we needed someone else in that position soon or I was going to go absolutely crazy.
Kyle is all business once we step into the huge building on the magnificent mile of Chicago. His company takes up an entire floor and it's immaculate. The problem is that it's my phone and email that's blowing up every day and not his. He has a million and one requests and I have to handle those along with everyone else. It's not easy being me, not that I'm complaining.
I headed for the shower and prepared for the day. I put on the pencil skirt and white business top that he liked, and paired it with

a simple pair of back Jimmy Choos. The shoes felt like they were making love to my feet. I had no idea what I was missing before I met expensive shoes. I smiled as I put on my understated gold jewelry and my gold day-collar. Most wouldn't know that it's a collar because it looks like a simple necklace with a circle as a charm.

When Kyle and I get to the office, he is all business. Our relationship isn't public because he doesn't believe that it's the right time to reveal that he is screwing his assistant. We're much more than that but that's how the situation will be assessed. He introduced me to his family 3 months ago and I was ecstatic. Now I want more. I'm not sure if that's just me being greedy or if it's a reasonable request. At the end of the day I have to trust that he loves me enough to not keep me as a secret to the world. When the timing is correct, he will make the announcement I am sure of it.

The question is what will he announce? We have a great relationship but I wonder if making it public will change the dynamic of what we have. Rocking the boat hasn't been worth it to me so I've put that conversation on ice for another time. I just want to enjoy what we have and he has been spoiling me absolutely rotten. It was hard to get accustomed to at first but he doesn't take no for an answer.

I headed into the office and prepared for my cluster fuck of a day. So many people want to get into meetings with him and I have to balance that with the people that he actually needs to see.

"Camille, my coffee," Kyle said.

"Yes sir," I said as I headed for the cappuccino maker. Nothing but the best for my boss.

My work day flew by because that's what happens when you go a mile a minute without stopping. I walked into Kyle's office to straighten up his desk for the evening. I heard him walk in behind me and close the door. My pulse raced because I knew what that meant for me.

"You young lady, have done a very good job," he said in his smooth voice that always got my engine revved.

"Well I aim to please," I responded.

"Good, because I've wanted to spank that ass all day, pull up your skirt and bend over the desk."

I don't know if I'm ever going to get used to following his commands. It's not that I don't want to; it's just that every time it is just as exciting as the last. My body has the same reaction over and over again, I'm addicted to it and I'm addicted to him. I made sure to do as he commanded and just the way that I know he likes it.

I pulled up my skirt, pulled my panties down towards my knees, spread my legs, placed my hands flat on the desk, and bent over so that the side of my cheek was resting on it.

"Hardly any hesitation, you're getting better as time goes on."

"I'm trying Sir," I said as my breathing became ragged.

I heard him walk across behind me and I braced myself for his touch. His hand rubbed my ass slowly and I melted against his touch.

"You like that Camille?"

"Yes Sir," I whispered.

This earned me a loud and resounding slap on my ass and it stung like hell.

"I can't hear you when you whisper, speak up when I ask you a question," he demanded.

I took in a deep breath and mentally bitch slapped myself for forgetting to speak up. That's one of his major commands to me. He doesn't just want me to speak up during play or sex, but in our relationship in general. Kyle is a huge fan of open and honest communication. One of his pet peeves is when I'm upset and I refuse to tell him what I'm thinking. So when I'm really upset with him, I use silence as my weapon. I know it's a little childish but I get my point across and that's all that matters.

"Yes Sir," I said louder.

"MMMmm that's better." He slipped his hand between my legs and cupped my sex. My pussy was still puffy and swollen from our activity last night. He slowly parted my lips and dipped his middle finger inside of me.

"Yessss," I moaned.

"You're so greedy, haven't you had enough?"

"I don't know if I can ever get enough of you," I admitted.

He pulled his finger from me and swatted my ass in slow hard smacks to the fleshy part of my bottom. I lifted my head up when my ass began to heat up.

"I don't think so," he said pressing my face back down onto the desk, "Not until I'm finished."
I went slack under his touch and waited on him to finish. His slaps got faster and they stung a lot more. My legs began to shake, I shifted my weight from one foot to another, and my ass felt like it was on fire. Just when I was about to plead for him to stop, they stopped. I tried to catch my breath and then I felt his warm breath against my pussy.
"Kyle," I moaned.
"Shhhhhh, I want to savor this," he said as his mouth sucked hungrily at the lips down below. There was a sensation of pain and pleasure that went through me. I wanted his mouth to continue its slow assault on my inflated lips. He darted his tongue inside of me before licking my lips again and licking my clitoris with the flat of his tongue. I felt like his favor flavor of ice cream on a hot summer day.
I lay relaxed on the table while he orally enjoyed me. I made sure to stay in the position that he liked so that he would make me cum. I've made the mistake of moving in the past and as a result he would bring me to the edge and then leave me hanging. That's always felt like one of the worst punishments ever. That feeling of needing to cum, but being denied.
My clit began to pulsate, my head start spinning, and my body went into spasms. I erupted like a volcano and he savored every drop as promised.
"I want to fuck you again but we're going to have to wait, you're too swollen," he said.
I heard him walk towards his couch and take a seat.
"Come here and return the favor," he commanded.
I licked my lips, lowered myself to the floor, and crawled over to meet his request.

***

Walking into my apartment seemed so odd to me because I hadn't been there in weeks. I had to come home to collect my mail, dust, and take a breather. Being with Kyle all the time is intense and I really enjoy it but sometimes I need a little bit of a break. I crawled into my bed and moaned at the nostalgia of it all. My apartment had been my safe haven away from the world that I escaped before.

My peace would be short lived because Cynthia and Sandy would be coming over soon. They hadn't seen me in a while and they were on the verge of stalking. Sandy actually threatened to call the police because she was sure that I had been brainwashed and kidnapped. She can be so damned dramatic sometimes. But the truth is that I've missed my friends just as much as they've missed me. My schedule is ridiculous because I work most of the day and then I crash at Kyle's place, not just because we're together, but because it's convenient.

Kyle is hanging out with a few friends tonight and I have the luxury of hanging out with two people that I care about. I am looking forward to it. I peeled my work clothes off and slipped on my new Dolce & Gabbana track suit. He had even upgraded my lounge wear and I felt expensive no matter what I was wearing. This man is ruining me for any other relationship.

I picked up the phone to order us some pizza, and walked over to my bar. My friends loved food and alcohol and so I had to provide these things so that I could avoid scrutiny. I wasn't a big drinker because of my mom. I watched her drink herself into a stupor way too many times. She would drink heavily when she couldn't afford drugs and that's why I can't stand the smell of beer to this day.

I can't begin to count the number of days and nights that I had seen my mom completely out of it. She always chose drugs over me and now I spend most of my time avoiding her. She never wants to spend any quality time with me or talk to me to see how I'm doing. The only reason she ever calls me is to beg for money. I used to do my best to provide for her but I can no longer handle that burden. She has to take care of herself the same way that I've taken care of myself since I was 7.

I looked out the window and saw the car arrive. I watched as they walked to my door and I buzzed them inside. I heard Sandy's loud mouth all way from down the hall. Cynthia was telling her to hush. That was pretty much the dynamic of our friendship. We all met as freshmen in high school and have been inseparable since. Sandy is loud, Cynthia is mild, and I'm *"bougie"*, according to them anyway. But we have a bond that's unbreakable. I know that I can emotionally depend on them when I need to and they know that they can get the same from me.

"Get your ass in here Sandy before my neighbors call the cops on you," I scolded her.

"That's what I've been tryin' to tell her. But you know she doesn't know how to keep her mouth shut," Cynthia said as she sat her purse down on my couch.

"Screw the both of you heffa's," Sandy said as she made a bee line for the vodka sitting on my counter. "Ummm, you said that you were going to feed us too," she said expectantly.

"Be patient, the pizza will be here soon. You know I'm going to feed you."

"That's right," Cynthia said, "We were beginning to think that you don't love us anymore."

"You all know that you're my girls. Nothing is ever going to change that."

"So what has been going on with you and Mr.Billionaire white boy anyway?" Sandy asked, "I've wanted to mind my business but it's hard. I know you've met his family finally. Has he told anyone else outside them yet?"

"No not yet. He says that it's not the right time to let everyone know. I sort of agree with him on that because once he opens his mouth, people will question his relationship not just with me, but with the other assistants as well. He's the boss but no one wants to deal with ridiculous gossip."

"But is it gossip, if it's true?" Cynthia inquired.

"It's our business, and we don't want people in it," I responded.

"Touchy touchy," Sandy laughed, "Put away those claws, you may hurt someone," she said as she mocked a cat's hiss.

"I know, I'm just a little defensive over our relationship. It's new and I don't want anything to ruin it. We already have the cards stacked against us. He's ten years older, crazy rich, and the whole interracial thing. I want to take it slowly and not rush," I said.

I got quiet as I examined my feelings and realized that the words that I was saying were true. The slow method for he and I was for the best. Who knew what kind of shit storm I would walk into once we went public? Our relationship couldn't handle that kind of scrutiny just yet, we were still getting to know each other.

"I still say, that it shouldn't matter what other people think about your relationship. When a man loves a woman he wants everyone to know. I just want what's best for you and I don't want to see you being used," Cynthia said.

"Thanks for being honest about how you feel. Those are the kind of things that I need to hear. I just know that I'm not ready. So don't entirely blame him for this situation because its working both ways."

"Wait one damned minute," I heard Sandy yell. She looked over towards my door and saw my black pumps. "Are those Jimmy Choos!?"

I playfully rolled my eyes, "Yes they are."

"Can I touch them?"

"You're so silly! Of course you can touch them. We wear the same size, you can even test them out."

She wasted no time and she was strutting around my apartment in the shoes in under 30 seconds.

"I swear she acts like she doesn't have any home training," Cynthia laughed, "Girl, we can't take you anywhere."

"I know how to act like I have some sense. When I went to the rooftop party, I fit in just fine. Well if you completely ignored the fact that Camille and I were the only black people there that weren't working. But there were so many fine white boys and I bet they were loaded. When is the next party? I better be invited."

"I don't know when his family is hosting another party. At this point the parties aren't anything special. He and I are always at some kind of event and I have to make sure that I'm rubbing elbows with the elite."

Sandy smacked her lips as she posed in front of my full length mirror, "I think you're just trying to keep all of them to yourself. Cynthia and I want to upgrade too."

"Speak for yourself," Cynthia interjected, "I have a man and I'm happy."

"I stand corrected, I want to upgrade and Cynthia NEEDS to upgrade."

We all laughed as Cynthia threw one of my pillows off of the couch at Sandy. I didn't care for Cynthia's boyfriend either. I wasn't going to openly agree with what Sandy was saying but I wasn't going to disagree either. Her man has 3 children by 3 different women and was working at UPS at night. He was hardly making any money and she had to struggle for everything. A man should be a help not a hindrance.

Her self esteem was way too low in my opinion. She was a size 12, with a pear shape, light complexion, and natural hair that makes her look regal. She has been trying to get me to stop perming my hair for years but I need my "creamy crack." We all have different preferences and I preferred my hair straight, and with 18 inches of extensions sewed into it.

My phone rang and it was the pizza company. I headed down to get our dinner and I knew that tonight was going to be a great one.

I really love my girls.

#Chapter2

"A weekend in the city of love will do us both some good."
Kyle

Wow, it has been a crazy few months since I first met Camille.

My buddies had been railroading me about how I've been missing in action. It was nice to take some time out of my schedule and hang out with them for bit while Camille is seeing her girlfriends. Beer, Burgers and NFL talk is always a good stress release for a guy. Good friends are irreplaceable and I've had my fair share of bad ones. In my business I can't afford to surround myself by anyone who isn't authentic. It's a waste of my time.

My loft felt empty without Camille here with me. I wanted to call her and to have her come back but I had a feeling that she needed the space. She's earned it. She's been working her butt off for months and a part of me feels bad about it but I like having her all to myself every day. Waking up next to her and having her in my office has been the greatest feeling.

Her smart mouth is one of her best qualities, although I'll never tell her that. I love how raw she is. I've been working on finding a balance between her keeping her individuality and her adjusting to meet my demands. She's been trying so hard, and I still have to stifle a laugh when she hesitates to do as I ask. I can almost see her mind yelling at her and telling her not to. But she always complies. She has given me such a great gift. Her submission means everything to me, so much more than what I've gotten from others. She has a very strong will and she's not a naturally submissive woman, yet she honors me in the way that I ask. In the beginning I know it was my looks and my money. But when she walked away from me, I knew that she couldn't be bought, and that her self-respect means a lot to her.
She's so different from the other women that I've owned and dated. When they walked away they weren't walking back into

poverty. They all came from well to do families and would be just fine without me. Camille left me and didn't have much, it bruised my ego but it made me respect her even more. I also know that I can trust her and that she wants me for the right reasons.

Even with all of these thoughts in my head, I miss her. She is a huge part of my life now and I can only hope that she knows how I feel. I will admit that I'm not the most vocal when it comes to my feelings but I'm working on changing that part of myself. She makes me want to be better and I really want to show her how much she means to me.

I decided to sit down with my laptop and found myself searching for cruises. I wondered if she'd ever been on a cruise. She and I were long overdue for a vacation. It's time for me to pull out all of the stops and show her just how generous I could be. It's easy to want to do things for a person that doesn't expect them or need them to be happy. I love watching her eyes light up when I surprise her with gifts.

I settled on a cruise with Crystal Cruises and couldn't wait to tell Camille that we were going to Australia and New Zealand. Even if she's been on a cruise before, I know that she's never been on one like this. Traditional cruises that most people go on have rooms that are like boxes, even their highest rooms are small. I booked us the best suite that this cruise had to offer and it was about the size of her current apartment. But I had to book that 2 months away from now but I am looking forward to it.

I also wanted to do something for this upcoming weekend. A trip to Paris should suffice, and she can shop until her heart is content. A weekend in the city of love will do us both some good and she'll be able to relax. I will make sure that she leaves her work phone in the U.S.A. Work will be the last thing on either of our minds when we're there, that much is for sure!

I decided to call it a night so that I could see Camille in the morning. She was going to flip, in a good way, when I revealed what I had in store for us. In two days, we would be far away from here and kissing on top of the Eiffel Tower.

My phone rang and my heart jumped. I hoped like hell that it was Camille but it was a number that I didn't recognize. I answered warily, I hate getting personal calls at this time of the evening from unknown numbers.

"Hello?"

"Kyle?" A familiar timid voice asked.

"Yes, who is this?"

"Hey, It's Charlotte."

The phone went quiet and I was at a loss for words. I hadn't spoken to Charlotte, my last submissive, since the day that she decided to leave. I honestly expected to never hear from her again. I tried to contact her on multiple occasions but my calls and emails had been ignored.

"What a pleasant surprise, how can I help you?" I said in the voice that I use for clients.

"I'm sorry for calling you so late, but I wanted to speak to you. Is that okay?"

"I have a few minutes; I was getting ready to go to bed."

"Oh good," she said with a sigh of relief, "Can you tell the doorman to let me upstairs?"

"Sorry what? You're here? What's going on Charlotte?"

"I'm sorry this was stupid. I didn't even take into account that you might have someone with you."

"I'm here alone but that's beside the point. You know it's rude to come by someone's home unannounced."

"You're right; I'm so stupid for doing this. I won't bother you again."

She then hung up the phone. I sat on my couch completely dazed by the events that occurred. I hadn't seen or heard from her in months and then she just pops up to my loft? I was more shocked than upset. She sounded like she really needed to talk and this was once a girl that I bound and fucked for months. I was very fond of her and I couldn't allow her to leave without figuring out what she wanted or needed.

I redialed her number and she picked up.

"I'll let Donald know to let you through; I'll see you in a few minutes."

"Are you sure?" she asked.

"Yes I'm sure, that's why I called you back."

I called down to the security desk and let him know that I was expecting company. I could hear the scrutiny in his voice because he was a huge fan of Camille. I groaned on the inside because I didn't want him thinking that I was betraying Camille. I wouldn't do that because I consider myself to be an honorable man. Camille and I made a verbal agreement to be exclusive. I don't want another man touching what belongs to me and the feeling is mutual. She made sure to let me know that if we we're going to have any kind of sexual relationship; it would be a monogamous one.

I heard my elevator open and I walked to meet her. She stared at me nervously with her big brown doe eyes. I hated to admit she still looked pretty good.

"Come in and have a seat," I said as I ushered her to the couch in my living area.

"I don't plan on staying long; I just wanted to clear the air between us."

"It seems to be a little late for that and I'm not saying that because it's almost midnight."

"I know you're right," she sighed, "But I felt so horrible after I left. I realized that I let Amanda chase me away. I should have come to you if I was having a problem with her. I didn't trust you enough to take care of the situation."

"So, you came here to apologize?"

"Yes, I came here apologize and I came here to be a little nosy."

I raised my eyebrow, "Oh?"

"Well, I heard that Amanda is working for your biggest competitor now, does that mean that you fired her or did she just leave also?"

I was expecting her to ask about Amanda but I didn't expect to hear what she said about her. Amanda had directly violated the terms of her contract and I didn't want to drag her through the mud with a court case but I couldn't afford to allow her to work for a competitor so soon after she'd worked for me. I tucked that piece of information away and would get that dealt with later. I kept my face as straight as possible on hearing the news as it is important never to let on when something alarms me. In the meantime, I was intrigued at what other information Charlotte may have.

"How she left is none of your concern," I said, "but it's true that she didn't leave on the best of terms."

A slow smile spread across her face, "That makes me so happy to hear. She was such a bitch, you have no idea just how evil and conniving she can be."

"Oh trust me, I have an idea. I know exactly how she can be. I liked that quality in her until she turned it against me and the people that I care about."

She got really quiet and stared at me as if she wanted to ask me something but was having second thoughts.

"Spill it," I said.

"Can I come back and work for you? I miss my job.... every part of it," she said suggestively.

I should have seen this scenario coming from a mile away. What other reason would she have stopped by at such an odd hour? She was a great assistant but I couldn't allow her back into my life in that capacity. I could no longer trust her within the realm of a BDSM relationship and I was already very happy with Camille.

"I don't want to overstep my boundaries with you, but I really enjoyed what we had," she said quickly, "I'm still kicking myself for letting Amanda chase me away, I should have known better."

"Just like you, I'm sorry that things ended the way that they did. I was surprised when you left me high and dry that way. But when I paid you out of your contract and your car, I was letting you go. You know how I do business; I don't bring people back on board after they've made the decision to leave."

She looked hurt by what I said and I wanted to comfort her but what she needed to hear from me was the truth.

"Wow, business? We weren't all business Kyle, or was our relationship a transaction for you too?"

Her words were filled with spite and her voice wavered as she spoke.

She continued, "I really cared about you, and I wanted to be with you. I wanted to be more to you than just your sub. Just give me another chance and I'll show you."

"I'm sorry, but I already have another assistant."

"Yeah, I heard that you have a new assistant, the black girl, but I was wondering if my position is still open."

"No. I just told you that your position was filled, every part of it.." I said sternly.

The realization of what I was saying hit her like a ton of bricks. I don't know if she was shocked that I replaced her so fast, or that she'd been replaced by a black woman. We're in the 21st century and people are still shocked by interracial relationships.

She tried to recover from her shock, "Well can I have Amanda's job then? I know that things have to be crazy at the office and that's a lot more than one assistant can handle. I already know the job so no one will have to teach me and you know that I can handle it."

"Why do you want the position?"

"Well I originally applied for the position because it could further my career. The part with you was an added bonus. You pay well, and, well, I need the money." she said in a matter of fact way.

She was right about the training portion. That's the part that always took the longest when bringing another assistant on board. If I brought her back she could just fall in line and it would be business as usual. It was an offer to give some serious thought to because I couldn't afford to have Camille training another girl when I needed her. That would make Camille even busier then she already is and we would have even less time to spend with each other. If Charlotte comes on board I could then see Camille more often. There were quite a few cons to this situation and one of them being that Camille may not like the idea one bit. But this wasn't Camille's call and if she was going to be with me then she needed to get used to me calling the shots. I couldn't properly think the situation through with me being so tired and with Charlotte in the same room with me.

"I don't know Charlotte, it's something that I'll put some thought into. I will have to think about it and get back to you."

"Is there a time frame?"

"I will know for sure by Monday," I said rising to my feet as a cue to her that it was time to leave.

She reluctantly stood up.

"I look forward to your call. I promise that you won't have any more drama coming from me and that I'll do my job to the best of my abilities."

"That's great to hear, and I'll take it into consideration" I said as I walked her to the elevator.

We waited for it to arrive and she stepped on.

As the doors closed she said, "I've really missed you."
I brushed my hands over my face and walked towards my
bedroom. I was going to need some serious rest tonight. I also
needed that vacation now more than ever. Paris with Camille was
the perfect escape. Over the weekend, I'm sure that I would have a
much better idea about what I was going to do about Charlotte.

#Chapter3

"Spill the beans Mr. Kane." Camille

I had to rush to work in the morning because the girls and I had way too much fun. It was a night filled with gossip, food, and drinking. I even had a few glasses of wine. I needed that time to unwind to reconnect with the girls that I loved. Both of them were still at my apartment passed out because they didn't have to work until later that day.

It felt nice to have an 8 to 5 job that I had to be at. It made me feel special, and I wasn't sure if that was a good or a bad thing. I just know that I've been able to use all of the skills that I crafted from my less than ideal background. I just know that few things get my blood pumping like being able to help him close a huge client.

One thing I hated was driving downtown. The commute in the morning was absolutely horrible and everyone drives like complete idiots in the morning. We're all trying to get to work but some seem to think that they deserve to get there faster than I do. I try to keep my road rage under lock and key but it's difficult.

I finally arrived at our floor of the building and I headed towards Kyle's office. I closed his door and sat in his lap.

"Good Morning," I said before I placed a kiss on his lips.

"MMMM Good morning indeed," he said before he leaned in for another.

"I know that today is hectic so I won't waste any time, I'm going to get your coffee, make some calls, and then head to assess the new venture for you."

"You make my life so much easier," he said grabbing my thigh.

"Well that is my job," I giggled before standing to my feet.

Seeing him put my mind and body at ease. I loved hanging out with my girls but I feel like I'm back where I belong. He has become my home. I never have to worry about anything as long as he is around and it's comforting. I've spent so much of my life worrying about finances and security and with him I don't have to do any of those things. Some may consider me to be a gold digger but I really don't care as I know the truth. It's him that I want; I could have been his assistant without the strings attached. I would have missed out on one of the greatest things that has ever happened to me.

I happily went to the cappuccino maker and prepared his with French vanilla. He was in a great mood today and all of his positive energy radiated though me. I was looking forward to getting through the day so that we could get back to his home. I wasn't sore anymore and I was sure that he was going to give my body the VIP treatment.

After delivering his coffee and making sure that his immediate needs were taken care of, I headed to my desk to get to work. I couldn't wait until we got a new assistant. It's time that someone else brings him his coffee, gets his dry cleaning, and etc. That way I would be free to take care of his actual business. I don't mind doing the grunt work but if I don't have to, that would be my preference.

After I returned to the office, I met with Kyle and his team to tell them about my findings. After he dismissed the team, I prepared to leave the conference room.

"Camille, don't leave, I have some things that I need to discuss with you," Kyle ordered.

"Okay," I responded and sat back down in my chair.

Kyle looked as if he was immersed in paperwork until the last person left the conference room. When we were alone he smiled at me.

"I have something that I want to tell you, and I was going to wait but I can't," he said.

"Oh yeah? Spill the beans Mr. Kane."

"Well, first I want to tell you that I booked us an amazing cruise in two months. I can't wait to show you the details. You've never seen anything like this before. Few people have."

I was ecstatic. I knew that anything he had in the works had to be wonderful. He's a very picky man and he doesn't settle for anything less than excellence.

"It leaves from Australia and goes to New Zealand," he added.

"Are you fucking kidding me?" I asked in disbelief.

"No, I'm not fucking kidding you," he said mocking my tone.

"Wow, that's so much more than I ever imagined. I expected a cruise to the Bahamas, Jamaica, or the Virgin Islands."

"We'll be heading to those places for sure, just not right now."

"Thank you so much! Two months can't pass by fast enough. I want to go now," I laughed.

"Well time can't go by too fast because then you'll rush our trip that's coming up this weekend."

"We have a trip coming up this weekend?"

"Yes we do, we're flying out to Paris on Friday night and we'll return on Monday morning."

I shrieked and hopped from my seat, and flew into his arms. I caught him off guard and we almost fell to the floor in his chair. I showered his face with kisses and then stood up before anyone could come in and see us.

"You are full of surprises today. When did you make these plans?" I asked.

"I made them last night. I missed you so much even though you were only away from me for a night. I decided that I wanted you all to myself in a place where we would be uninterrupted and I won't have to share you with anyone."

"Now you know how I feel. It's tough being me," I winked.

"Yeah I know," he said and his face began to look serious. "I just want you to know that you mean a lot to me. I love you. I've been hearing what you're saying and I'm making an effort to do more."

I leaned down to give him a chaste kiss on the lips, "I appreciate it and believe me, I'm noticing. I know that these things take time and that it's going to be a huge transition. Right now I'm just enjoying being with you."

"Good," he responded, "Head to my office and prepare it for tomorrow. I don't know about you but I'm ready to get out of here."

"I've been ready since this morning," I grinned.

"I hope so, because ready or not, here I come."

***

Coach and first class are two very different things but First class and private jet are in two totally different stratospheres. I was made a believer last night, well today. We left yesterday at 7p.m and it's now 10a.m in Paris. To say that I'm jet lagged would be an understatement. However, there is no way I'm going to bed and missing a full day in Paris. Sleep would have to wait.

When we arrived at our hotel I was speechless. I had only seen places like this in movies and photos. Le Pavillion De La Reine pulled me back in time to a world that I've never had the pleasure of visiting.

"We are in Place de Vosges, in the heart of Le Marais, one of the most famous and historical districts of Paris, isn't it beautiful?" Kyle asked. I loved the French accent he used when saying the French words.

"Beyond beautiful," I confirmed.

We checked in and I walked around the grounds. I developed an appreciation for the immaculate boutique hotel. I sighed as I walked out to the courtyard. The building was covered in lush leaves and I was surrounded by grass and flowers.

"Can we stay here forever?" I asked Kyle as I lay my head on his shoulder.

He chuckled, "You haven't even seen the suite yet."

"OOH there's more?" I asked.

"The best is yet to come, let's go to our room."

I followed him to the second floor and we entered our suite. It was just as great as the rest of the area. There were two floors and a balcony directly off the first floor, giving us a spectacular view of the courtyard. We walked around the rest of the area and we were both very pleased. I've heard about how small rooms can be in Paris but these were a really good size. I'm sure that this is because of the amount of money that Kyle spent.

I fell in love as soon as I saw the claw footed bath tub. It was deep and I felt so icky from the plane ride. As if on cue, Kyle began to fill the tub with water and used the bubbles on the sink to create a nice foam.

"I've always wanted to get inside of a bathtub like this one. There's something about it that looks so relaxing and comforting."

"Well now you'll have your chance," he said as he began to pull my clothes off.

"You're spoiling me rotten," I said as I lifted my arms to assist him in pulling off my dress.

"That's the general idea. I love spoiling you; it's something that I enjoy. I want to make you as happy as you make me."

"You make me happy just by being yourself. It's you that I want."
He got quiet after I made my declaration. We stood in the
bathroom embracing each other and I wondered what he was
thinking. I would hope that after the time that we've spent that he
would know that it's not the money I'm after. You can't put a price
on being with a person that makes you feel this good.
The tub was filled halfway and he assisted me with getting into the
tub. I didn't need his help but it was nice to have it. The whole
scene felt very intimate.
"I feel under dressed," I pouted, "Can you take your shirt so that I
don't feel so exposed," I said as I blinked demurely.
He gave a hearty chuckle, "I don't want to make you feel exposed
so I guess that I can accommodate you."
I shamelessly watched as he pulled off his v-neck graphic t-shirt. I
have to admit that when he put the t-shirt on before we left to go to
the airport I was a bit surprised. It's rare that I get to see him dress
down even on the weekends because he still has business to attend
to. I would have to get him to wear t-shirts more often because his
body looked delicious in them. But, I prefer him not wearing
anything. His six-pack, muscled chest, and rippled arms were
enough to give my eyes an orgasm.
The water was warm and the tub felt as if it was made for my
body. It was so deep that I could hardly see over the edge. Kyle
knelt behind me and massaged my shoulders with his large hands. I
moaned and leaned back against him as he kneaded out the kinks
in my shoulders.
"You're incredibly tense," his thumbs focused on a knot around
my shoulder blade.
"I know but you're making it all better," I looked up at him and
kissed him on the lips, "Get in with me? There's more than enough
room in here for you."
"I thought that you would never ask."
He relieved himself from the rest of his clothes and climbed in the
tub behind me. I leaned back against his chest and inhaled and
exhaled slowly. This was the life that I wanted and I never thought
that it would happen for me.
"What's on your mind?" he asked.

"I was just thinking about how you're my dream come true. You're a dream that I didn't even know I had. I just feel very fortunate to be here with you right now."

He grabbed a towel and began to lather my body.

"I can't focus when you touch me," I moaned.

"You have to work on it because if you stop talking to me then I'll stop what I'm doing," he said against my ear.

"Now that doesn't seem fair at all," I said as I wiggled my backside against his hardening erection.

"Who is playing dirty now?" he chuckled.

"There's so much that I want to see in Paris but I don't want to leave this suite. I love knowing that we're beyond the reach of our world. I have you all to myself."

"We'll see a few things while we're here but we won't rush it. We will come back again soon if you like."

"That's something that we'll have to do," I admitted. "We are going to spend a lot of quality time in this hotel."

"You have no idea," he whispered against my ear again, "I packed some fun things for us."

My heart began to race again because I knew what kind of "fun things" he was speaking about. We had a lot of fun together and it was clear who the dominant in our relationship was. However, we haven't had a lot of opportunities to play as much as he or I would like recently. The bottom line is that we both are busy and tired by the time we get home. We still have our dynamic but we want to get off and go to bed. There's nothing wrong with this and I'm just happy that we have sex as often as we do.

"I can't wait to see what you have in store for me."

We finished up our bath, stepped into the shower for a few minutes and went to the bedroom. We drifted off to sleep within minutes. I wasn't the only one tired from the plane ride. I was awakened to find one of my wrists being handcuffed to the bed post. I tried to move my other arm but it was already cuffed. My eyes shot open and I saw Kyle was standing above me with a blind fold. He tied it sharply around my eyes.

"Good afternoon sleepy head. I figured that I would take advantage of your vulnerable position while I had the chance."

"Wow, really?"

"Yes really," he said mocking me again. That seemed to be a favorite pastime of his.

"You enjoy making fun of me," I said with a frown.

"Not at all baby, I just really love the way that you talk. It has a touch of a southern accent. I hardly get to hear it in the office but I love when you let your guard down and it comes out."

"Most of my family is from the south. So the accent has been passed down from my grandmother. Are we really having this conversation while I'm handcuffed and blind folded? What are we about to do?"

"I see that someone needs to learn patience. When I handcuff you or tie you up, it's because that's what I want to see. I may want to use you, and I may just want to see you spread out and vulnerable."

"Aww come on," I whined, "There is so much for us to see. What time is it?"

"It's only 2 o'clock and you know that Paris lights up at night and so we'll see plenty tonight, and then go shopping tomorrow."

"Shopping?" My ears perked up.

"I knew that would make you feel better," he said as he took one of my nipples into his mouth."

I gasped as he teased my nipple. He ran his tongue all over it and then pulled it between his teeth. He gave me a slight pinch before soothing it with his tongue again. My body was walking the line of pleasure and pain. His hands worked their way down my body, and rested between my legs. He cupped my center and slowly massaged there.

"See you're feeling better already," he said in a hushed tone.

I wanted to touch him. I wanted to caress his face as I kissed him. I hated not being able to touch him but I also loved that he could have his way with me. I never worried about what he was going to do me, not in a scared for my life kind of way. Some of the things that he does can be painful but he never takes it too far. He knows my threshold and he's only crossed it once. He felt like complete crap after and it took me 3 days to convince him to play with me again. He made an honest mistake, but all he kept saying was that it's his job to make sure mistakes don't happen.

The greatest torture for me is having to wait and he knows that. I'm an impatient person and I want it all and I want it quickly. I squirmed against his hand, trying to press my clit against his palm for greater friction.

"Be still Camille," he said in a firm voice.

Being still is easier said than done. I wonder how he would feel if I told him to be still while I was sucking his cock. He would realize that it's not so easy. Now that's an intriguing idea. I wondered if he would ever let me tie him up. He doesn't seem like the kind of man that would, but it won't hurt to ask at a later date.

I felt him climb onto the bed and place himself between my legs.

"Your skin is so fucking beautiful; I don't think that I can ever get enough of touching it and looking at it. I suggest that you grab onto your cuffs because this is going to be a bumpy ride."

I bit my bottom lip and prepared to be impaled by his rod. He could be so gentle one moment and then a beast the next. I enjoyed not knowing what was coming next. He grabbed my legs and put them on his shoulders and lifted my hips from the bed. I felt his massive cockhead placed at the damp entrance of my pussy. He pushed inside of me in one swift motion. I gasped at how full he felt; with one stroke he ignited a fire within my entire body.

My entire body went rigid as he took long and hard strokes inside of me. He pulled out all the way to tip and pushed deep inside of my tunnel, giving me every unrelenting inch. My head thrashed back and forth as his cock coaxed moans from lips.

"Kyle pleasseeee faster."

He withdrew from me and I laid there in anticipation for what was going to come next. Seconds felt like minutes.

"Kyle?"

"Lick your lips for me," he demanded.

I slowly slid my tongue across my bottom lip and repeated the process with the top one. I made sure that I did it teasingly and then I slightly bit my bottom lip just the way that he liked.

He groaned, "You're trying to drive me insane. I have to get inside of your mouth."

He straddled my face and rubbed his cock against my lips. I loved to feel him inside of my mouth but I was disappointed and horny. My cunt was begging him to finish what he started but he'd already made up his mind and I knew that I couldn't change it. If I did, I would have to pay for it later. He would probably deny me orgasms for a week and there was no way in hell that I wanted that to happen.

I opened my mouth and sucked him deep inside. He pumped in and out in unsynchronized movements. He grabbed my head and took control, and he had no mercy on my mouth. I gagged and he continued to chase his own orgasm. He plunged inside of my mouth one more time and then erupted. I loved it!

I went to the bathroom to freshen up after he removed my handcuffs and blindfold. He stood at the entrance watching my every move.

"Is there something that I can help you with Mr. Kane?"

"I think that you've already helped me just fine," he laughed. "But what I find interesting is that you're sexually frustrated and you haven't said a thing."

"Would it have made a difference?" I asked with more attitude than I intended.

"Probably not," he admitted, "I want you to be on edge tonight for a reason."

I walked back into the room and there was a pair of black lace panties on the bed with a device inside of them. I walked closer and they began to buzz. I jumped slightly and I heard Kyle laugh and show me the remote control in his hand.

"Today you'll be wearing this as we go out on the town, I hope you don't mind," he grinned.

My pussy jumped when I saw the sinful look on his face. He planned on having way too much fun tonight and it was going to be at my expense.

"I'm a little nervous because you can be downright evil. I wouldn't put it past you to make me orgasm during dinner."

"Then you know me very well," he said as he slapped my ass.

I inserted the stimulator inside of my aroused hole. I gritted my teeth as he turned it on to the lowest setting.

"Bend over," he commanded.

I stared at him in disbelief because he was being such a tease.

"Bend over; I shouldn't have to say it again."

I loved him being dominant but it sure could get on my damned nerves sometimes. I wanted to cum so badly and he was playing around. It all felt very unfair.

"Fine," I said as I bent over and placed my hands on the bed.

He walked to one of his bags and pulled out some lubrication and his favorite anal plug for me. It had a pink jewel on the end. He was determined to drive me absolutely insane.

I almost pushed out the toy that was inside of me and it was on purpose.

"Hold it in there, or you won't like what happens if it hits the ground," he said as he pushed it in deeper.

It was keeping me on edge. My entire body felt warm and it stroked the flames of my arousal. However, it wasn't strong enough to make me cum. He lubricated my ass hole and slowly pushed the plug inside. I groaned as it made me clench onto the toy inside of my pussy tighter. He kissed each of my cheeks and helped me into the black lace panties.

Today was going to be a very long day.

***

Paris is such a beautiful place and I can see why it's the city of love. I had been wined and dined all day. I was almost too full from pastries to enjoy dinner. We took strolls through beautiful gardens and had a leisurely day. Nothing felt rushed and it's hard to adjust for a person who is used to walking fast everywhere that they go.

Kyle kept grabbing me by the waist and asking, 'What time do you have to be there?"

But after a few hours I learned how to be present in the moment and to take everything in. What good is a vacation if you're rushing through it to see the next landmark? According to him, we would be back and so I didn't have to rush. That also could have partially been due to the constant buzzing that was happening inside of me. He hadn't played around with the settings at all. We made one stop to the rest room and he switched out the batteries. My pussy was soaking my panties.

The highlight of the night had finally arrived. We were on the lift of the Eiffel Tower, and I was beyond excited. One thing that no one tells you about is how crowded it is. In hindsight I should have expected it because of how huge of a landmark it is. As we got to the top the vibe inside of me started to pulsate faster. My eyes almost rolled into the back of my head and I looked at Kyle with a panicked expression and he responded with a grin.

I wanted to implode but it still wasn't enough to cause me to get there. I was on the verge of tears because I was so sexually frustrated. He escorted me out onto the tower once we reached the top. The view mixed with my frustration made me well up with tears. He grabbed my hand and led me to the railing. The view was spectacular and I was happy that he made me wait until the sun went down to go.

Tears streamed down my face as I grinded uselessly against the seat of my jeans.

"Please," I said as I pressed back against his body.

I felt completely surrounded by him as he stood behind me. His arms were around my waist and his chin rested on my shoulder.

"What do you want," he whispered into my ear.

"I want to cum," I said in a low voice, hoping that he could hear me.

His hand went to his pocket and the vibrating went on super power. It was sending waves of pleasure throughout my entire body. I tried to turn around to face him so that I could hide my pleasure as I stood against his chest, but his hands kept me firmly in place.

"No, I want you to keep your eyes open, look out on this beautiful city, and cum for me," he said huskily.

His words sent me over the edge. I tried to comply with his wishes and keep my eyes open. My hips moved back and forth, against the seat of my panties, causing the toy to press against my g-spot. My body was overtaken with pleasure as I exploded with the pleasure that I'd been denied for hours upon hours. The buzzing finally stopped and an intense calm settled over my body. I leaned my head back against his chest as I looked up at the city of lights.

"You feel better?" he asked.

"So much better," I responded.

He turned me around and looked into my eyes with an intensity that I've never seen before. His lips met mine and I kissed him hungrily. I slowed down once I felt the fire inside of me begin to rekindle.

"Dinner and then back to the hotel," he said as his erection pressed into my belly.

We headed to straight to dinner afterwards and it was delicious. Everything is so cramped here and it forces you to be close to the person you're with. I was happily seated next to Kyle at a restaurant and we were surrounded by others but only we mattered. We couldn't keep our hands off of each other and I'm sure that it may have sickened those that didn't enjoy seeing PDA. He kept kissing me and touching me. I was in pure heaven.

Our waiter came and brought us the check as Kyle kissed my cheek. The server gave us a condescending look and I couldn't figure out why. Kyle removed his arm from around my waist once the waiter walked away. I was baffled and hurt. Why would he stop just because someone didn't like what they saw? He and I were keeping it PG-13 and there was no reason for the waiter to give us such a dirty look.

In that moment I became aware of my skin color. That had to be the reason behind the look. There were other couples here as well and I doubted if they were on the receiving end of the waiter's scrutiny. Why would Kyle respond to such a thing? Was he ashamed of our relationship? Am I going to be his secret forever? "Let go babe," he said after he paid for our meal.

I tried to not read into the situation too much so that I could enjoy the rest of our trip but it did play on my mind somewhat.

#Chapter4

"What did I do to deserve that look?"
Kyle

This weekend has gone by like a whirlwind. We're already back on the plane and prepared to head home. I didn't want to leave Paris because I was enjoying Camille so much. It was nice to have uninterrupted time with the woman that I love. Being able to show our affection for each other in public without having to worry about who is lurking around the corner was absolutely refreshing. I was already looking forward to our cruise in two months. We would have 2 and half weeks of time together.

We ended up having to buy extra suitcases to bring home because Camille had such a great time shopping. I purchased everything that tickled her fancy. I love spoiling her like she is my princess. She was going to need to use the extra room in my place as a closet. But that's a habit of hers that I don't mind supporting because she has great taste. I love watching her strut around in her heels, tailored suits, and expensive underwear.

We were heading back to reality and I'd made my decision about Charlotte. I had been avoiding the subject all weekend because I didn't want to ruin our trip. I have no clue how Camille will react to the situation. She doesn't come across as the jealous type but I couldn't blame her if she felt a twinge of it in this situation. But the bottom line is that we're in need of a new assistant that doesn't need to be trained. Charlotte is perfect for the position.

I looked across at Camille and she looked radiant and beautiful. Paris did her well and I could see that she was refreshed. She was peacefully reading away on her Kindle device and she looked like she was enjoying it. I guessed it was probably one of those *Lena Skye* novels that all the women are going crazy for these days.

I sighed and leaned back into the comfort of my seat as the plane took off.

"I don't want to go home," she said.

"I agree with your sentiment but it's time for us to get back to work."

She looked out the window and didn't respond. She had been a little distant over the last day. I didn't have much of a clue as to why. She wasn't disrespectful or unpleasant, just a tad different. I didn't like it at all but I still enjoyed the comfort of her presence.

"Camille, there is something that I want to tell you."

"Uh oh," she said with a slight smile, "Should I be nervous?"

"No you shouldn't be nervous but it's definitely something that we need to discuss before we get back to Chicago."

My throat went dry and as if on cue, the stewardess came by with two glasses of water and mimosas. I skipped the water and drained the champagne flute and requested another. This was going to be so much harder than I thought.

"Okay," she said as she watched me intently.

"Well, you've made it quite clear that you are in need of help at the office. You want another assistant on board to help. I completely agree with you and I think that you deserve to have your load lightened."

Her face lit up as I talked and I could tell that she was happy with what I saying.

"I think I like where this is going," she said, "When do we start the interview process?"

"That's the thing; there won't be an interview process. I already know exactly who I'm going to hire."

Her face went neutral, "Oh yeah? Who is it?"

"Her name is Charlotte."

"Charlotte? As in your ex personal assistant Charlotte? As in one of the girls that Amanda chased away?"

I took another long sip of my mimosa, "Yes that Charlotte. But I can assure you that she will only be my personal assistant, nothing more. I have you and that's a boundary with her that I will not cross."

"I don't really know what I'm supposed to say at this point," she admitted.

"Feel free to say whatever is on your mind. If you have questions, I'm more than willing to answer them."

"How am I supposed to be sure that you and her won't cross the line."

"I guess that's something that you will just have to trust me on. You are the woman that I want and I no longer want her in that capacity."

She shook her head, "How did all of this even come about? Why is she coming back?"

"I know that you wanted someone on board that could actually help you. Charlotte knows the job and I know that she would be willing to come back and work. You don't have time to train a new assistant right now."

For some idiotic reason, I decided to keep Charlotte's late night visit over to my house a secret. Nothing inappropriate happened but I wanted this conversation to go as smoothly as possible. That wouldn't happen if I disclosed that piece of information to her. I don't imagine that any woman would be happy about her boyfriend's ex stopping over at an odd hour of the night.

"So in the midst of all of this, you still aren't going to go public with our relationship?"

Her question seemed to come out of left field as if she'd been holding it in for a while.

"Where did that come from?"

"You said that I could ask whatever I wanted, and so I'm asking."

"If you're concerned about Charlotte, I will let her know about our relationship. She knows how to maintain discretion."

She rolled her eyes and gave me the stare of death.

"Whoa, what did I do to deserve that look?"

She opened her mouth as if she was about to let me have it and then closed it.

"Tell me," I said.

"I just feel like a secret. I feel that you're never going to tell everyone about us and that you're ashamed of our relationship. I love you and I want to be with you but I'm getting a little tired of hiding."

I wasn't entirely sure as to how I should respond. I noticed that she was extremely frustrated and she did have a point. I wasn't ashamed of our relationship but I wasn't ready to deal with the backlash that could come from it. Although my family knew about the both of us, they didn't completely accept it. They wrote it off as a phase that I'm going through and they don't take it seriously. I haven't told Camille because I didn't want to hurt her.

My father suggested that I keep it quiet until I've made up my mind about what I permanently want. The social circle that I'm a part of is very judgmental and they believe in maintaining the status quo. I've been taught to go along with what's needed to get what I want and to achieve results. My father warned me I could potentially lose clients over my relationship with Camille. I didn't want to lose them or her and so I was in quite a predicament.

"I understand that you're frustrated. But trust me; this is for the best right now. When the time is right we will go public. Aren't you happy with me?"

"Of course I'm happy with you; I wouldn't be here if I wasn't. Sometimes it just gets difficult and I think that this trip highlighted it. I had such a good time and I wish it could be like that all the time," she said.

I breathed a sigh of relief because she was beginning to soften. I reached across the table to grab and stroke her hand.

"Please never doubt my feelings for you. Give me a chance and I'll show you how great things can be," I pleaded.

"I will, and I hope that it all works out. You are where I want to be and I'll stick it out for as long as I can. Just please don't make me regret it. I've had my share of bad relationships and I don't want to do it anymore. I would rather be alone than be mistreated. I appreciate everything that you do for me, but it's how you treat me that makes me stick around."

Her admission warmed my heart and I wanted so badly to be the person that she was challenging me to be. I wasn't in the position to freely be myself right now. I still had a lot to prove as the CEO of the company and something like this could force my father out of retirement. He's so damned stubborn and he's been watching my every move.

"Believe me; I hear everything that you're saying. You lighten up my life in more ways than one. I have no intentions of letting you go at all. I love you, so please stick it out with me."

A big smile spread across her face, "I'm here for you and I'll do my best. I will try to take your business into consideration as well. I know that things aren't as black and white as they may seem."

"That's my girl," I responded, "Now how about we make use of the room that's in the back," I said as I wiggled my eyebrows.

She giggled, "After you Mr. Kane."

***

It was back to the daily grind on Tuesday. My conversation with Camille went better than I expected. I wasn't sure how she was going to take the news about Charlotte, but she did her best to stay level headed. I inducted her into the mile high club before we got off of the plane, and we haven't spoken about it since.

Things have been a little tense this morning because Charlotte will come in to complete her paperwork. I've called a meeting so that the three of us can have a firm understanding about my expectations. Camille also needs to be assured that nothing is going to happen between Charlotte and me. I would probably never tell her that Charlotte would like for us to be a lot more, but that's because I want to keep the peace between all of us.

I called Charlotte shortly after our plane touched down and told her about my decision. To say that she was excited would be an understatement. She promised that she wouldn't bring any drama to my office and that she would do the job to the best of her abilities. For her sake as well as my own, I hoped that was the truth.

"Check your email at your earliest convenience, I've copied you on the itinerary that I've sent out to the staff for the meeting tomorrow," Camille said as she walked into my room.

"Thank you Camille," I said.

"Also Charlotte is here, her paper work is finished, and I think she's ready to come to your office so that we can get the ball rolling," she said with a sigh.

"Okay, bring her in and let's get this over with, but first shut the door and come here," I said.

She raised an eyebrow at me and did as I asked.

"Is everything okay?"

"Yes, everything is fine. I just wanted to take the time to assure you that I love you," I said as I walked to her and pulled her into my embrace.

She relaxed against my body and placed her had on my shoulder, "I know you love me, but it's always nice to hear it directly from you."

"Of course," I said as I placed a kiss on her forehead. "I'll do my best to get along with Charlotte. As long as she's nice and respects the both of us, then we will get along fine. I'll keep my claws put away."

"Great, now bring Charlotte in," I said and then gave her a light smack on her rear.

I took a deep breath to steady myself before we started the meeting. I wasn't exactly sure what to say once they both were in front of me, but I knew that we had to have a talk before we all worked together.

"Good morning Kyle," Charlotte said in an upbeat tone. A huge grin was spread across her face, "It's good to be back."

I gave her a brisk nod, "It's good to have you back, I'm sure that you've already met Camille. Please take a seat, the both of you," I said as I motioned to the seating area in my office.

They both took a seat on opposite ends of the couch. They're body language showed that they were tense and unsure of what was going on.

"I wanted to bring the both of you into a meeting today so that we can move forward and be as productive as possible."

They both nodded and looked at me intently. I felt my palms begin to sweat. I've lead meetings with some of the most influential people in my industry without sweat. I would rather stand before a crowd of 5,000 than in this room, but it needed to be done.

"Camille will continue in the capacity that she's in," I said to Charlotte.

"May I ask what capacity that is?" Charlotte asked.

"She handles communication with clientele, maintains my schedule, and is the first point of contact when people want to get in touch with me. She is my representation when I can't be somewhere."

"So what will I be responsible for?"

"You will handle my day to day affairs. You will get my coffee, laundry, do the set up for my meetings, create correspondence, and other duties as assigned," I said. "The bottom line is that we will all work closely together, the two of you are my eyes and ears and so it's imperative that you get along. Do either of you feel that this will be a problem?"

"That's not a problem for me; I look forward to working with you Charlotte. I'm glad you're here because doing it all on my own was driving me nuts," Camille laughed softly.

"Well that's what I'm here for. I hope to make both of your lives easier. I'm so grateful to Kyle for giving me another chance. I'm here strictly for work and if I can ever help you with something, please let me know. We're a team now," Charlotte said brightly.

"Well that's settled then," Camille said with a tight smile.

She obviously didn't care for Charlotte's choice of words, and I found myself second guessing my choice. I wouldn't know how it plays out until I gave it a chance.

"Charlotte we will see you bright and early. Camille has compiled a list of the things that need your immediate attention. Charlotte I need you to get Donald Alexander on the phone and route it to my office."

"I'll get on that right away after I give Charlotte the list," Camille said as she rose to her feet.

"I look forward to getting to work in the morning; I will see the both of you in the a.m." Charlotte said as she followed Camille out of my office.

I walked over to my crystal decanter and poured myself a short glass of my favorite scotch. I got through it, and I was happy that it was over. That was easier then I thought!

***

The sunlight shined brightly through my window, and I woke up to find Camille in the kitchen cooking me breakfast in one of the satin gowns that I purchased for her in Paris.

"I love the weekends," I said as I hugged her from behind as she cooked my steak.

She gave me a quick kiss on the cheek, "I love the weekends too. Now sit down, breakfast is almost ready."

I took a seat at the island in the middle of the kitchen and looked at all of the food.

"Are we expecting company?" I laughed.

"No, I just wasn't sure what you wanted so I decided to make everything."

"I think I'm going to eat a little bit of all of it. This is a breakfast that's fit for a king, now you're going to have to cook for me all the time."

"Don't get too comfortable," she said, "I was just in the mood this morning."

"Please tell me what I did to deserve this, so that I can do more of it."

She placed all of the food on the table before me and got us plates and utensils. I loaded up my plate with eggs, French toast, steak, and grapefruit slices. My stomach gave a deep growl in anticipation.

"I just wanted to let you know how much I appreciate you. Things have been going pretty smoothly over the last 3 month with Charlotte. I wasn't sure how things would go, and I was very skeptical about it all. But you've made the transition really smooth. I won't lie and say that there aren't times where I'm jealous because she gets to be with you so much, but I know that everything is kosher."

Her words warmed my soul. I was doing my best to be as transparent as possible about everything that was happening with Charlotte. I didn't want to give Camille any reason to feel threatened. Charlotte tried to flirt every now and then, but I put an abrupt end to it. It seems that all of us were settling into a comfortable flow, and they were working out in the way that I hoped.

"That's what matters babe, you mean the world to me and don't you ever forget that," I said.

She beamed at my statement and began to eat her food. I was one lucky man. I had the opportunity to wake up next to her on most mornings. She was my submissive, but she possessed an inner strength that was intoxicating to be around. She submits to me because it's what she wants to do, and she's doesn't shrink under my leadership. I've watched her flourish sexually and professionally, and it's been wonderful to watch.

She wears my collar around her neck everyday, and she never complains. In the beginning I would request that she put it on, and

I no longer have to ask. She belongs to me, and I'll cherish her for as long as she allows me to.

"What are you staring at?" She asked as she stuffed a piece of pancake into her mouth.

"I'm looking at you, I'm allowed to do that you know."

"Well if you're going to look, then you may as well touch," she said flirtatiously.

"Oh I'll touch you alright; I think your ass is still sore from all of the touching that I did last night."

"You may have a point," she grinned coyly.

"I know I do, so you may want to think twice before you challenge me."

"Oh believe me; I'm going to take that into consideration. It's already hard for me to sit down after you had so much fun with the flogger last night."

"Good."

#Chapter5

"Your head is on the block for this"
Kyle Kane Senior

My weekends always go by so fast, if it was up to me they would last forever. I've never looked forward to my weekends as much before I met Camille. She forces me to leave my house and to see what Chicago is all about. People assume that because of my wealth that I have a great quality of life. The truth is that I was a workaholic before I met her. I worked most weekends, and I fit sex into my schedule.

With Camille, I carved time out specifically for her, and I wanted her all to myself. She makes me feel selfish and protective. It's a different feeling, and I liked it. I wanted to be able to officially express my feelings for her, but running the company was holding me back from doing so.

I was already looking forward to going home because I wouldn't get the chance to see much of Camille. She was out tying up some loose ends for with a few clients and putting the finishing touches on a charity ball that would take place the next month.

"Good morning Mr. Kane," Charlotte said as she strolled into my office with my morning coffee.

"Good morning Charlotte," I responded after I took my first sip.

"Do you have some time this morning to speak with me?"

"Sure, I have about 20 minutes."

"Great," she sighed.

"Is everything okay?"

"Yes, everything is fine but I just wanted to warn you about Amanda."

"What do you mean?"

"Well apparently Amanda is super pissed off about the fact that she had to leave her job after she was served by your lawyer."

I nodded, "Well that's not my problem."

"Well it may be your problem soon because she's starting to spill the beans about you and Camille's relationship. She's also telling people about the kind of relationships that you've had with your previous assistants."

My blood began to boil, and the asshole inside of me wanted to completely ruin Amanda. I would call my lawyer today to start the proceedings against her. I wasn't just upset about her telling my personal business, but I was upset that this could hurt Camille. No woman wants to be portrayed as a man's sexual secret. She deserved better than that and people should have found out under different circumstances. I felt partially at fault, but I was determined to not let it stain Camille's reputation.

"Well thank you for letting me know Charlotte," I said to her coolly. You always have to look cool despite your inner feelings, that is just what an alpha male does.

"You're welcome; I had to be the first to tell you because I still care about you."

"I care for you as well, that won't change."

"I love working with you as closely as I do; it takes me back to before I left. I wish that things could be that way again."

Is she fucking serious? I leaned back in my chair, and I was instantly put into a bad mood, "We've gone through this and I thought that we had a clear understanding of what was happening between the both of us."

"I know I know," she said, "but you can't blame me for trying. I miss the way that you took control of me, fucked me on your desk, and tied me up. I don't know if I'll ever find another man like you."

"You should have considered that before you chose to leave. Now this is the situation that we're in, and nothing will change."

"I'm telling you right now, that you can have the both of us. I would never make you choose," she pleaded.

"I've already chosen. Can you please go get a pad of paper and a pen, I have some things that I need you to do today," I said.

She looked as if my words slapped her across the face. Her cheeks flushed and she had the decency to look embarrassed. I didn't want to be harsh to her, but she didn't seem to get the memo. Tough love was that she was going to understand, and if this didn't work then I would have to let her go. I didn't want to let her go because she was great at the job, and she was a nice person.

After I told her my needs for the day, I set about calling my lawyer. I didn't want things to get ugly with Amanda, but it seems that she wasn't going to be happy until we had a bitter court show down. If that's what she wanted, then I would crush her. I tried my best to avoid it, but it seemed to be inevitable.

The rest of my day went as expected and I rushed home to be in the arms of the woman that I loved. She was without a doubt the best part of my day. When I entered the house she was naked and sipping a glass of wine. Yum!

"Oh well good evening to me," I said to her.

She smiled when she saw me walk into the front room.

"Hello sir," she said as she rose to her feet to greet me with a kiss and a hug.

She smelled like lavender, and it instantly calmed me. Her body molded perfectly to my own.

"I feel overdressed," she said as she unbuckled my belt, "We're going to have to correct that."

Within seconds I was naked like her, and she got to her knees before me. Her warm mouth enveloped my cock. I moaned as I enjoyed the feeling of her mouth surrounding me, she hungrily sucked me as if she's been waiting for this moment all day. I grabbed her head and pushed deeper into her mouth. I was serenaded to the sounds of her slurping my cock; I pulled away before I came prematurely.

 I sat on the couch, and she straddled me. I looked at her in the eyes and pushed her hair back from her face. Her perfect dark complexion was stunning, and her almond shaped eyes drew me in. She guided my cock to her tight entrance, and I took a quick intake of breath in anticipation of what was to come. She slowly lowered onto me; my cock invaded her velvety walls, forcing them to spread apart to accommodate me.

Her head lay against my shoulder, and I could feel her breath on my face as she rode me to in a slow sensual rhythm. I grabbed her ample hips and lifted to meet her thrust for thrust. Her body was supple, and I would never get enough of touching it. She was larger than all of the women that I've ever been with, and I don't think that I could ever go back to a size two.

Her pace increased, and she was no longer with me. She was in a place of her own ecstasy, but I was reaping the benefits. I leaned my head back against the couch I pushed deep inside of her, and her pussy convulsed on my cock as she imploded around me. Her creamy coating covered me, and I joined her. My balls tightened, and I exploded inside of her warmth.

We stayed in that position for what felt like minutes in complete contentment.

"You sure know how to greet a man," I laughed.

"You inspire me," she smiled.

***

I finished up a meeting with my executive staff, and headed for my office. It had already been a long day but it was about to get even longer.

"Kyle Kane Senior is in your office Sir," Charlotte said as she went to help Camille on a project.

I wondered what would cause my father to drop by unannounced. He's the master of protocol and would call for an appointment if he was going to see me during the work day. I knew that there must have been something important that he wanted to discuss.

"Hi father, this is a surprise."

"Hello Kyle," he said curtly sitting in my own seat, "Come and have a seat," he pointed to the chair across from him.

I was transported back in time, back to when the office used to belong to him. I suddenly felt like this was no longer my turf. Technically everything still belonged to him. He was the owner, and I'm the acting CEO, but I'm accustomed to having full reign.

"What's going on?" I said as I sat down.

"Why haven't you told me about the trouble that your old assistant Amanda has been causing?" he asked.

"I didn't want to trouble you with petty information like that," I said, "It's being handled and so there was really no need."

He gave a slight grunt, "No need my ass, obviously there was a need. If this information got back to me then that means that she's a problem. She's leaked information. You took it too easy on her, and she ran her mouth. Your head is on the block for this Kyle.."

"Like I said, I'm handling it. I was doing my best to be civil and that didn't work so I'm working on a different approach."

"Maybe you've been too busy with other, erm, things."

My temperature went up a few degrees because I knew that the "things" that he was referring to was Camille.

"Now that you're here dad, I've wanted to talk to you about that. I plan on going public with Camille."

"There is no need in going public with someone you're not serious about," my dad scoffed.

"I thought that I've made it quite clear that I'm serious about her. I've let you, and the rest of the family know just how much she means to me."

"Oh you mean that little charade you pulled months back? We didn't think that you were serious; we figured that you were just trying to keep her around. I can't say that I blame you; she's a hot little number. If I were 30 years younger I would do the same... But you can't go public with this relationship; I think that it will be a potential disaster. The shareholders are nervous enough as it is at the moment."

"I understand that people may not like it at first but they will get used to it."

"I really don't understand why you're trying to parade your girlfriend around. The both of you seem to get along well enough, there's no need for the rest. You're staying together, and she works with you every day. You give her the best of everything from what I hear. What more could she possibly want?"

"She wants all of me, and I don't want her to be a secret. I should be able to let people know who she is to me. I don't want to hide it anymore, I'm not going to hide it anymore," I said as my pulse raced.

Me and my dad sat and stared each other down. I seldom opposed his wishes; he was a dad that led his household with an iron fist. He was used to complete compliance from his children, and we usually obliged him. But I couldn't let him walk all over me when it came to my relationship with Camille. I had to stand up for my relationship or he would try to dictate to me forever.

"Listen here son;" my dad said slowly, "The bottom line is that it's too risky of a situation. I allowed you to take over because I thought that you would do a good job despite your youth. Being the boss means putting the company before your own personal interest. I had to make huge sacrifices in order to get where we are today. Now it's time for you to make some sacrifice as well, and this isn't a big one."

I listened intently to his words and understood what he meant, but everything within me was saying it was the right thing to do. I needed to listen to my heart for once in my life.

"Trust me dad, I understand all about sacrifices. That's what I've done all my life to get to this position. I've worked my ass off to be worthy of taking over the company. But I plan on moving forward with this. I think that it's best for me, I love her."

"Kyle, you are not listening to me. This is a critical time for the company, and because of you and your personal life getting out of hand, our competition is trying to poach clients from us. It looks like some of them may succeed," he said raising his voice. "We have an image to uphold and that's all American. Can you imagine what they'll think if they find out whom you're dating? To make matters worse, she's your assistant too. This entire situation looks sleazy and this will not represent well on the company."

I tried to contain my anger. My father had a lot of nerve to speak about my life. It was a well known fact that he had more than a working relationship with his assistants. If Camille was white he probably would have no problem. He had no right to judge me or to tell me how to live my life.

"There is nothing sleazy about my relationship with Camille. I told you what I planned on doing out of courtesy, and I'm not asking for your permission."

My dad sighed, "I didn't want it to come to this, but if you push me I will replace you Kyle. I gave you this position, and I will remove you. Do not test me. You think long and hard about what you want to do. Now, what's your decision?"

I was in between a rock and a hard place.

For now, it was probably best to just agree with my father and work out a plan later on. He clearly was not going to take no for answer right now.

#Chapter6

"I know you want my man."
Camille

Two steps forward, one step back. That's how my relationship with Kyle felt sometimes. I was really happy with him, and he was being so attentive. I had everything that I wanted except public recognition. I hated that small feeling inside me that I was just his little "secret" and he would be ready to drop me for the first hot white blonde that comes along. No matter how much I tried to tell myself to get over it, I just couldn't. But my love for him kept me around. He was so good to me, and he asked me to be patient, so I was determined to give him the time that he needed.

So now I'm here in the conference room confirming the guest list for the gala with Charlotte. She and I weren't friends, but we weren't enemies either. I had the suspicion that she was still in love with Kyle. You can never trust the intentions of a bitch that wants your man. She reminded me of Amanda, and I wanted to bring it up to Kyle but then I would seem like I was causing drama. You can't tell a man that his judgment was bad two times in a row. That would be too much for his ego to take.

"So how are things going with you and Kyle?" Charlotte asked.

"What do you mean?" I responded.

"You know what I mean," she laughed, "We've never talked about it but I know about your relationship with him."

I felt dread settling in the pit of my stomach because I knew that the conversation wasn't going to turn out well for either of us. There was a reason that I never discussed my relationship with Kyle with her. It wasn't her business, and it wasn't appropriate.

"I know that you're privy to our relationship, I just don't understand why you want to know about it. It just seems inappropriate for you to ask me a question like that."

She gave a sly grin, "Aww come on, don't be like that. I was just checking to see if he treats you the same that way he treated me. I figured that we could compare notes you know…girl talk."

One thing that every black girl knows is that you don't talk to another woman about your man. You definitely don't tell his ex about our relationship. Charlotte must have thought that I had stupid and naïve written on my forehead. She was proving to be the manipulative bitch that I pegged her for.

"There will be no girl talk," I laughed, "I know you want my man." She looked taken aback by my forwardness, and I could see the wheels turning in her head. She was trying to figure out what to say next.

"Well, even if I did want him it doesn't matter. He made it quite clear when I was at his apartment that we would have a business relationship."

Her words cut into me like a knife. I know that she intentionally tried to hurt me with her admission, and I chose not to go for her jugular. But I had to know when she was at his place.

"When were you at his apartment?"

"Oh, It was the week before he hired me, I came to his apartment around midnight and we had a long conversation. The next Monday he hired me. I was hoping that we could be more, but he has you," she said with disgust.

"You're right he does have me."

"You know that the both of you are never going last right? He's using you and as soon as he gets tired, you're going back to where ever your came from. It has happened a million times before..."

"You sure are bitter for someone that claims to know her place," I said.

"I am a little bitter because you're only around because I chose to leave. Kyle and I were happy, and we can be happy again if you would just go away. We're meant for each other, he and I can have a real future, and you're messing it up. Do us and yourself a favor by going away."

I closed my eyes and took a deep breath. Her words were full of a lot of my insecurities, and I couldn't let her know that she was getting to me. I was afraid that Kyle wasn't going public with our relationship because he was ashamed of me. There was no way that a man like him would settle down with a woman like me. We were opposites in so many ways and not just in skin color. My background and upbringing was so different, Kyle would be shocked if he knew the truth about what I used to get up to when I was younger.

"This conversation between us is over, and you better tread lightly. You don't want to suffer the same fate as bitter Amanda. I'm not going anywhere, but you're expendable, so don't you ever forget that," I said as I rose to my feet.

I walked out of the conference room, and I was happy to have some space between her and I. She was safer while a door was between us. I had to find Kyle to tell him what was going on. I needed to vent, and I needed some answers from him. Like, why would he allow her to come to his apartment at midnight and never tell me? He had plenty of opportunities to tell me what happened but he never told me the truth. This worried me.

I walked to his office, and the door was cracked. I was about to open it to see if he was alone, but I heard another voice from the inside of the door. He wasn't scheduled for a meeting so I was a little surprised. I was going to walk away, but I heard my name mentioned.

"Well I am glad you agree son. No one outside of the family needs to know about your relationship with Camille."

"Yes sir," Kyle said.

"I'm happy to see that you're thinking with your brain again and not the part down below," his father laughed.

"Well at the end of the day, I want to do what's best for the company. Nothing means more to me than that. It's my legacy, and I'll do whatever it takes."

His father sighed, "If it was anyone else, I would have allowed you to go public. But we just can't afford a move like this one."

"Okay dad, we don't have to talk about it anymore. Let's talk about what's next for us."

I stood frozen outside of the door. I couldn't hear what was being said anymore. I was lost in my own thoughts. He was never going to tell anyone about me and our relationship wasn't going to go anywhere. My fears were proving to be true. As much as I didn't want to admit it, Charlotte was right. The color of my skin was a huge barrier between Kyle and I, and it was one that we wouldn't be able to cross.

***

Getting through the rest of the day was torture. I had to smile and pretend like everything was okay but inside I felt sick. I went to Kyle's apartment in a separate cab at soon at the clock struck 6 p.m. I wanted to gather my things and take them back to my apartment. But I had to speak with him before I chose to leave. I wouldn't storm out like I did before; he deserved a chance to prove me wrong. I hoped like hell that he would surprise me but I did not feel confident he would.

I sat nervously on the couch and waited for him to arrive. It felt like the longest half hour of my life. He and I had grown so close over the time that we've been together, and I didn't want to throw it all away. But I could no longer compromise my wants and needs to be with him. His father didn't respect our relationship, and I was willing to bet that his family didn't either. I felt like a complete fool.

I heard the elevator open, and Kyle walked in, he looked downtrodden, and my instinct was to hug him, but I couldn't put his feelings over my own.

"Hey," he said, "It would have been nice if you told me that you were leaving. I had to find out from Charlotte. She said that you were upset. What's wrong?"

"Why didn't you tell me that Charlotte was here in your apartment?" I asked.

He stared at me, and a myriad of expressions flashed across his face.

"Camille, any other day I could tolerate this kind of conversation but today I just can't. It's been a long day and I just want a drink and I want to relax. We can have this conversation later."

"No, we have to have it now. I need to know why you kept it from me Kyle."

"So Charlotte told you that she was here huh?" he asked in disbelief. "She promised that she wasn't going to bring any drama to my damned office. I'm such an idiot, again," he said to himself.

"That doesn't answer my question."

"I didn't keep it from you to hurt you. I kept it from you because I didn't want you to feel insecure about it. Nothing happened between the both of us and so there was no need for you to worry about it. I don't want her, I want you, and that's why you're here with me instead of her. I thought we had been through this.." he said with a hint of annoyance in his voice.

"Kyle I-I can't do this anymore," I said.

I felt exhausted, and I didn't want to fight with him. I didn't want to feel hidden anymore. I wanted peace in my life and it wasn't with him. I deserved to be with someone that wasn't afraid to tell everyone about me. Even if it meant going back to my loser ex at least I would feel respected.

"What do you mean when you say that?"

"I heard the conversation between you and your father," I admitted, "I can't be your secret anymore. I deserve more than this."

"You promised that you would stick it out with me."

"For how long Kyle?" I yelled, "Because it seems like you're asking me to do it indefinitely."

"You know that I would never do that you," he responded.

"Do I?" I asked, "Prove it to me then. Let everyone know who we really are to each other, and I'll stay. I'll stick with you through everything; nothing will be able to keep me away. I'll give you all of me, but first I need to know that you're willing to do the same for me."

Kyle went completely still, and it looked like he was fighting a war within himself. My heart felt like it was about to beat out of my chest, as I waited for him to respond. What was he thinking? Why wouldn't he give me what I needed?

"I love you Camille, but that's just something that I can't do right now. I'm sorry that we can't work this out, but the fact is that things just have to be this way. If you can't stick through it with me, then we have to end this part of our relationship."

"Really? That's what I get? A dismissal as if our relationship is a business transaction. I'm done Kyle. I'm done with everything, I can't take anymore."

I reach up to my neck and undid the clasp of my necklace, I sat it on the coffee table and walked away to gather my things. I only grabbed the items that I purchased with my own money. I didn't want any reminders of him inside of my apartment.

"I hope that we will be able to work together without this affecting our work relationship."

"You really don't get it do you?" I asked in disbelief, "I'm resigning as your personal assistant. I can't be around you every day and not be with you. All I ask from you is that you give me a good personal reference. I've delivered quality work, so please don't screw me over. I won't work for any of your competitors, and I won't expose our secret relationship to anyone."

His face showed a pained expression. He looked like he had so much to say, but he didn't let me know what he was thinking. He just watched me helplessly as I packed my clothes and sat them by the door. I called downstairs and asked for them to bring my car to the front.

"Camille, please don't do this," he whispered.

"Are you going to give me what I need?" I asked.

"I can't right now," he responded.

"Then there really isn't anything left to say."

I walked to him and kissed him on the cheek, grabbed my bags and walked to the elevator. My heart sank with each floor, and my walk to the car felt like I was walking the green mile. The life that I saw for myself was getting the electric chair. I climbed in my car, and released the tears that I'd been holding for most of the day.

I mourned the life that I wanted, but now I would never have.

#Chapter7

"I don't really know what to say."
Camille

The last month has been complete torture. The only thing that has held me together has been the love of my friends. The first week I didn't leave my apartment and I was surviving on takeout food and wine. Did you know that you can get some stores to deliver to your door these days? That was right up my alley.

A ridiculous amount of money showed up in my bank account, and my car note was paid off. I knew that Kyle did it and I was grateful but it all made me feel so damned cheap. I wanted to apply for jobs again but I couldn't bring myself to do it, and at this point I wouldn't have to work for a while if I didn't want to. Not that I would but it seemed like a good though right now.

The first people that I contacted were my friends and within a week they were in my apartment grabbing my clothes and telling me that I was coming with them. I fought it at first but then I realized that it may be best for me. Hell, at least they cooked and they were on a health kick, so it would keep me from eating so much crap.

My life felt like it had come full circle. I was back on the West-side of Chicago and I saw a lot of familiar faces because Sandy refused to let me stay in the house all day. We went shopping, got our hair done, nails done, and went to local bars whenever she was off work and at home. I was a crying mess whenever she wasn't there with me, and then Cynthia would show up and keep me occupied. I wasn't sure if it was a good or bad thing. A part of me felt like I needed to cry and another part of me felt like I'd cried enough.

I missed Kyle so much and my nights were the worst. He always held me so tight at night, and I'd come to find comfort in his embrace. I didn't realize how much I needed him; I couldn't even get a good night's sleep. He'd tried to contact me but I avoided his calls. I took the first few with the hope that he'd changed his mind about us but he was singing the tune. He wanted to be with me and he was asking me to be a patient and wait until the time was right. Whenever that would be.

I wanted to run back to him but I couldn't allow myself to do it. I deserved to not be someone's secret, and if he was going to be with me, then it had to be out in the open. I deserved better then that. My stomach still twisted when I thought of the words that his father said. It was clear that he didn't respect me and that hurt because it was purely based off of the color of my skin and my background. I didn't have control over those things but I was actively working to better myself.

None of that mattered to him though. He was more interested in looking like an "All American," and that image didn't include a person like me. The way that his father felt about me hurt, but what hurt the most was that Kyle didn't take up for me. He was just like his dad, and the bottom line was the most important to him. I understood that they may lose some clientele but they wouldn't go bankrupt. They would still be filthy rich and they may even get a different customer base because of their level of diversity.

But I refused to plead my case to the either of them. If they didn't want me around because they were ashamed of me, then I wasn't going to fight to stay. I have too much self respect and dignity for that. There is no amount of money that could make me compromise my self-worth. I would have to learn how to live my life without Kyle.

"Come on Camille, it's time for us to get out of here," Sandy said while opening the blinds of the room.

The sunlight poured into the room and my dark Oasis was a distant memory. I wanted to lash out at her for ruining my solitude but I knew that she was doing it because she loved me. I sighed and sat up in my bed.

"What do you want to do today?" I asked groggily.

"Today I want to rearrange my front room furniture so that I can buy a new couch. The one that's in there is being put out back today. It's time to upgrade darling,"

"I hope you don't think that I'm going to help you move that big ass 1980's couch to the alley."

She smacked her lips, "Shut up, don't talk about my couch. My granny gave it to me and I'm a little sad but it has to get out of here."

I laughed, "Fine, I'll leave your granny's couch alone. But you still didn't answer my question."

"Well that's the thing, I don't really want to tell you and that's why I was avoiding the question," her eyes widened and it was filled with amusement and nervousness.

"So you think I'm about to risk a hernia trying to help you get that couch out of this house?"

"Of course not," she said, "Marcus and his friends are coming to move it," she said quickly and then covered her face with her hands. She peeked out to see my reaction.

I flung myself back onto the bed dramatically, "Why would you do that Sandy? You could have called anyone else. Why would you call my ex-boyfriend?"

"I tried to call around to see who could help me today but no one was available during the day. He was the only one that was willing to come by here and bring people, for free. I need him Camille, I'm sorry. You can stay in the room if you want and you'll never have to see him."

"Does he know that I'm here?" I asked.

"Everyone knows that you're here. People have been seeing you out and about with me and Cynthia, so of course it's already gotten back to Marcus."

"I don't need this drama right now, I'm mad at you."

"I know you're mad at me but hopefully I can make it up to you by taking you to Pink Berry after we find my couch?"

"Don't think that you're getting off that easy skank. You're going to take me to Pink Berry before we find you a new couch, and then we're going to Cold Stones after."

"Deal," she said quickly.

I suddenly thought that I let her off of the hook too easily.

"When will they be here?"

"They'll be here within an hour."

I gave her the stare of death and pulled the covers over my head. Sometimes friends sucked. I decided that I didn't want to be around at all while Marcus was at the house. I rushed to the bathroom to freshen up and make myself presentable to the world. I was going to go to the diner that Cynthia worked at and have breakfast.

I walked out of the door and Marcus was coming up the stairs. I fought the urge to run past him to my car.

"Hey Cam," he said with a crooked smile.

"Hi Marcus," I said as I continued down the stairs, "Where are your friends?"

"They'll be here in a few minutes."

"Oh okay, it was good seeing you," I said as I walked past him towards my car.

"So it's going to be like this between the both of us now?"

"Like what Marcus?"

"Like this. Like you not talking to me. I thought that we were friends, we've been through too much together to let it all go to hell."

"I don't know how to be your friend anymore. I just don't think that's a feasible option for us."

"Oooh 'feasible,'", he said mocking me.

"Whatever Marcus, don't rip on me just because my vocabulary is bigger than yours."

"Hanging out with that white boy has really fucked your head up. Bet you think you are better then all of us now don't you??" he spat.

"Ah, there we go. The real Marcus is coming out. I changed long before I ever met him actually and so don't act like he's the reason that we aren't together. You made your choice, now go run back to your raggedy low class baby mama."

He gave an evil grin, "So white boy didn't choose you either huh? That's why you're here right?"

I opened my mouth to say something but then closed it. Tears welled up in my eyes and for the first time in a month, I let someone see me cry. Marcus' words pierced my heart and they hurt like hell.

"Screw you," I said and walked to my car.

"Wait," he said as he grabbed my arm and pulled me into his embrace. "I'm so sorry; I never should have said that bullshit. I was just trying to hurt you because I miss you so much. I really thought that we would end up getting back together. And honestly, my life sucks without you."

I sniffled against his shirt and accepted his comfort. His body enveloped mines and I continued to ball. My body was wracked with tears and I began to shake uncontrollably. All of my emotional hurt and pain washed over me like a tsunami.

"Whoa, Camille, so what happened with you and him?"

"He doesn't want me," I cried, "Not in the way that I want. He wants to keep me a secret. I gave him an ultimatum and he didn't choose me. What's wrong with me? Why am I never good enough?"

"That's not true," he said as he smoothed my hair with his hand, "You're more than enough. You are what every man wants and needs in his life. You are a diamond baby. What's fucked up is that men don't appreciate it until they lose it. But don't ever say that you're not good enough."

I slowly regained my composure and pulled away. I was reminded of why I loved Marcus. He could be an asshole to the outside world but on the inside he was kind and compassionate. He took great care of me and I didn't know where I would be without his presence in my life when we were younger.

"I'm sorry that I didn't respond to your calls or texts. But I didn't know how to tell you that I couldn't be in a relationship with you anymore. What you did hurt me and I can't recover from that. I can't be with you and you had a baby with someone else. You also aren't showing any signs of giving up your lifestyle."

"It's hard for me to admit," he sighed, "But you're right. I would hate myself if anything happened to you because of my life. I have a baby and I have to provide for him and this is the only way that I know how. I also know that you don't want to have to deal with my "raggedy low class baby mama". I don't fault you for that."

"I'm glad that you understand."

"If I could take it back I would. I would have appreciated you a lot more when I had you. I can't take my choices back but please know that I'm sorry. If you ever wanted to give the two of us another try, I would do it in a heartbeat."

"You can't give me what I want, a life free of drugs and illegal activity."

"I would if I could but this is my life. I've built it from the ground up and the money is damned good. I have to live."

I wanted to tell him that he didn't have to live that way. I didn't want to run down the statistics on men that lived their life in the way that he did. In my heart I knew that he would end up in prison or dead within the next ten years. But every person in the drug trade thinks that they're untouchable and that they won't end up like all of the men and women before them. I didn't want to ruin our moment and so I let it go.

"I understand. Just know that I care about you and that won't ever change."

"That's good to know," he said as he kissed me on my cheek.

I walked to my car, fixed my face, and went to the diner. I could use a good meal at this point, and I wanted a drink too but they didn't serve alcohol.

Sometimes a girl can't have everything.

***

"That's great," Cynthia said, "You and Marcus really needed a heart to heart. It was long overdue. Everyone knows that you love each other and so I'm happy that the two of you made up. You will probably never be the best of friends, but there's no need to hate each other."

"I agree. I just can't believe he made me cry like that. I hate that he still has a hold over me."

She laughed, "You're right about that but then he turned into a big ass softy as soon as he saw your tears. You can be pretty rough too Camille, so I know you said some mean stuff to him too. He was just striking back."

"You're right, I called his baby mama raggedy and low class," I laughed.

"See what I mean."

"Well the hoe is raggedy and low class. She's gutter trash and everyone knows it. I don't know what he was thinking messing around with her."

"It seems like men flock to those kinds of chicks and then they want to come back to us after they've had their fun."

"Exactly, and I'm not going to put up with it. But I wish him and her all the best. I'm sure there will be a lot of broken windows and slashed tires in his future," I giggled.

"She slashed the tires on his Audi two month ago and he was super pissed."

"Now you see what I mean," I said in disbelief, "If I was with him, she would be slashing my tires and I would have to kill her. I don't want to be ghetto but she would bring it out in me and it wouldn't be pretty."

"True and you're too pretty to act so ugly."

I laughed and looked at my phone. I had 4 missed calls and they were all from Sandy. I read her text message.

To: Camille
From: Sandy
Girl get back here as soon as you can. It's like a circus outside.

"I have to go," I told Cynthia.

"Is everything okay?" She asked.

"I'm not sure, but I have to see what's going on at the Sandy's."

"Okay, my break is over anyway but call or text me as soon as you can. Keep me updated on what's going on. You're worrying me."

"I will," I said and kissed her on the cheek before I headed out of the door.

I tried to call Sandy back but she didn't answer her phone. I drove faster than I normally would to get back to her place and prayed that nothing horrible had happened. What was it now? A rape? A murder? A drive by?

I had to get my friends out of that shitty neighborhood. We deserved to live a life without fear of getting shot and killed every damned day. I cursed myself for not getting them to move sooner and asked God to take care of everything.

When I pulled up to her house there were at least 5 reporters with cameras outside of her house. Thankfully, no cops. My stomach dropped because I didn't see her anywhere. I barely parked my car, pulled my keys out, and ran past the reporters and up the stairs. I needed to find my friend.

"Camille! Camille!," the reporters yelled.

How in the hell did they know my name? I turned to them.

"How does it feel to be the love interest of a billionaire?" One of them yelled.

Cameras flashed and I couldn't tame my stunned expression. What in the hell was going on? I used my key and entered the house.

"Thank God you're here!" Sandy exclaimed, "They've been out there for a half hour."

Relief flooded my body when I saw that my friend was alive and well.

"What is happening?"

She gave a grin, "You have a visitor."

I looked behind her and Kyle was sitting on a chair in the corner. My throat went dry and I was speechless.

"Hi Camille," he said as he stood up.

"What are you doing here?"

"I came to talk to you."

"How did you find me here?"

"It is always easy to find someone when you have my resources..."

"What in the hell are all of those cameras doing outside? I was thinking that something happened to my friend."

"I'm sorry about that," he said, "But I wanted to let you know just how serious I am about you."

"What do you mean?"

"I just want to say that I'm sorry for being such a damned coward. I did stick up for us with my father but I folded under all of the pressure. I shouldn't have done that. You're the best thing to ever happen to me and I let money and the potential loss of power get in the way of us being together. I've realized that none of that matters if I can't have you."

"I need for you to spell it out for me, I don't want to get my hopes up and you're just asking me to wait some more."

"Geesh Camille, I have the media outside," he laughed, "It doesn't get any more public than that."

"You have a point," I smiled.

Was this situation real? Everything was happening so fast. Over an hour ago I was crying in Marcus' arms about how Kyle didn't want me and now he was here and willing to give me what I wanted.

"I don't really know what to say," I admitted.

"Say yes," he said with a whisper as he got down on one knee and presented a ring to me. Not just any ring but a huge ring that looked vintage. My eyes widened when I saw it.

"It was my great grandmother's, and my grandmother gave it to me. She told me to give it to the woman that I planned on spending the rest of my life with. This won't be easy Camille. Some people won't like that we're together and we'll have some obstacles, but I'm willing to do it for you. I can promise that I won't allow anyone to disrespect you and that I'll always stand up for our love."

"If you don't say yes girl, I'm going to marry him," Sandy mumbled.

"Hush," I said in her direction.

"Yes kyle. Of course, I would love to marry you." Tears began pouring down my face for the second time today, this time for a good reason.

He placed the ring on my finger and my heart swelled. I was going to be Mrs. Camille Kane, and the thought absolutely blew my mind. Tears streamed down my cheeks and he rose to give me a kiss. Our lips meshed together perfectly and I melted into his body. I was where I belonged again and life couldn't get anymore perfect.

"Whoooooo!!!!!!!" Sandy shrieked, "I gotta call Cynthia. She's going to die when she finds out."

"Okay," he said as he grabbed my hand. "Are you ready?"

"Ready for what?" I said in confusion.

"To go out there," he motioned towards the door.

I forgot that the media was outside. I got nervous because I had no clue what to say to them.

"Don't worry, I'll do the talking. You just smile and look pretty for the photos. This will be front page news in a lot of the press tomorrow. So you want to be looking good!" he said, partially soothing my fears.

"Okay, then I'm ready," I gripped his hand tighter and we walked outside to let the entire world know about our love.

I could not believe it. I was engaged to a billionaire.

My dreams were finally coming true...

Epilogue

Posing for the press was an amazing experience. I really felt like a celebrity.

Waking up the morning, next to the man I loved was the best thing ever. He held me tight all night and I woke up to him showering my body with kisses. His personal chef came by to cook us breakfast. I enjoyed my mimosa and stuffed French toast.

"I'm the luckiest man in the world," he exclaimed.

"That makes two of us. I must have done something right in my past lives. You mean so much to me."

"I still can't believe that you left all of your stuff here," he laughed, "That was pure torture. I had to take all of your clothes and put them away so that I could get through the day."

"Well I couldn't take it with me, I didn't want any reminders of you. My life was hard enough without seeing parts of you everywhere."

"Oh," he said changing the subject, "I just want you to know that I've fired Charlotte."

"And another one bites the dust," I said as I rolled my eyes.

"I have a new personal assistant and I'll have to hire one more."

"So I won't be getting my job back?"

"No, you won't be getting your job back," he said. "I would rather you open your own business and do something that belongs exclusively to you."

My eyes widened, "Are you serious? I don't even know what I would do."

"Well you have time to think about it but I think that you would make one hell of a consultant. Businesses will be fighting to get your advice on how to enlarge their client base."

"I don't know, I feel like I want to get formally educated first."

"No amount of school can beat what you have in experience. But if you want to go back to school then do it. Pick any one you want, that's in Chicago."

An entirely different world was opening up to me and I was excited for my future.

"Wait a minute, who is your assistant. I'm going to have to meet her. We haven't had the best of luck with your choices."

"Fine, you can meet *him*," he said.

"It's a male?" I said in disbelief.

"Yes, his name is Jacob. I figured female personal assistants are just trouble for me. I either fire them or end up proposing to them." Kyle laughed. "I figured that you could hire the second one."

"Now that I can definitely do," I said as I beamed from ear to ear.

"Babe I'm going to get in the shower because I'm still all sticky from last night," he grinned. "Feel free to join me after you finish eating."

He kissed me and then headed for the shower.

I reached for the newspaper and flipped my way through it. In the local living section there was a huge picture of me and Kyle, not quite the front page but it will do.

My mood instantly changed when I saw the headline that was written alongside it. I was shocked. Horrified. Sick to my stomach.

I could not let Kyle see this so I ripped it up and threw it in the garbage.

I sighed as I knew that this would not get rid of it for good. This would only delay the inevitable. I had to face up to the reality that my past was now going to come back to haunt me.

And I don't think Kyle will like what he is going to discover...

The End

#Book3

SUBMITTING TO THE
THE
WHITE BILLIONAIRE

#Chapter1

"I suddenly wished that I was holding a glass of vodka instead of caffeine."
Camille

Some say that relationships tend to drift before they end but I still remember the precise moment I knew that me and Marcus were definitely over...

"So what did he say?" Marcus asked me.

"He said to meet him at the lakefront on 43rd tomorrow at 10 pm. and he'll get it to you then."

I watched Marcus give a huge sigh of relief.

"I swear you're my lucky charm," he said as he gave me a passionate kiss once we stepped into his apartment.

"Well you know that I've got you. Jay is going to be pissed that we stole his connection though. Are you ready for that kind of heat?"

"That's not for you to worry about," he said as he began to prep a bowl of weed.

My nerves were on the edge because I'd just finished a meeting with one of the largest distributors of crack in the city. I didn't want to go, but Marcus was convinced that it needed to be our next move. The problem was that we had to steal that connection from our largest rival. My body was tense, and I couldn't wait until Marcus finished packing the bowl. I needed to feel the calm that only the drugs could provide.

"I know that it's not my issue, but I worry about you. I'm scared that you're getting in over your head. I don't want to lose you to some bullshit Marcus, you know I love you."

He shook his head dismissively and placed the lighter to the bowl before taking a long pull. He motioned for me to come over, and he placed his lips to mine. I slowly inhaled as he released the piney pungent smoke into my mouth. I closed my eyes and held my breath for a few moments before I exhaled.

"See baby, I've got this. You just continue doing your part and I'll do mine. Now let's take a seat, finish this bowl, and then really celebrate," he grinned as he cupped my center with his free hand. "That sounds like a plan," I replied as I took the bowl from him and sat on the couch.

I tried to mentally shake the image of him dying from my head. I knew that it wasn't the right time to discuss something like that with him. We were now into the drug game way too deep, and it was something that we promised we would never do. I stared at the huge smile on his face, and I knew that I was losing him. I knew I could not continue doing this.

***

My mind drifted back to present day reality and my stomach twisted and turned as I thought about the life that I led with Marcus. I couldn't help but wonder if all of those things would come back to haunt me. I'd done my best to distance myself from that life, but it all has a way of creeping back to bite you on the ass. I just wanted to live my life with Kyle and to continue to make positive choices for myself.

Reading the papers hasn't helped me in this endeavor. The headlines served as a constant reminder of where I've come from. Pictures of me have been pulled from my Facebook page, and I've been dubbed the "*Urban Cinderella*" in the newspapers and on blogs. I never thought that I would regret the club photos that I'd taken with my friends but now they are a source of shame. They depicted me as if I was some sort of ghetto hood rat. The "*Urban Cinderella*" title was one of the milder headlines. The headlines weren't outright racist, but the undertones screamed from the pages.

"Good morning babe," Kyle said as he stepped into the dining area wearing nothing but a towel.

I quickly folded the papers up and sat them to the side, closed my laptop, and sipped my coffee. Looking at him made me give a slight smile. I loved to watch him walk around the house half naked. But not even that would cheer me up because my mind was occupied with thoughts of the media. I didn't feel comfortable talking to him about how I felt regarding what everyone was saying. I wasn't ready to verbally acknowledge it yet.

"Good Morning Mr. Kane," I responded as I rose to my feet and kissed him on the cheek.

He wrapped his arms around me, and I relaxed within his embrace. His arms had become my solace and my safe place. I didn't need to be protected from the world, but it was nice to have a place to rest when I needed it.

"You had breakfast without me?" He asked.

"I'm sorry but I wanted to get an early start on the day. It's beautiful out, and I'm just going to get some girly stuff done."

"Alright, don't stay out too long. I have plans for us today."

"I know, I'll be back by 3."

"Good, I'll see you then. I'm looking forward to our day out."

"Me too," I said as I gave him my best smile.

I rose from the table, gathered my belongings, and headed out of the door. The truth was that I really just wanted to be able to look at everything in peace. It was some sort of cruel torture that I was putting myself through, but it was a compulsion. I had to read everything that people were saying about me. I settled at a local coffee shop, ordered a cappuccino, and took a seat in one of the comfortable seats in the corner.

I pulled out my iPad and began to read the news stories that dealt with my relationship. They all had the same tone. They were surprised that a billionaire was marrying a lower class black woman. Everyone wanted to know where I'd come from, and they all highlighted my background. My own mother was even quoted in a few of the stories. She spoke about how hard it was to raise me in an impoverished area, but she did her best. She went on to say how proud she was of me and then she credited her parenting.

I gave a shake of my head. My mother was a terrible parent, and she was the reason I had to help Marcus sell drugs. I'd gotten to where I was in spite of my mother, not because of her. She was too preoccupied with being an alcoholic coke head to bother with her parental responsibilities. She had a lot of nerve speaking to the press about me. But the only reason that she was being favorable was because she was hoping that I would give her some money.

I still wasn't in the place mentally to deal with her. Now that she'd figured out that I was marrying a billionaire, she probably thinks that I'm going to be her cash cow. Kyle offered to give her a place and a monthly spend, but I declined. She'd never taken care of me so why should I take care of her? The only thing that I would invest in for her was a quality rehab program. I knew that it was something that she would most likely refuse. She wasn't ready to give up her vices, and she would probably never be. I've come to accept that about her, and it no longer bothers me.

I checked my local twitter trending topics, and I saw that *Kyle Kane* was trending. My heart lurched as I read the things that people were saying. It was mainly young girls calling me a slut and saying that he could do so much better. Some even tweeted me personally to express their disdain. I suddenly wished that I was holding a glass of vodka instead of caffeine. I hoped that my life wasn't always going to be this way. I didn't plan on falling in love with Kyle, and I shouldn't have been attacked for it. My head was telling me that they were just jealous bigots, but my heart was hurt. I wondered if Kyle had read any of the negative press that we were getting. I had to assume that he was because he wasn't hiding beneath a rock. He was always aware of things that were going on. I opened the Kindle app on my iPad to read a *Lena Skye* novel to take my mind off of things but even that was not working. I put my iPad away and decided to get a pedicure and a manicure.

Sometimes a woman just needs to be pampered, and this was one of those days. I wasn't ready to pull myself from my sullen mood yet, and I would need some more time before I faced Kyle. I picked up my phone and called to see if Sandy was willing to meet me at the spa. She always lifted my spirits, and she would give me the "*fuck the world*" speech so that I could feel better.

#Chapter2

"I see this as more of an opportunity than a crisis"
Kyle

A blind man could see that Camille was stressed out about something.

The only reason that I let her leave so easily is because she obviously needed personal space. It was hard not to press the issue, but she needed some time to herself. She and I had just taken a huge leap of faith together and maybe she just needed to process it all. I sat down at the table and took a sip of my coffee. My stomach grumbled in anticipation of eating the bountiful breakfast that was before me. Camille and I had a long night, and I needed sustenance. I decided to start with the pancakes.

After my immediate need for food was taken care of I checked my phone for news updates. My phone was set up to give me all the news that involved me or my company. A handy feature called *Google Alerts* will let me know whenever we are mentioned anywhere on the web. Camille and I were really popular because our faces were plastered all over the 'showbiz' sites and apparently my name was trending on Twitter. I read the comment sections of the news articles and people were being pretty harsh overall.

Most women had taken an immediate dislike to her. I expected a backlash over our engagement, and so I wasn't surprised. However, I should have prepared Camille for it and I regret that now. I gave myself a mental smack when I realized that this was probably why she was so depressed this morning. She was reading the paper and on her laptop before she left. She can seem tough as nails, but she was a sensitive woman, and I couldn't imagine what was going on in her head and heart as she read those things about herself. It all boils down to the media and the public being assholes. They'll be happier with your loneliness than to see you happy.

I decided I needed to cheer her up somehow. It was time for me to whisk her away again. Granted we had a huge cruise coming up in over a month but she needed some time away from all of this. We both needed some time away from our reality. I would whisk her away to California for a few days, and we would have the opportunity to enjoy each other without the stress of the media.

I opened the laptop to find a nice hotel for us to stay in. Before I could pull up my search engine I heard my elevator door open. I was shocked that Camille had come back so early. Except it wasn't her, it was my father, and his face was a special shade of bright red. When I saw him I stood to my feet and secured the towel around my waist. He gave me a look of disgust.

"Good morning dad. To what do I owe the pleasure?" I asked with a hint of sarcasm in my voice.

"This is not the time to fuck with me Kyle You know damned well why I'm here."

"I have a pretty good idea," I said.

My indifference only incensed him more, but I refused to let him get to me. I knew the risk that I was taking when I went against his wishes and asked Camille to marry me. My father doesn't like being ignored, and he doesn't take being disrespected lightly.

"You've given me no choice. Effective immediately I'm removing you as CEO of the company. I can't believe that I trusted you to do the right thing."

"I did do the right thing. I love her and so I asked her to marry me. There is nothing else to say."

"Do you understand what this means?"

"Yes I understand what this means," I replied.

I was telling the truth when I told him that I knew what it meant. I hadn't talked about the consequences of what we'd done yet because I knew that she would feel guilty. That's part of the reason why I knew that she couldn't come back to work for me. I wouldn't have a place for her to return to.

"You're such a fool," he sighed.

"I'm not a fool. I'm doing what feels right and at the end of the day this will make me a lot happier. Love means more to me than that business."

"So you're willing to give up the family's legacy for her?"

"I'm not giving up anything, you're taking it away. That's a decision that you're making, but I'm not going to try to change your mind."

"What has that girl done to you?" He laughed harshly.

"She's not a girl, she's a grown woman. At this point I'm going to have to ask you to leave."

"Are you fucking kidding me?"

"No, I'm completely serious. Don't come back until you can respect me and my future wife. This is our home, and I won't have it."

I watched his jaw tighten, and I stood taller so that he wouldn't get any ideas. I was no longer interested in hearing what he had to say. Our conversation had come to a close. He got the idea and turned on his heels and walked out without another word. I gave a sigh of relief as I watched him leave my penthouse. We both needed some space and hopefully in time he would cool down but if he didn't, I was okay with that too. I was over allowing him to run my life.

After he left, I went to my closet and got dressed. I had quite a few things that I needed to get done before Camille returned from her outing. It also gave me time to think about what I wanted to say to her when I saw her again. The wheels in my head were already turning. Money was never going to be an issue for me in my life, but I was accustomed to working. It was time for me to think of a game plan.

That afternoon Camille returned, and she looked like she was in much better spirits. It was great to see a genuine smile on her face again. I wanted to keep my news a secret for a little while longer, but it was time to put the cards on the table.

"How was your trip?" I asked.

"It was great, I hung out with Sandy and it was just what I needed," she smiled.

"I'm a little jealous that I wasn't able to put a real smile on your face. What does she have that I don't?" I said playfully.

"I just needed some girl time," she said as she playfully hit my shoulder.

"I need some girl time to," I said as I brushed my cock against her plump ass and wrapped her in my arms. I rested my head on her shoulder as we swayed contently from side to side.

"You've had plenty of girl time," she giggled as she pressed against me.

"I don't think I can ever get too much when it comes to you."

"The feeling is mutual," she sighed.

"I'm sorry, and I don't want to put a damper on things but I need to talk to you about something."

"Uh oh," she said as she tried to pull free of my embrace.

I tightened my grip on her so that she couldn't move, "No I want to tell you just like this. That way you can't run away and we can actively talk about it."

"I don't know if I can handle any bad news," she said.

"It's not bad news; it's just a major change."

"Okay, so what is it?"

"Well," I started, "My father stopped by today and he fired me."

I felt her entire body go rigid, and I held her tighter.

"Oh my god, I'm so sorry to hear that. This is all because of me isn't it? What are you going to do?" She asked quickly.

I chuckled, "Calm down, it's not the end of the world. A huge part of me knew that this was going to happen, and so it's no surprise. I now have the chance to build my own company and to do it the way that I want. I want you to be a part of it, and so I see this as more of an opportunity than a crisis."

She turned in my arms so that she was facing me, "Are you serious? I would love to be a part of whatever you have going on. I'm honored that you would even consider me for something like that."

"You're my partner in crime and I trust you. I know that you'll learn the ropes and help me get things off of the ground. I've already been in contact with a few people and I have some meetings set up for next week. This is something I actually always wanted to do."

She gave me a full kiss on the lips, "I'm excited, and I can't wait to hear about this new business."

"We will talk about it later because right now we have more pressing matters to discuss."

"More wonderful news?" She asked sarcastically.

"Yes actually. You and I are going to LA tomorrow. It will be good to get away while the dust settles. Besides, it's not as if I have to go to work tomorrow."

"Are you freaking kidding me?"

"You don't want to go? I can always give our trip away—"

"Don't you dare! I can use some California sun right about now."

"Then it's settled. In the morning we're Cali bound. Now go get dressed I have plans for us."

"I have to change?" She asked?

"Well unless you want to go rock-climbing in those 5 inch stiletto boots then yes."

"Say no more, I'm going to put on something a lot more comfortable."

I slapped her on the ass as she made her way back to the room, and I admired the view. Camille wasn't what you would consider to be a big girl, but she was larger than what was considered standard beauty. You wouldn't find her body type in Vogue, but she was so much sexier. I loved her ample curves and the feeling of her plump flesh beneath my hands. My cock hardened as I thought about it, but I ignored it because we would never get out of the door if we went down that road.

#Chapter3

"I can't believe that we just did this."
Camille

I had a sense of deja vu as I sat next to Kyle on the plane. It seemed like not too long before we were returning from Paris, and he dropped the bomb on me about Charlotte. I smiled to myself because I had no clue that my life was going to change so drastically. He and I were worlds away from that place, and I was the future Mrs. Kane.

Now that I felt more at ease I was able to speak to Kyle about how I felt regarding all of the things that I've seen. I casually brought up the news and asked him if he'd seen any of it. He quickly admitted that he had.
"Well what do you think?" I asked.
"I think that they're lonely assholes that don't have anything else to do with their time," he said plainly.
"Really? It's that simple for you?"
"Yes, it really is that simple for me."
"I wish that I was so easy going about all of this. All of that stuff really got to me, and I haven't known how to deal with it."
He grabbed my hand and looked into my eyes, "Listen to me. You are the only thing that matters to me. Please stop worrying about what everyone else thinks of us because it's none of their business anyway. The life that we'll have together has nothing to do with them, and none of it affects how I feel about you. I love you, and we're in this together, right?" He asked.
A huge grin spread across my face, "Right, we're in this together."
"Good because I'll be heartbroken if you leave me hanging," he said.
"I won't do that. I believe everything that you said, and I'll do my best not to let it get to me."

"To help you with that, I'll be taking your phone for the remainder of the trip," he said.

"You can't be serious," I said in disbelief.

"I'm very serious. I don't need anything to ruin our trip, and you seem to have an odd compulsion to check everything online. Don't worry; we'll get an amazing camera when we arrive so you can still take photos."

I opened my mouth to protest, but then I closed it quickly. He had a very valid point because I probably would have spent most of our trip obsessing over the things that people were saying about me. I wanted to have a great trip and the only way that I was going to do that was if I handed my phone over to Kyle. I reached beneath the seat in front of me, grabbed my phone out of my purse, and handed it over.

"I expected a lot more fight from you," he laughed, "You surprise me more and more each day."

"See, I'm learning," I laughed.

I felt free the moment I handed my phone to him. I knew that it was the right thing to do as soon as he tucked it away in his pocket. We would return to Chicago soon enough, and we could deal with the crap when we returned. For now, we were just an engaged couple that was going to party in LA. I still had no clue as to where we were staying. He had the wonderful habit of surprising me, and I trusted his taste so I wasn't worried.

*

Kyle's taste proved to be impeccable once again. We arrived at the Chateau Marmont, and my breath was taken away. It was located in an enclave that hovered above Sunset Strip. I'd admittedly never heard of it before, but I doubt if most people in my circles had. It was the kind of place that you only knew of if you could afford, at least that's how it seemed to me.

"This hotel is modeled after a castle from the French countryside," Kyle explained, "You'll notice the Gothic and bohemian influence. This is one of the best hotels here and so I knew that you would love it. Maybe we'll see a celebrity or two," he winked.

"I honestly don't care if we see any celebrities," I laughed, "I already feel like one. You're spoiling me rotten."

"That just means that I'm doing my job. I want to give you everything you want and more."

"You've already done that," I said as my heart swelled inside of my chest.

It was moments like these where I had to make an attempt to shake my feelings of inadequacy. I had an overwhelming feeling of unworthiness. I appreciated everything that he was doing, but I hated feeling as if I didn't belong with him. He'd given me so much, and it seemed as if I had nothing to truly offer him in return. Kyle was so far out of my league, and I wondered what he truly saw in me.

"What's the look for?" He said warily, "Give it to me straight, I want to know what's on your mind."

I laughed, "How do you do that?"

"Sometimes you're very easy to read. It's clear that something is bothering you and I want to know what it is."

I toyed around with brushing over the subject, but I knew that if he and I were going to make it then I needed to be honest.

"I just feel like I don't deserve you," I admitted.

His eyes softened as he looked at me.

"Please take our bags inside, and we'll check in shortly," he said dismissively to the bellhop.

Without a word the bellhop did as he was asked. I felt a little twinge of guilt because I didn't like it when people spoke to people in customer service that way. I also knew that Kyle was going to give him an amazing tip. He wasn't rude, just standoffish and he was probably used to it anyway. I made a mental note to talk to Kyle about that kind of behavior later.

Kyle laughed, "And that is why I love you so much."

"What do you mean?" I asked in confusion.

"You want to tear me a new one for talking to him that way don't you?"

I wrinkled my nose, "You think that you know me so well."

"That doesn't make it any less true. Do you know how many women wouldn't have had a problem with the way that I spoke to him?"

"We'll I'm not them and I just think it's important to treat everyone with some respect."

"Exactly, you care about others even when you don't have to. You're compassionate, feisty, beautiful, intelligent, and you go after what you want. Hell, sometimes I don't feel like I deserve you. You're the best thing that's ever happened to me, and I'm so fortunate to have you in my life."

I searched his eyes for the truth, and I could tell that he really believed what he was saying. I smiled and let his words wash over me. He was so much better than marijuana, and he provided me with a natural high.

"Thank you," I said as I kissed him.

"No, thank you. Now please let me spoil you," he said as he ushered me into the hotel.

When we got to our room I went from room to room and my eyes lit up like a child on Christmas day.

"This penthouse is ridiculously huge," I exclaimed.

I walked out onto the private terrace and closed my eyes as the sun kissed my face. I was getting exactly what I needed. I silently wondered if Kyle would consider moving here. It's not as if he had to stay for the company anymore, and we could use a change of scenery.

"You know, we can get naked out here and have some real fun," he whispered into my ear as he trailed kisses down my neck.

"No sexy time yet," I said as I pulled away from him, "If we have sex now we'll be in bed all day."

He gave a mock pout, "You're right. You just can't seem to get enough of me."

"That goes both ways sir," I laughed.

"I'm still sir?" he said playfully.

"You'll always be sir to me," I said as I playfully batted my eyelashes.

"Since we can't have any fun here then we have to head out before I take advantage of you. I have just the thing that will make your panties drop to the floor."

"Now you have my interest," I said.

"First change into bikini and put on a pair of shorts."

"You're really particular today."

"Well it's the Cali uniform, and I want you to feel at home," he laughed.

"I don't have a problem with that in the slightest."

I hastily got redressed, and he did the same. We were Cali ready in less than ten minutes. We hopped into another cab, and it was easy to see why people in California were so carefree. Everything about it was relaxing. I leaned into Kyle, and he wrapped his arm around me and he told the cab driver where we were going. We arrived at our destination 20 minutes later. We arrived at a boating dock. I gave him a puzzled expression.

"Oprah loaned me her yacht," he said with a smile.

"You've got to be shitting me," I said in disbelief.

"I am," he laughed, "But my family's yacht is docked here, and I arranged for us to take it out for the evening."

I pinched him, "You play too much. I really thought that you were serious."

"I know you did and that's what made it such a great joke."

"Yeah whatever," I mumbled.

"I promise that our humble yacht will make you forget all about Oprah."

"Knowing you, I'm sure that it will," I said as I beamed at him.

Kyle delivered in spades on his promise. His family's boat was absolutely stunning. I'd never stepped foot on such a beautiful boat in my entire life. It was massive, and the interior was a mixture of white and light blue. It was larger than some of the houses that I'd been in and consisted of three floors. I was a little overwhelmed by the decadence of it all. I walked from room to room the same way that I had with the hotel. There were two huge bedrooms that had a master bath, a full kitchen, dining area, living room, small theater, and a massive hot tub on the deck.

"There's a bathtub out on the deck upstairs," he said, "So what do you think?"

"I'm wondering why we're staying in a hotel when you have all of this?" I said as I gestured wildly at our surroundings.

He gave a hearty laugh, "Would you like to stay here for the remainder of our trip? If you let me know I can arrange for another captain to meet us tonight because the one that we have now can't stay. I can also have a crew come and cater to us for the next few days."

I shook my head in disbelief, "All of this is so unreal. There's no way that I can ask for you to do that. You've spent all of that money on the hotel, and we can't let it go to waste."

He shrugged, "I'm not a wasteful man but if you want something, then I'm going to get it for you and I'll spare no expense."

"No, we'll enjoy the boat today and head back to the hotel," I said.

I knew that he was being honest, but I still couldn't bring myself to waste that kind of money. It all just seemed too exorbitant. He's a billionaire, but I wasn't raised like that. There was no way that I was going to allow a huge penthouse sit empty just because I wanted to sleep somewhere else. I would get over it quickly.

Kyle disappeared into the kitchen and re-appeared with a cart. On it was plates that were covered and bucket of champagne.

"I had everything prepped before we got here," he said.

"I'm convinced that you think of everything."

"I try."

We walked outside and set everything up on the dining table. I watched in awe as we saw the coastline slowly disappear. There were other boats around, but it felt as if we were in our own private world.

"So how is life without your phone?" He asked.

"What phone?" I asked.

"That's what I like to hear," he said as he popped the cork on the champagne.

We had a wonderful lunch out on the water. The conversation was great, and we laughed and talked about trivial things. I got to learn more about his family, and I saw the sad gleam in his eye when he talked about his father.

"Your dad will come around," I said.

"I don't know if he will," he admitted, "My dad is a stubborn asshole, and he doesn't like anyone that he can't control. Now that I've stepped outside of his will, he won't be happy with me."

"That's true, but he'll learn how to respect you. Men like him don't respect people that cater to their every whim. It will be tough, but I think that your relationship with him will get better."

"I really hope so, and you may be on to something there," he said.

"Well I know something that will make you feel better," I flirted.

"I'm open to whatever suggestions you may have."

He and I were a really good distance away from everyone at this point, and I was feeling adventurous. I stood to my feet and removed my shorts and my bikini bottoms.

"I think that I feel a little better already," he grinned.

"I would feel a lot less lonely if you joined me in my naked crusade."

He rose to his feet and mirrored my actions. We both were completely naked, and I closed my eyes as I felt the warm air lick my flesh. When I opened my eyes he was seated once again in his chair, and his cock was standing at full attention.

"Don't mind me," he said, "I'm just enjoying the view."

I carefully straddled him without inserting him inside of me. His rod rested against my ass as I rubbed my breast against his bare chest. I loved the way that he felt. He wasn't completely shaven, and he had a light sprinkle of hair. The friction was causing feelings pool inside of my lower belly.

His hand grabbed me possessively behind the neck as his mouth claimed mines. I eagerly gave in to his mouth's demands. His tongue traced my lower lip before he gave it a slight nibble. I whimpered against his touch, and the only way that I was going to be satisfied was if he was inside of me. I lifted and guided him to my wet slit. I slowly lowered myself onto his throbbing shaft; he stretched and filled me in a way that felt like perfection. He was a wonderful mixture of pleasure and pain.

His huge hands wrapped around my waist, and he lifted from his chair to give me all of him. I cried out in shock as I bit into his shoulder. His arms wrapped underneath mines so that his hands gripped my shoulders.

"I want to fuck you just like this, is that okay with you?" He groaned.

"Mmhmmm," was all that I could manage to get out but that was encouragement enough for him.

We began a slow and hard rhythm that kept my senses on high alert. His thrusts inside of me were deep, and the head of his cock pressed into my womb. Tears pricked at the back of my eyes, and I was rendered speechless. Our sex was indicative of the roller coaster ride that we'd been on since I met him. It was bittersweet, but the pleasure outweighed the pain, so I didn't want it to stop.

His cock felt so deep that I was sure he would pierce my soul. I lifted and rotated my hips each time he pressed deep inside of me. I felt like a goddess as the sun kissed my skin, and he worshiped my body. My orgasm hit me unexpectedly, and my entire body tensed as I imploded around him.

"Fuck Camille," he groaned as his body jerked and mimicked my own.

His grip became so tight that it bordered on painful, but I didn't mind. Our breathing was ragged, and we stayed entangled for a few quiet moments.

"WOOOOOOOOO!!!!!!!!!!!!!" I heard several people yell excitedly, and I quickly looked up.

Not that far away from us was a smaller yacht filled with young adults that were cheering us on.

"Oh shit!" I said panicked.

"It's okay, don't move. That way they won't be able to see anything," he said as he held my body closer to his own.

I laughed, "I can't believe that we just did this."

"Me either," he admitted, "but damn it was fun."

We drifted further away from the party boat, and they were still hooting and hollering so I gave them a timid wave.

"Yes, it's been a lot of fun," I said into his ear.

#Chapter4

"I know you're not going to play me like this,"
Camille

The next few days went by in a blissful blur.

It was filled with shopping, food, and amazing sex. Every time my eyes lit up at something, we were carrying it out of the store. The shopping in LA was absolutely amazing, and I couldn't wait to strut my stuff back in Chicago. Provided that I didn't have to go back to all of the drama. But it was hard to worry about everything that was going to be waiting back at home when I had Kyle sitting next to me on the plane holding my hand. He was my anchor and being with him without any other distractions helped center me. I once again remembered why I was going through all of it. The temporary scrutiny was worth a lifetime with the man that I loved and adored.

I squeezed his hand during takeoff like I usually did. I wasn't sure if I would ever get used to the sensation. It wasn't entirely unpleasant, just odd. Humans just weren't meant to fly, and my body knew this all too well.

"You okay?" Kyle asked with a concerned expression.

"Yes, I'm fine," I said as I took a deep breath.

"You'll get used to it."

"Tell my body that," I laughed nervously.

He chuckled and kissed the back of my hand. I always liked how he allowed me to be myself. He didn't spend the next few minutes trying to convince me that I would get over it. He made it easy for me to have my own feelings and that's something that's hard for men to do. In my experiences they always tried to tell you how to feel or what to do about your feelings. That's incredibly annoying.

After we were in the air we sat in a comfortable silence. I rested my head on his shoulder and closed my eyes. I wished that we could have stayed in California forever. I wished that we didn't have to return to all of the chaos but the sooner that we jumped right in the better.

"I'm excited to get this new business venture going with you," he said breaking into my thoughts.

I had totally forgotten about the business portion. He'd done a better job than I thought with getting my mind off of all the drama.

"Are you finally going to tell me exactly what it is?"

I sat up straight and looked at him, he gave me a sheepish grin, "Well I'm about to start a string of high end restaurants and clubs. We can test the market by playing around with a few different concepts and then the ones that are successful can be duplicated in other parts of Chicago as well as other states."

My eyes widened at his suggestion, and I realized what a huge undertaking this was about to become. My heart began to race because we had a lot of work ahead of us.

"Well what part do you want me to play in all of this?" I asked.

I suddenly felt extremely inadequate because I didn't have any clue about the restaurant or club industry. Sure, I'd been to quite a few but that probably wouldn't help me much in that arena.

"You're going to be my right hand. I'm learning about this business just like you are. So don't feel as if you're at a disadvantage. I'm bringing in some of the best of the best in the industry and so you'll be sitting in with me to learn about what it's going to take. We'll navigate all of this together. So I hope you're ready for the ride."

I gave a small sigh of relief. I knew that if someone spelled things out for me then I could figure it out. Some concepts may go over my head, but I would spend some of my personal time figuring it out.

"I'll admit that it's going to be a little out of my element but I'm going to do my best. We're in this together babe." I said.

He brought my hands to his lips and gave my knuckles a long slow kiss and it went throughout my entire being. He had the ability to create a flame where there wasn't any. I gave a content sigh, and it caused him to laugh.

"But that's what I like to hear. You're easily one of the most intelligent people that I know, and it comes naturally for you. What you don't have in formal education you make up for in instinct," he said.

"I still would like to get my formal education. I just think that it will make me a lot more confident in the long run. I've always wanted to do it, but I didn't have the time or money."

"Well, consider it done. Pick a school and that's where you'll go, you already know how I feel about that. We can get the ball rolling as soon as possible, and you can be in classes next semester," he assured me.

"You don't waste any time," I said in amusement.

"Life is too short to waste time Camille. If there's something that you want to do, and you have the means then there's no reason to wait."

"I like the way that you think Mr. Kane."

"I love the way that you think, future Mrs. Kane," he said.

"Speaking of getting the ball rolling, it's time for us to start organizing the wedding. Have you given any thought to where you want to get married?"

Did he seriously ask a woman a question like that? I'd been planning my wedding since I was seven years old. I always knew that I wanted it to be a very laid back ceremony because that matched my personality.

"I've always wanted to get married on a Caribbean island. I want to be completely relaxed with the warm air caressing my face. I envision walking down the sandy beach as I approach you at the altar. " I said dreamily.

"That sounds wonderful and I will make that happen for us. We'll start scoping out locations so that we can pick a date and send out invitations. Right now our main priority will be to get our new venture off of the ground immediately."

"I'm looking forward to our wedding and I agree with you. We have a lot on our plate right now and we have to focus on the immediate issues."

His arm went around my shoulder, and his head rested on mines. That moment in the air with him seemed perfect.

*

Our meetings with the advisers seemed to be endless. My brain felt like it was going to explode from all of the information that I was being inundated with. But we'd finally made a decision about the first 3 ventures that we were going to move on. Kyle had assembled his team and some of them were from his father's business. I knew that wasn't going to go over well with his dad, but they were well within their rights. The employees signed a non-compete agreement, and this business was in a completely different arena.

I was exhausted, but I was on my way to see Sandy because she seemed like she just needed a friend. I refused to allow my new life to cause me to abandon those that I loved. On my way there, Marcus called me. I was going to ignore the call, but I picked up out of curiosity.

"Hello?"

"Hey Cam, I need to speak with you," he said in a smooth tone.

"Okay, what's up?"

"I need to speak to you in person."

"What is it about?" I asked.

"Like I said, we need to speak about it in person."

"It's that important?" I asked in disbelief.

"Yes it's *that* important," he said in annoyance.

I shook my head at my phone, but I knew that I couldn't ignore his request. I considered him to be my friend and at the end of the day I trusted him. If he said that something was important then there was a high likelihood that it was.

"Okay, I'm headed out your way now. So I'll be at your place in about 20 minutes."

"Alright, come to the one in Oak Park."

"See you soon," I said before I hung up.

My mind began to race with all of the possible things that he could want to talk about. I sincerely hoped that it wasn't an attempt to get me back. I'd been very clear about where I stood on that subject. He'd ruined any chance for a future with me because he'd made his choice about the life that he wanted to lead. Marcus chose drugs and money over me. I then began to think about my mother, and I hoped that she was okay. I didn't want her to be a part of my life but I didn't want anything bad to happen to her either. I increased my speed so that I could figure out what he wanted sooner because I was going to drive myself crazy with my theories.

I finally arrived at his house, and his door was wide open. He was expecting my arrival and so I walked up his stairs and entered his house. From the outside it looked like he had a simple family home. Once you entered his home, it looked like a rich playboy was living there. Everything was expensive, but there was no real style. There weren't any photos on the walls, and there was no warmth. His hardwood floors shined brilliantly, and his white butter leather section sat in the center of his huge family room towards the 70 inch television.

He rose to his feet once he saw me.

"Hey Camille," he said as he greeted me with a hug.

I returned it and made sure that our lower halves had some space between them. Once we parted he shook his head and grinned.

"Hey Marcus," I replied.

"Come on and take a seat."

I walked in and took a seat on the opposite end of the couch. I stared at him because he didn't seem in a rush to tell me what my visit was about.

"Okay you've freaked me out enough and you know how I am. So please tell me why I'm here," I said.

"I just wanted to tell you the press has been blowing my phone up. They want me to sell them a story on you," he laughed.

My stomach dropped because I never expected them to contact my friends or ex-boyfriends. All of the peace that I still had from LA had drained from my body.

"But don't worry baby girl, I told all of them no," he said.

I gave a huge sigh of relief, "Marcus thank you so much for that. I appreciate you being a real friend because a lot of people would have sold me out."

"Well I told them no at first, bu then, they called back and offered me $5k if I sold them a negative story," he said before I was finished thanking him.

I closed my eyes and hugged my arms to my body. That was the absolute last thing that I needed. They were offering a pretty good chunk of change for information about me. Even if Marcus didn't tell, someone would. Most of the people in our neighborhood knew about my past, and it's something that I've never disclosed to Kyle. I inwardly cringed when I thought about the field day that the media would have if they knew of my illegal activity. It would justify everything that they've ever said about me. I wondered if he would leave me over that news.

"But you aren't going to give them the story right?" I asked to clarify.

He shrugged, "Honestly I could use the money right about now. I can't afford to turn down 5k."

"What do you mean you can't afford to turn down $5k? You wipe your ass with that kind of money," I said incredulously.

"Times are hard and I have bills to pay. But of course you wouldn't know what that was like anymore now that you're with white dude."

"That white *dude* is my fiancé, so don't act as if he's some random man."

Marcus angrily stood to his feet, "Look, I'm going to give them their story unless you give me 5 grand. It is as simple as that."

"You can't be serious Marcus! I can't get that kind of money."

He gave an angry laugh, "I don't know who you think you're trying to food but we both know that he will never miss that money."

I stared at him as he stood over me. I tried to find the man that I once knew in his eyes, and I didn't see him. The look that he gave me was one that he never directed towards me. It was the way that he looked at people that he despised. I didn't realize how badly my new relationship had truly hurt him. I found that to be funny because he was the one that went off and had a baby. Now I was the bad guy because I was about to marry my prince charming.

"I can't just take 5 thousand dollars without him noticing," I said.

"I suggest that you figure out a way because I want the money by this time tomorrow or I'm going to be forced to call them and tell absolutely everything. I bet everyone would love to know what the ghetto Cinderella was like before she went from rags to riches."

I stood to my feet so that I would not feel so intimidated by him. I refused to believe that the man that I grew up with and loved would do that to me. We'd been through everything together, and we never betrayed each other. That would go against everything that we've ever stood for.

"No," I shook my head quickly, "You wouldn't do that to me. You're upset, but you still wouldn't do that to me."

"That just goes to show how little you know. Get my money or your face is going to plastered in every local newspaper and I bet some stations will want to pick the story up as well"

"And what does that mean for you?" I asked, "I'm no longer doing any of those things. My hands are a little dirty, but your hands are extremely filthy. You're tied to everything bad in my past, and you're still apart of this life. If you ruin my life Marcus, I'm taking you with me."

"See now you're pissing me off," he said as he grabbed me by the throat.

I gasped from shock and yanked myself from his grip. He didn't grab me hard enough to do any damage but it was clear that his jealousy had driven him insane. Marcus had never put his hands on me before.

"Don't touch me ever again," I said in an even tone.

"Just get me my fucking money," he demanded through gritted teeth.

"Whatever," I said as I headed towards his door.

"I'm looking forward to hearing from you." His tone had changed to one that you would use with a friend.

I walked to my car in disbelief. Our friendship was completely shattered, and I never thought that was a real possibility for us. Tears streamed down my face as I opened my car door and got in. For the first time ever, I was afraid of him. He always promised to never put his hands on me and to never disrespect me, but I guess all bets were off. I'd seen him act this way with other people before and this treatment was reserved for those that he felt betrayed by. I finally came to terms with the fact that he wasn't bluffing.

I picked up my phone and called Sandy. I would have to reschedule our girl time because I needed to think my way through the predicament that I was in. I headed back towards the penthouse and took that time to decide what I was going to do. My thoughts went to the pre-loaded debit card with $8,000 that Kyle offered me in case I ever wanted to go shopping on my own. I'd never used it because he already got me everything that I wanted, but it was my get out of jail free card for the moment. I breathed a little lighter, and I was happy that I had a temporary solution to my problem.

Now I would just have to ask him for the card. I wasn't looking forward to having to lie to him over something so damned stupid. My past was haunting me, and I hated the feeling. I wanted to just crawl into the bed and snuggle with Kyle. He would make me feel better and chase away the feelings that I was harboring.

The following morning went much like the ones that we usually had, but this time my stomach was in knots. My hands shook a little as I ate a bite of my delicious Denver omelet. Kyle looked at me and gave me his winning smile and my heart melted. He was such a wonderful person, and I wondered why he chose me. I was full of drama, and I had a horrible past. He could have picked anyone that he wanted but yet he wanted me. I felt fortunate and guilty. But I still had to do what was necessary.
"Can I have the debit card to go shopping?" I asked.
"Sure," he said as he rose to his feet and headed for the room.
His lack of hesitation made me grin from ear to ear. He didn't bat an eye at my request or grill me over where I was going. I added that to my list of reasons why I loved him.
"You want me to go with you today?" He asked as he handed me the card.

"No," I said quickly, "I'm going to get my hair done and a whole bunch of other stuff. It's going to take a while, and I don't want it to bore you.

"Alright, say no more," he said.

I smiled and kissed him on the lips and finished my omelet. I drank my mimosa and tried to let it soothe my anxiety away. But I knew that nothing was going to make me feel better until I put everything at rest.

I left the house at about noon to meet Marcus. I went to the ATM and was severely frustrated because I could only take the money that I needed off of the card in $500 increments. Once I was finally finished I headed towards his house. He was at home and waiting for me. Once again his door was open and I walked in. He was seated comfortably on his couch and was playing basketball on his gaming console.

"Look at you, being all reliable and shit," he said sarcastically as he placed his controller on the table.

I rolled my eyes and handed him the wad of cash. He slowly counted all of it and made a big show by putting it into 5 piles on his table.

"You did really good baby girl," he said.

"Then we're good?" I asked.

"Yes, we're good for now."

"I know you're not going to play me like this," I said.

"Play you like what? Play you the way that you've been playing me?"

I knew that arguing with him was going to be fruitless and possibly cost me much more than I was willing to pay.

I sighed, "Okay, you have your money. I'm leaving."

Before I could turn around he said, "There is one more thing that I want you to do for me."

"What is it?"

He grabbed his crotch with his left hand and leaned back against the couch, "Suck it for me just like you used to."

"Fuck off," I spat before I hastily retreated out of his door. I could hear his laughs as I made my way down his stairs. I found myself wondering what I ever saw in him to begin with.

#Chapter5

"I don't know what's gotten into you but I think I may like it,"
Kyle

I always miss Camille whenever she's away from me even if it's only for hours. I've become a pathetic sap, and I've loved every moment of it. She's been a catalyst for me changing my life, and she's enriched it in the process. That's why I wanted to go out for dinner tonight. I took her to one of my favorite steak houses. *Joe's* was one of the best in my opinion, and we hadn't had the opportunity to go yet and so it was overdue.

I looked over the table at her, and she was gorgeous. Her makeup was done flawlessly and so was her hair. However, I didn't see any evidence of all of the things that she claimed to have gotten done. She looked the same, but there was no way that I was going to say that. Because if she'd gotten a lot of things done then I would be labeled as unobservant. No man needs those kinds of problems.

She kept biting her bottom lip and shaking her leg nervously. I wondered what was going on with her because she'd been acting weird since the day before. I was trying to not think of the worst scenario, but I wondered if she was having second thoughts about the wedding. She took the fact that we were going to wait to plan the wedding really well. Maybe she didn't want to marry me anymore. It was possible that all of the bad press was getting to her. I wanted to shield her from it, but it wasn't realistic. She would have to grow a thick skin if she was going to be a part of my family.

"Camille, what's going on?" I asked.

"What do you mean?" She asked as her eyes locked onto mine. I could tell that I had just pulled her from her thoughts, and I was hoping that she would share them with me.

"You're acting a little off and I want to know what's going on with you."

"I'm sorry," she said, "Things have just been so busy, and my brain is going into overload. I keep thinking of all of the information that I need to retain. I'm sorry if I seem a little spaced out, I didn't realize that I was doing that."

I looked at her suspiciously but chose to take her at her word. We got through the rest of dinner, and she was a lot more talkative. Something was still bothering her, but she was pushing through it, and I was going to give her the space to work it out.

When we got back to my house she couldn't keep her hands off of me. I was surprised, but I wasn't going to complain about her level of enthusiasm. I would take any opportunity that I could to be inside of her. As soon as we entered the apartment and got through my door she dropped to her knees and pulled my cock out.

Her mouth was warm and wet around my dick. Her tongue teased my cockhead before she tried to take all of me into her mouth. I closed my eyes and let out short groans as the velvet walls of her mouth, and her tongue worked their magic. She created a nice tight suction as if she was milking my cock for cum.

"I want to be inside of you," I groaned as I felt myself about to erupt.

She came up for air, "You're already inside of me."

Her mouth got really wet, and she grabbed my hand and placed it on the back of her head. I squeezed my eyes shut as my balls tightened, and my legs shook. My seed spewed into her mouth, but she didn't slow down her momentum. I twitched as she continued working on my overly sensitive flesh. I pulled away.

"I don't know what's gotten into you but I think I may like it," I panted.

She gave a naughty laugh, "I sure hope so because in a few hours you'll be awakened to my mouth on your dick so that I can ride it."

"Such a dirty little mouth," I said as she stood to her feet, "I wouldn't have it any other way."

#Chapter6

"Leave me the hell alone and get over it, I don't want you,"
Camille

I know that I should have felt better over the next few days, but I felt like I hadn't seen the last of Marcus. That made my work experience with Kyle a lot less enjoyable. I jumped every time I got a text message or a phone call. Kyle would look at me suspiciously, and I would make it my business to cause him to forget later. Him and I had been humping like rabbits because it was one of the few things that I could do to make me feel better about having to lie to him. It was therapeutic even if the feeling was only temporary.

Kyle was moving at a lightning speed with the new ventures, and we'd already chosen the venues for each place. Contractors had gone over each one and placed their bids. We would be choosing the following day and within 3 weeks we would be ready to open the doors of each one. Money had the ability to get things done ridiculously quickly. I was amazed throughout the entire process, and it made me feel good to see our ideas come into fruition. Kyle beamed with pride each day that we got closer to opening.

While I was in the bathroom my phone rang, and it was from Marcus. I picked up the phone quickly.

"Hello?" I said in a hushed tone.

"Hey baby girl, it's Marcus."

"I know who it is."

"Of course you do," he said in amusement.

"What do you want?"

"I've been speaking to a few of my boys recently and they confirmed my thoughts. They said that $5k is kind of low considering everything that I know about you and how much you have now."

"Don't do this."

"Don't cut me off when I'm talking," he said edgily. "As I was saying before I was rudely interrupted, it's a low price. I could tell the press about how you used to sell drugs. I could even feel a little nostalgic and show them the photos and videos of the evidence."

"How in the hell do you expect to get away with this without bringing yourself down idiot?" I asked.

"Well I'm going to do it anonymously and only show the photos with you," he said in amusement.

"If you think that's a good idea then you're dumber than I ever knew you were," I said.

"Don't forget that I still have our sex tape. You know, the one with you posing with drugs, guns, and money. The world will know just how kinky you can really be. I am sure white boy would not be impressed."

"Just shut up," I hissed.

I was mortified as I thought of all the things that I'd done on photos and video. I was young and stupid when I'd done all of those things. I was really just a teenager, but the press and Kyle wouldn't see it that way at all. They would be all over it like ants at a picnic. But I couldn't continue to fold under the pressure that Marcus was applying. I knew this game, and it would never end. He would own me until the day that I died if I kept giving in to him.

"I've given you enough money. Leave me the hell alone and get over it, I don't want you," I said before I hung up.

That wasn't going to be the last of Marcus, and I would have to think of a permanent solution before everything got completely out of hand. I didn't have many options at my disposal, but one of them was going to have to work.

#Chapter 7

"He has us by the fucking balls!"
Kyle

I could hear Camille talking in the bathroom. I lay in the bed and thought about what I'd overheard. She'd told whoever it was that she'd *"given them enough money"*, and she seemed strained. She hadn't mentioned anything to me about giving someone money, but I decided to keep it to myself. Once she emerged from the bathroom she crawled into bed and made me forget all about the conversation. I was sure that if it was anything really important then Camille would have come to me for help.

Later that morning I sipped my orange juice and read the papers at the table. I was wishing that Camille was with me, but she was still in the bed. She tossed and turned all night and so she really needed the rest. I perused though the papers and then I saw a horrible headline. It had a big photo of Camille under it, and it talked about the '*Chicago gang connections*' that Camille had. I read further as my heart pounded, and it said that she was involved with people that were selling drugs as well as other criminal activity.

I shook my head in disbelief. I could not believe the blatant lies they would print. The press would stop at nothing to ruin Camille and all of this had gotten really out of hand. It was time that I actively made a move to stop the madness. I called my legal team and instructed them to call the paper to retract their story. If they didn't agree to pull the story I was going to completely ruin them. Unable to wait until Camille awoke I walked to the bedroom.
"Camille," I said from the doorway a few times until she opened her eyes.
"What's up?" She asked as she stretched and yawned.
"We have to talk. I didn't want you to find this out on your own and so I have to be the first to tell you."
Her body went into full alert, and she sat up straight, "Is there something wrong?"

I told her about what I read in the paper but did my best to assure her that I was taking care of it. I then apologized about being so quiet with the press and letting it get out of control. She started to bite her lip again as she hugged her legs to her chest and rocked.

"I am so sorry Kyle, but it's true," she interjected.

My breathing became labored with the shock of what I thought that I'd just heard.

"What do you mean?" I asked.

"It's true Kyle, all of it" she said as tears streamed down her face.

My heart softened when I saw her tears, and all I wanted to do was ease her fears. I walked to the bed and placed my arms around her.

"I know that's not who you are anymore," I assured her, "You have nothing to worry about."

"I'm so sorry that I didn't tell you, but there never really was a right time," she said.

I kissed the top of her head, "I can see how you would come to that conclusion. I don't think that I would have shared something like that either. It's all going to be okay."

She shook her head, "I can't believe that my ex actually sold them the story."

"No, it wasn't your ex. My legal team said that it was a female that sold the story to them. I don't have a name yet."

Her body began to shake, "It must have been one of the girls that I knew when I was younger. Any one of them could have sold my story to the press because it wasn't exactly a secret. They probably called and volunteered the information."

"So is this what your conversation on the phone was about last night?" I pried.

She gave a slow nod, "Yes, I gave Marcus $5k to be quiet and now he's trying to blackmail me for more."

"Hold on, you did what?!"

A rage that I didn't know that I had bubbled up, and I became extremely pissed. How could she do such a stupid thing? I backed away from her and stood to my feet.

"Seriously? You gave him $5k of my money? Are you fucking kidding me?" I asked.

"I didn't know what to do," she said in her defense.

"You could have come to me! Now you've given him my money, and I'm sure that will probably fund more drug selling. That directly implicates me. You have possibly ruined everything that my family and I have worked for. Can you imagine how bad this looks? Giving a known drug dealer $5k? I could do time for that."

"I'm so sorry," she said, "I wasn't thinking like that. I just wanted to give him the money so that he would go away for good."

"Right except now he isn't gone for good. Now that you've given in to him, he has us by the fucking balls!"

"It will be fine," she said.

"It could have been fine. It could have been fine if you would have come to me in the beginning. Now it's not fine, it's so far from fine that I'm ready to completely flip my lid."

She grabbed her legs tighter and inched away from me as if I was going to get violent with her. I felt bad for scaring her because I would never do something like that, but I wasn't in the mood to comfort her either. I couldn't look at her anymore, she was not who I thought she was.

"I don't know if I can trust you anymore," I said.

Her bottom lip trembled, and a fresh set of tears spilled from her eyes. I wanted to hug her, but all I could hear was my father in my head. He may have been right about everything after all. I was sure that I would be hearing from him soon because this had become my family's problem.

"Kyle-"

"No," I said cutting her off, "You need to leave."

She shook her head quickly, "Please just listen."

"Now really isn't a good time to speak to me because I'm finding it hard to be rational. I need you to leave my house. I have a lot of damage control to do because of you. Get your things and go."

Her shoulders slumped in defeat, and she rose from the bed. I quickly put on my clothes and left the apartment. I couldn't bear to watch her gather her things to leave my loft. I wanted her to stay, but I was so angry with her. I knew that she was from the poor part of Chicago and that she'd had a rough life, but I never thought that she would have been caught up in drugs and gangs. She'd never lied to me about her background, but she never volunteered the information either.

I told her that I understood why she didn't tell me, but I wasn't quite there yet. I wanted to understand why she kept it from me, and I was willing to work through it. But the last straw was when her actions began to threaten the livelihood of my family. I didn't agree with a lot of things that my father did but on that point I agreed with him. I couldn't have someone in my life that made poor decisions.

Her giving her ex my money completely threw me off guard. I overheard her the previous night, but I didn't want to believe that she was doing something like that. I hoped like hell that the press wouldn't figure out that she'd given him that money. If they did, they would be all over the story and create connections where there aren't any. Would not surprise me if they implied I was funding all the drug dealers in Chicago.

I walked to my car and decided to take a drive alone lake shore. I needed some downtime on the beach alone before I was ready to fully face the day. I should have been moving forward with my business venture but instead I was going to have to spend the day cleaning up the mess.

My phone rang continuously, and I saw that it was my father. I groaned and hit ignore. I would deal with him after I had my morning coffee and not a moment before.

I did not want to lose Camille but it would be very hard for me to trust her after this. I needed to think of a plan.

#Chapter8

"It's funny how we sometimes want comfort from the person that's caused us pain."
Camille

To say that my heart was hurting would have been a severe understatement.

The shit had finally hit the fan, and I didn't come out unscathed. All I could think was that it was way too early for this. My tears flowed over my cheeks as I drove aimlessly around the city. I contemplated driving back to my apartment in South Holland, but I knew that being alone wouldn't have been good for me. I'd spent far too many days and nights crying in that apartment over my dating and financial woes.

I called the first person who popped into my head, and that was Sandy. She was a little surprised to hear me burst into tears once she picked up the phone, and she told me to come over. She was working the night shift so I'd gotten lucky because I needed to speak to her. I didn't want to go back into the same area as Marcus, but I hoped that no one spotted me. I didn't want to see him, and he probably couldn't wait to rub everything in my face.

My phone had already been called a few times and it was reporters asking for an official statement from me. They wanted to know if there was any truth to what had been alleged in the papers. I refused to answer any of their questions and hung up. I probably wouldn't take any more calls for the rest of the day. I didn't need any bad news, and I definitely didn't need anyone prying into my business.

I arrived at her house shortly, and she greeted me with a big hug at the door. I seemed to be leaning on my friends a lot lately. The truth was that I really needed them.

"Girl what the hell is going on? People are talking, and I saw the paper," she said as she plopped down on her couch.

I sighed and left my bags at the door and joined her, "I don't even know where to begin."

"The beginning," she said. "I've been trying to get a hold of you because the media has been trolling and wanting me to tell them info about you. They even offered me money, but there's no way in hell that I would sell you out like that."

"I'm happy that you feel that way, and honestly I've never thought that you would. Thank you for being a real friend."

"So what in the hell is going on?"

"Marcus is what's going on," I said.

"What do you mean?"

I started from the beginning and told her about my interactions with Marcus over the last few days, and she stared at me the entire time with an open mouth.

"He put his damned hands on you?" She yelled, "What did Kyle say about that?"

"I haven't told Kyle," I said.

"So let me guess, that's why you're here instead of with your man?" She asked without a hint of sympathy in her voice.

I didn't realize how bitchy I was feeling until I imagined me slapping the condescending look off of her face. Just as quickly as I thought about it, I felt bad. She'd opened the doors of her home to me, and I was imagining hurting her. I closed my eyes and took a deep breath.

"Yes that's why I'm here," I said through gritted teeth.

"I would have never allowed Marcus to come between me and my rich man. He's a fucking peon, and you're about to be royalty. Why didn't you go straight to him and tell him? Money rules everything; I bet he could have put an end to all of it immediately. Kyle is like a giant and Marcus is an ant," she ranted.

I stared at her as she went on about what a stupid decision I made. I wanted to be upset with her, but she was absolutely right. I should have known better, and I should have trusted Kyle with my past and with the things that were going on with me. It was unrealistic to think that I could keep it from him. I'd possibly put an end to what truly mattered most to me. He'd become my companion in every sense of the word and now I wasn't sure if he was done with me or not. I wanted to call him, but I wasn't going to ask him to make a decision when he was so upset. It wouldn't turn out in my favor.

"I already know that you're right," I said in frustration.

She took a moment to end her scolding and took a real look at me.

"You know that I'm just trying to keep it real with you," she said, "I wouldn't be your friend if I didn't tell you the truth."

"I already know the truth. I know it better than anyone, I'm the one that got put out today," I said as my tears pricked my eyes again.

I took a moment to calm myself and to put a halt to my tears. I wondered if it was such a good idea to come and speak with her. She wasn't being very helpful at the moment. I didn't want her to be a parent; I wanted her to be my friend.

"I'm sorry, I know that it's not what you want to hear right now but someone has to tell you. I would hate to see you give up such a good thing over bullshit. Leave the ghetto shit here and don't let it leak into your new life."

"OKAY SANDY," I yelled.

"No need to get pissy with me," she rolled her eyes, "So do you think Marcus told?"

"Of course I think he told," I said.

She shook her head, "I always knew that he was evil, but this is just beyond evil. The fact that he would do something like that to *you* shows just how crazy he really is. He is off of his rocker, and everyone around here has been talking about it."

"What do you mean?" I asked.

"People are really starting to become scared of him and you know how that goes. Someone is going to silence him soon. He lives too close to where he does dirt to act so crazy," she disclosed.

"There was a time where I wouldn't have wished anything bad on him but now I just don't know anymore. He's pushed me to a place where I really don't care."

"I don't blame you."

"I think he's completely ruined my relationship," I said.

"Kyle didn't ask for the ring back and so he's probably thinking things over. When men are finished with you, they love to ask for their ring back."

"I really hope you're right," I yawned.

"I'm always right," she grinned, "Now take your ass in the room and get some rest. I'll wake you after I've made lunch. I'll also bring your bags."

I rose to my feet, "Thank you. I really appreciate it."

"You're my girl, even when you're hardheaded."

I laughed sleepily and walked back to the room. She and I spent the day together, and she didn't mention how crazy she thought that I was for the rest of the day. I was happy that she was able to pick up on my mood and leave it alone. I didn't think that I could take much more of her unasked for advice. I watched the clock because I couldn't wait for her shift to start at 7pm. It was her house, but I wanted the peace and quiet. I wanted to be able to cry without her coming in trying to make me feel better. I could have done it at home, but it would have felt so much lonelier.

"Alright Cam, I'm about to get out of here for work. Don't sit up all night crying, I know how you are. You're way too cute for those puffy ass eyes that you rock after a long night of tears."

I smacked my lips, "Bye Sandy, I'll see you in the morning."

She gave me a big hug and left the house. I went straight towards her freezer and grabbed a strawberry shortcake ice cream bar. I couldn't wait to tear into it and so I was halfway finished with it before I reached the guestroom. I sat on the edge of the bed and finished it as I enjoyed the silence. After I threw it away I crawled in the bed and cried. I was able to release everything that I'd been feeling over the last few days into the pillows.

I thought that I would drift off to sleep, but I was up for hours thinking about my future that was up in the air. Kyle had every right to longer want me, but I wouldn't be able to walk out of his life without trying to get him back. I just hoped that what I had to say would be enough to keep us together. I was finally experiencing the love that I'd always wanted, and I ruined it with my lack of trust. I was bringing back old habits into my new relationship, and it put everything in jeopardy. Kyle took my past so much better than I'd expected, and he was willing to still be with me. What he didn't appreciate was that I'd given money to Marcus. The feelings of guilt plagued and tormented me all night.

When I wasn't feeling guilty, I was feeling angry. I wanted to confront Marcus, but it would only make him happy to see me so miserable. He'd shown me exactly how much he truly cared about me. I didn't buy into the idea that a woman sold me out, he probably put someone up to it. I was willing to bet that it was his child's mother. Charity was a vindictive hood rat that chased after cheese. She was attracted to shiny objects, and when a man flashed his cash or gold in front of her, he could do whatever he wanted. I couldn't stand her.

I awoke to the light coming in through the blinds. I should have thought to close the curtains before I went to sleep, and I was paying for it. I pulled my phone from beneath my pillow and saw that I had a few missed messages, but the only one that I cared about came from Kyle. He asked me to come to the loft. The bitch in me smacked her lips because he'd asked me to leave. He just couldn't decide when he did and didn't want me around. We were engaged and if we were going to be together, then putting me out wasn't an option. But he could have asked me to come over so that he could request his ring back. He wasn't the kind of man to break up with a person over the phone. He was much more direct than that.

I climbed out of the bed and freshened up within 10 minutes and headed for the door. Sandy was home, but she was sound asleep from a long night at work. I didn't want to wake her, and I figured that I would text her later. Besides, if she wanted to reach me she would call. I couldn't get to my car fast enough. I was ready to see where I stood with Kyle because the waiting was killing me. Navigating my way through Chicago traffic in the morning absolutely sucked. Traffic was crawling, and I was exhibiting some true road rage. No one was driving fast enough, and no one deserved a license in my opinion. I would have driven along the shoulder of the road if I didn't think that I would have gotten a ticket. I took the opportunity to text Kyle and let him know that I was on my way. His response was short a short 'See You Soon.'

I finally arrived at the loft, and when I got there I saw that his lawyer was sitting on the couch in our living area. When I walked in he stood up and greeted me.

"Always a pleasure to see you Camille," he said as he extended his hand.

I instinctively gave him a firm handshake, "Nice to see you too Bill," I said cautiously.

Kyle met us in the room, and I gave him a confused look. I wasn't sure what to say because I didn't understand why his lawyer was there. He and I weren't married yet and so I didn't see the need for any lawyers. I wondered if I was in some sort of legal trouble with him.

"What's going on?" I asked.

Without saying anything he pulled me into an embrace, and I happily accepted it because I wasn't sure if it would be my last from him and because I just needed it. It's funny how we sometimes want comfort from the person that's caused us pain. He pulled away and kissed me on the forehead.

"I'm happy that you came. Bill is here because I need to discuss something really important with you. Please take a seat," he said.

I sat in one of the single chairs, "Okay."

"I've done quite a bit of thinking," he began, "And I need to know that I can trust you. The only way that I can do that is if we turn your ex in to the police."

My eyes widened in panic, and I shook my head no quickly, "Do you know what he'll do if we make a move like that?"

"You think I'm afraid of him?" Kyle asked in an offended tone.

I stared at him in shock. What Sandy said came to my mind, and I realized that she was more correct than I originally thought. I'd never thought of a world that was free of Marcus and in my world he was one of the most dangerous people that I knew. When I took in the big picture I grasped that he wasn't a force to be reckoned with. He was a petty thug that had achieved a small measure of success through illegal means.

"I don't think you're afraid of him. I just don't want you involved in this, you don't deserve your name being tied to this any further," I said and I surprised myself because I meant every word.

"You're going to be my wife," he said sternly, "If someone is blackmailing you, then he is blackmailing me, and I won't stand for it. So I'm asking you to help me put this fucker away. I could go after him without you, but I don't know enough about him to make anything stick. With your help we can ensure that he's away for a long time."

I was proud to be engaged to Kyle in that moment. He was standing up for me, and he still planned on marrying me. I didn't want him to walk away from our relationship, but I wouldn't have been surprised if that was the route that he took. Some people just weren't equipped to deal with the kind of baggage that I brought to the table. I silently thanked God and he was probably surprised to hear from me.

I didn't want to be a part of bringing Marcus down because he and I were originally in it together. He was the reason that I'd made it through my childhood with the things that I needed and wanted. We were partners in crime, and he took care of me when no one else would. Not a lot of girls have had a boy take care of them in that way. I never had to worry if I was going to eat because Marcus always made sure that I did. Turning him in really was betraying him.

But hadn't he betrayed me? He didn't get to where he was without my help. But yet he'd cheated on me when I wanted to make a legitimate living, and he got another woman pregnant. To add insult to injury, he then left me to be with her. I felt like he ripped my heart out of my chest and stomped on it. When I'd moved on he then chose to blackmail me. I warred with myself for minutes in silence. Snitching on someone is definitely not something you do when you are on the street but, fuck it, I am not on the street anymore. I am not a part of that life. Kyle has been the best thing to ever happen to me and I am not going to let this slip away because of "street honor".

"What do you think?" Kyle said.

"Let's do it," I said.

It was time for me to let Marcus go. I didn't owe him my loyalty anymore. He not only blackmailed and disrespected me, but he choked me as well. We were at a crossroads, and it was either him or me. I didn't want my life to be ruined, and I was saddened that it had to come to that point, but I had to make the tough decision. I wanted to prove to Kyle that it was all behind me, and this was a good way to do it.

Kyle looked relieved, "Are you sure?"

"Yes I'm sure. I want to be with you, and this is something that needs to happen so that I can close that chapter of my life. I would have liked to move on without having to do it, but he hasn't given my any other option," I said.

"Okay," Bill interjected, "We've been in contact with the police, and we've come up with an action plan. We may not be able to get him for drugs, but we'll be able to get him for blackmail. When he contacts you again you'll give in to whatever his demands are and when you meet him you'll wear a wire..."

The lawyer gave me the entire game plan and all of it bothered me. I was raised in the environment of 'snitches get stitches." We were never supposed to do things like this to one another. If I went through with the plan then there was no one from that area would ever trust me again. My name would be mud in my old community. However, that community hadn't done anything for me and so I didn't owe it anything. I had to fight and struggle to beat the odds and if they didn't like me anymore because I wanted a better life, then screw all of them.

After Bill finished explaining the process to me I felt overwhelmed but I was determined to push through my fear.

"I'll be waiting outside with the police the entire time and when it's over we can have our lives back."

I smiled weakly, "I'm ready to have our lives back."

"Well the sooner we get this over with the sooner we can move forward."

#Chapter9

"I'm really sorry that it had to come to this."
Camille

Marcus was ridiculously predictable, and he did call back just the way that we all thought that he would. He demanded an exorbitant amount of money from me. He was so damned condescending and evil during our phone conversation that it was difficult to feel sorry for him. He wasn't expecting me to show up at his house and surprise him. I wanted to get it all over with and so we decided to push to end things a lot quicker.

I texted him and asked him if he was at home, and he said that he would be there in about an hour. I showed up to his home a little after that. The process of getting wired went a lot faster than I thought that it would and the officers gave me my instructions over again. I couldn't focus on anything that they were saying. I was way too nervous to listen to them. I hopped in my car, and I saw everyone drive behind me on my way to his house. I wasn't alone, and so that was a huge bonus. If he knew what I was doing then he probably would have tried to kill me.

I arrived at his house, and I didn't look to see if they were there behind me. I'd watched enough TV shows and movies to know that it was a bad idea. I walked slowly up his stairs and knocked on his door. I was surprised that it wasn't open already the way that it was usually. I knew that the mics worked because I tested them before I exited my car.

His door opened, "Nice to see that you've come to your senses baby girl," he said.

I walked into his house and jumped when his door closed with a loud thud. I was going to have to calm the hell down.

"So do you have my money?" He asked impatiently.

"I'm going to need time Marcus. Exactly how much are you asking for again?"

"Just when I thought that you were smart, you go and show me differently," he laughed, "Have my $100k to me within a week, or

I'm going to press and I'm telling them all of your dirty ass secrets," he said.

I gave a sigh of relief because I'd gotten what I'd come for. I was going to make my exit but before I left he stopped me.

"You know, out of all the shit that I've done…this feels the best. You would think that watching Solomon take his last breath after I shanked his ass for crossing me would have topped this but nope. This shit is way fucking better. You know that I own you right?"

"You don't own me," I said.

"Yes I do, and I always have. I made you, and now it's time for you to finally show me just how much you appreciate me. I can't wait to receive my payout; it's the first of many. I always wanted to be a pimp," he laughed sarcastically.

My stomach turned and if I didn't have the wire on I would have said some pretty unsavory things but I didn't want Kyle to hear me talk in that way. He'd giving the cops so much more than they ever thought they were going to get. He'd just admitted to murder, and he'd pissed me off so I wanted to push him further.

"Why did you kill Solomon anyway?"

"Let's just say that he was giving my product away for free, and I don't play like that," he said.

I gave a huge shake of my head, "I don't know when you became so cold but I hope you're happy."

"I've always been like this," he said, "I've just never had to show you. But now I just don't care anymore. You don't give a shit about me and so now that feeling is mutual."

"Well I'll be back later with your money," I said.

"Don't make me wait too long; you know the press be hounding me to get that story."

"I will have it to you as soon as I can."

"Looking forward to hearing from you. But honestly, I'm really sorry that it had to come to this."

I wanted to spit in his face, but I had more manners than that. He had a lot of nerve to say that after all that he'd put me through.

"I'm sorry that it's come to this too," I said as I headed out of the door.

I got out of the car and got into the car with Kyle and his lawyer. One of the officers was going to drive my car back to his place. The lawyer confirmed that the recording was good and gave the signal to send the police in. My stomach dropped as I watched the police rush in and raid his home. They had a warrant to search his home, and I knew that they were completely turning it upside down. A small crowd formed outside, and I pushed my inner panic down. I wondered if I'd done the right thing, but Kyle's grip on my hand soothed me.

Then they finally brought him out in handcuffs. Tears flowed down my cheeks when our eyes connected. Seeing him in handcuffs had been one of my worst fears since we'd first began illegal activity. I never thought that I would be the reason that he ended up in them. My soul ached over the loss of the friend and lover that I once had. It was over between us for a while, but our connection was completely severed. He was going to hate me for the rest of his life, and he'd done a pretty good job of making me hate him.

Kyle put his arm around me and squeezed me to his side, "I love you," he said into my ear.

I closed my eyes and allowed my body to melt into his body. I needed the comfort and the assurance that I'd made the right decision.

"I love you too," I whispered.

"We don't need to see anymore," Kyle told his driver and we started back towards the loft.

I don't know how I was able to contain so much guilt and joy within myself all at once. I was so relieved that Marcus wasn't going to be able to make my life a living hell anymore. I was also getting ready to enjoy life with the man that I loved.

#Chapter10

"I am going to kill him."
Kyle

It was early in the morning, and I missed Camille more than anything.

Spending the night without her had been exhausting; I wasn't able to get any rest. I regretted asking her to leave as soon as she got onto the elevator. I wanted to call her and beg her to come back, but the space was for the best. I could use the time to think, make phone calls, and to get a firm handle on what had to happen so that we could move forward. She looked absolutely distraught, but I had to keep myself from comforting her for the moment. She needed to understand that what she did wasn't okay.

I ignored my father's phone calls for the remainder of the day. I didn't want him to try to tell me what to do, and I didn't want to hear him gloating. I was determined to make my own decisions and to let the chips fall where they may. I called my lawyer, and he and I had a long conversation and he agreed to come over today. He assured me that we could get out of everything and still come out smelling like roses. That was why I hired him, he was a shark and he did whatever it took to make me look good.

Bill showed up before 6 am to my loft, and I went over everything again as best as I could. Bill always came prepared, and so he went over the game plan that he'd worked on the previous day. I was liking his plan so far, and it seemed to go in the right direction. "She's going to have to wear a wire," Bill said as he sat on my sofa.

I shook my head, "No, that's too dangerous. If he finds out that she's wearing a wire then we could put her into a lot of danger. I'm not going to put her in that position."

"There is no way that he's going to think she's wearing a wire. They have a long history, and so it's the last thing that he'll expect," he said making a valid point.

"I'm not sure if Camille will go along with something like this. She's an extremely loyal woman," I said.

She was also stubborn as a fucking mule, but I wasn't going to vent to Bill about her, I'd done enough venting.

He shrugged, "Well if you two want to put all of this behind you, then this is the most direct way to do it. Her helping to get him off the streets will give the both of you a lot of great PR, and we can put all of it to rest."

"I will see if she'll be willing to do it, but the last thing I want is to put her in harms way" I said as I picked up my phone and texted Camille.

I hoped that she would be on board for our plan. If not, I wouldn't leave her but everything would be a lot more difficult. I was going to eventually have to answer to my father, my family, and the rest of the world. Our relationship would face more scrutiny than she, or I was truly ready for.

Within the hour she sent me a message saying that she was on her way. She arrived at the loft while I was in the restroom. She was in the living area with Bill when I emerged. Before anything could be said I took her into my arms and hugged her to my chest. She'd been away from me for far too long, and I vowed to myself to never deal with another dispute by asking her to leave. That was just rude as hell, and I can't deal with shit that way when we're married, so I may as well get used to it now. I felt fortunate that she was still receptive towards me. I half expected her to slap me when I saw her again.

When she agreed to the plan I sighed in relief. She was on board with everything and that just solidified what I already knew about her. She was strong, she loved me and she was ready to move on, it was just hard for her to deal with that part of her past. I couldn't even begin to fathom the kind of childhood that she experienced. She was a diamond that had been through intense pressure, and I loved her even more for it.

I was happy when Bill left the loft so that she and I had time to reconnect. Reconnecting with her was starting to get pretty old rather quickly. I wanted to be able to enjoy her time and company with breaks. Life was dropping a lot of drama at our doorstep, and I didn't like it one bit. The sooner we got married the better. I knew that getting married wouldn't keep problems at bay, but it would be something solid between us. I wanted her to know just how much I truly loved her and for her to never doubt if I was going to stay. I planned on dedicating the rest of my life to that purpose. She'd put up with enough of my indecisive bullshit.

I spent the next couple of days immersing myself in work and in Camille. She really didn't have a clue about how intelligent she was. Her business instincts couldn't be taught in a classroom. Her suggestions were usually spot on, and her questions showed that she was really trying to get to know the business. I couldn't have chosen a better partner in this journey. She has come a long way from that nervous girl I first hired to be my PA. Many people say that you shouldn't work with your spouse, but I was hell bent on proving them wrong. My father kept my mother out of his business, and they both seemed miserable.

My mother wasn't happy, and she was usually very lonely. She busied herself with charity organizations and shopping. She'd done a ton of philanthropy work, but I've always thought that my father was missing out by not asking her about her opinions. Camille would never have to live her life that way. She would be at my side and never behind me.

Watching the officers attach the wires to Camille on the morning of "The Sting" had shattered my nerves. I hated the idea of sending her into the lion's den alone. She assured me that she was safe, and I could only take her at her word. If anything happened I would never be able to forgive myself because she was only doing it for me.

"Are you sure that you want to do this?" I asked before we headed to our separate cars, "If you don't want to do it anymore, we can call this entire thing off."

She gave a brave shake of her head, "No, I'm going through with it. If we don't end it now, there is no telling how long this will continue and I'm not going to put your family through that."

I gave a laugh, "You're thinking of my family right now?"

"And of us of course. I want you to trust me, and know that part of my life is over. Marcus made his choice when he blackmailed me. He brought this on himself," she said.

I possessively grabbed the back of her neck and brought my lips to hers. I wanted to communicate how much I loved her through my kiss. She inhaled deeply as she eagerly returned it. For a moment I forgot that we were surrounded by a team of officers and my lawyer. I heard someone clear their throat.

"So we're good to go?" One of the cops asked.

I hesitantly broke my hold on Camille and searched her face for the answer. She nodded at me to signal that we were still moving forward.

"Yes we're good to go," I echoed as I walked her to her car.

Driving behind her car as we headed to her ex's house was a sobering experience. I'd been to that part of the city only a handful of times, but I was now looking at it through a different lens. My Camille, the woman that I loved, grew up in that impoverished area. I was in awe of her, and I realized just how wonderful she was. I wasn't sure if she was the exception because I didn't know a lot of people from her walk of life, but I did know that she was special.

When we arrived to her ex's home, I hated seeing her disappear into his house, and I began to rethink my decision. My heart was pounding against my ribcage as she engaged in conversation with him. He told her that he owned her and suggested that she was his whore, I almost lost it. My hand flew to my car door, and I was about to get out of the car and storm into the house to knock him the fuck out.

"I am going to kill him." I yelled.

Bills hand tightly gripped my arm, "Do not do that, you'll ruin everything. I know this is rough but don't let it all be in vain."

I gave him a look of contempt and steadied my breathing. We had everything that we needed, and I wanted her to leave as soon as possible. But she kept going, and that miscreant not only confessed to murder, but illegal drug activity as well. I realized that Camille was doing it purposefully, and I was proud. I also made a mental note to never get on her bad side.

I was overjoyed when she exited the house and got inside of the car. She was completely shaken up, and I could see the undercurrent of emotions that were taking place within her. I wanted to ease all of her fears and doubts. Watching his home get raided, and him being brought out in handcuffs felt like sweet justice. I didn't feel sorry for him at all because of everything that he'd put Camille through. I didn't understand how he could be so damned evil to a woman like her, she didn't come a dime a dozen. I'd never felt as fortunate in my entire life as when we drove back to our loft.

#Chapter11

"Are you fucking kidding me?"
Camille

My life with Kyle was finally back on track, and we picked up where we left off. Every day we worked diligently to get the businesses up and running. We had a staffing agency on board to do the hiring, and the properties were coming along really well. But nothing beat the feeling of waking up next to *him* in the mornings. The situation with Marcus had occurred a full week before and yet it seemed further away. As if a huge weight was lifted off of my shoulders.

The way that Kyle treated me was different, and that wasn't necessarily a bad thing. I just knew that I was going to have a lot of groveling to do after what I put him through, but it never happened. If anything I felt like he appreciated me a lot more, I enjoyed the reaction although I thought it was strange as hell. I'm not accustomed to people being so forgiving, and so I've had to work on accepting it. I hate always feeling like the other shoe is about to drop. We've been on such an emotional roller coaster that it can feel like a setup when we're enjoying a great time.

But it was easy to ignore all of those feelings while his arms were wrapped about my body. I snuggled my naked backside against him and enjoyed the light as it came through the window. He kissed the hollow portion of my neck.

"Good morning babe," he said gruffly.

"Good morning indeed," I giggled as I wiggled against his hardening cock.

"Look at what you're doing to me," he said as his hand cupped my breast and gave my nipple a slight pinch.

I smiled contently as he explored my body. His phone buzzed on the night stand next to the bed, and we weren't in the position to be able to ignore calls. He groaned as he separated our bodies, answered the phone and walked out of the room. I fought my sexual frustration and enjoyed the feeling of the Egyptian cotton against my skin. Shortly after my own phone began to buzz, and I reached under my pillow to answer it.

"Hello?"

"Now you answer the phone!" Cynthia said in mock frustration.

"I'm sorry girl, I've been so busy but I know that's not a good enough excuse. I'm gonna do better."

"I would appreciate that, I miss you."

"I miss you too. It's been too long since I've seen you."

"Hell yeah," she said, "So what in the hell is going on with you? I've been hearing a lot of rumors, but I would love to hear it directly from the source."

I began to fill her in on everything that happened, and she let me know about what Sandy filled her in on.

"So what happens now? Is there going to be a trial?"

"Yes, there is going to be a trial. I know him, he's going to plead not guilty and there is a huge chance that I'm going to have to testify against him."

"Oh wow," Cynthia said, "How do you feel about that?"

"I really don't like it but he's put me in this position. So I have to do what's necessary."

"Absolutely," she said in an understanding tone, "Just be careful and don't worry about anyone's bullshit."

"You're right," I said with a hint of sadness.

"I know how you are Camille, and so I know that it's tearing you up inside. Just make sure that you're honest with yourself and with the man that loves you. Don't hold all of your frustration and sadness in. Kyle seems to love you a lot, and so you need to lean on him."

Cynthia missed her calling as a life coach and psychic. She was right about my mixed feelings, and I was having a hard time opening up. I didn't want Kyle to think that I was going to backtrack on anything and so I didn't share my feelings about it. I would let him know that it hurt, but I didn't let him know just how deeply it hurt. It just seemed to be a little ungrateful to me, but I was doing my relationship a disservice by hiding a part of myself from him.

"I'm going to try to be more open," I conceded.

"I'm happy to hear it. I just wanted to check in with you before I headed to work. I love you," she said.

"I love you too," I said before I hung up.

I hated that my friends worked at that crappy diner every day. They were so much better than that place, and the management sucked. I was going to talk to Kyle about hiring my friends at our restaurants, the pay would be a whole lot better, and they could even get management positions. I also didn't want them to live in that neighborhood anymore. I didn't really have a family, and they'd become my family. There was no way that I could just sit back and continue to let them live in those conditions. I think Kyle's good nature is rubbing off on me.

Shortly after I got off of the phone, Kyle came back to the room with a huge grin on his face.

"What's the good news?" I asked.

"Well my beauty, we no longer have to worry about the negative stories being printed in the major press," he said.

I raised an eyebrow, "How in the hell did you pull that off?"

"I've got connections baby," he said as he plopped onto the bed next to me.

I giggled, "What kinds of connections? Please don't tell me that you're dirty dealing."

"Nope, not this time. I just know someone on the inside, and he's taken care of it for us. Bill has been working with him, and we have an injunction against them. From now on the only stories they can print are positive ones."

"That's music to my ears. I think we've had enough negativity to last a lifetime," I said.

"I also have some information for you, but I'm not sure if you'll want to hear it," He said soberly.

His expression turned serious, and I wasn't sure how to take his sudden mood change. I wondered if I truly wanted to know the information that he had.

"How bad is it?" I asked cautiously.

"Honestly babe, it's pretty fucked up. However, I think it is important you know the truth." he said honestly.

I groaned, "Just tell me and get it over with."

"I found out who sold the story about your past," he said.

"It was Marcus right?" I said.

"Babe, no it wasn't Marcus. I told you that they said it was female," he said.

"Yeah, but I figured that it was someone that he had to do his dirty work for him."

"I don't think that's the case this time," he said.

"Well who was it then?" I said in annoyance.

"You're not going to like it," He said.

I picked up the pillow and threw it at him, "Come on, and just say it."

He looked at me in the eye, "It's your mother."

"Are you fucking kidding me?" I shrieked.

"I'm so sorry," he said em-pathetically.

"That's it," I yelled as I hopped up from my bed to get dressed.

"Where are you going?"

"I'm going to find her, and then I'm going to kill her."

"Calm down," he said, "I don't want you to go out there while you're so upset."

"I'm not going to kill her but I am going to speak to her. It's long overdue, and I can't take it anymore. My own mother sold me out!"

My blood was coursing with lightning speed through my veins. I was beyond pissed and extremely hurt. I knew that my mother was shady, but I had no idea that she would sink so low.

"You can't go see her Camille, but you can call her," he said in a concerned tone.

I gave him the evil eye and swallowed the impulse to tell him to fuck off. My temper was at an all-time high, and it may have been best if I didn't see her in person. There was nothing that she could say that would have made me feel better. If she stood in my face and made excuses I probably would have completely gone nuts.

I snatched my phone off the bed and dialed my mom's number.

"Wow I didn't know that you had my number," my mom said sarcastically as she picked up.

I realized how right Kyle was about calling her instead of seeing her. I probably would have slapped her. I know that it's wrong to physically assault your parent, but I just felt like she was asking for it. I wanted to see if she was going to lie to me.

"Did you sell that story to the media?" I asked completely ignoring her.

"W-what? I know you didn't call me with this bullshit. I haven't heard from you in forever, and you call me with this?"

"It's something that I really need to know," I said.

"Who told you that?" She asked guiltily.

"Why does it matter? Did you or didn't you?"

"If you would have called and took care of your mother then I wouldn't have had to sell that story. You know I've been struggling and so what was I supposed to do?"

"You can't be fucking serious," I yelled through the phone, "All I've done my entire life is take care of you."

"What have you done for me lately?" She said defensively.

"First of all, I took care of myself and that was your job."

"Camille, you have lost your mind. You know that times were hard, I was a single mother and I had to do it all by myself."

"No! You were a single junky mother. You were never there for me, and all you did was beg. I just needed you to keep your fucking mouth shut, and you couldn't even do that," I yelled.

"All I told was the truth. If you wouldn't have been involved in all that ghetto shit, I wouldn't have had anything to say," she countered.

I had figurative smoke coming out of my ears. I'd never unloaded on her, but I refused to hold back any longer. She'd crossed the line.

"You were the reason that I had to do all of that ghetto shit and you've been taken care of because of it. I swear, I should have left you to your own devices when I was fifteen. I only stayed around because Marcus didn't want to you see you tricking off in alleys for cash. I'm done with you," I said as I paced the floor, and I turned my back to Kyle in shame.

"So you're really going to turn your back on your family? All over some damned money?"

"You made that decision, not me," I said as angry tears pricked at the back of my eyes, "I wish you well mom, but I'm done."
I hung up the phone and walked out of the bedroom without looking back at Kyle.
I grabbed a bottle of wine and walked upstairs to the balcony. I grabbed a glass and the opener from the portable bar outside and took a seat. I should have been working, and I definitely shouldn't have been drinking because it was too early in the morning. I let my mother get to me, and it pissed me off. I knew exactly what was coming from her and so I shouldn't have been surprised. She'd been the same selfish bitch ever since I was young.
My hands shook as I poured myself a delicious glass of Malbec. Tears streamed down my cheeks, and I took a sip after sip. Looking out at Chicago from our balcony soothed me although I felt a little guilty as I watched everyone going to work. I was letting Kyle down, but I wasn't in the mood to think about anything.
"Are you okay?" Kyle said as he took a seat across from me.
I jumped because I didn't hear him approach.
"You scared me," I said.
"I'm sorry, I guess I'll knock first," he grinned.
I shook my head and gave a short laugh.
"So tell me what's going on with you," he said.
I was going to tell him that everything was okay, but I thought about the conversation that I had with Cynthia earlier. He and I couldn't have a relationship if I wasn't able to share this kind of stuff with him. Everything isn't roses all the time, and I have a lot of baggage. I'd spent a lot of time hiding my baggage from him, and all it did was drive a wedge between us. I wiped my face and took a deep breath.
"She didn't even apologize," I said as fresh tears streamed down my cheeks.
"I'm so sorry; maybe I shouldn't have told you."
"No," I said shaking my head, "I needed to know. Although I really thought that it was Marcus, and now I've turned him in."
"Don't upset yourself over that. You did the right thing, he was blackmailing you."

"I knew that she wasn't going to say sorry, but I really wanted her to surprise me. I just wanted her to own up to her shit for once in her life."

"Unfortunately, it seems that you're going to have to give yourself closure on that part of your life. I'm not saying that she won't come around because it's very possible, but she may not. You can't spend your life waiting on her to apologize," he said.

"What's fucked up is that I thought I was over it. That's why it's surprising that I feel this way."

"She's your mom, and I think its human nature to not give up on our parents. That doesn't make you weak, it makes you strong. Don't write your mom off but don't expect anything either."

"I'm going to work on that," I said as I took another sip.

"It takes time," he said as he grabbed a wine glass and filled his glass.

I raised my eyebrow at him.

"If you can't beat em'," he said with a smile, "How about we take it easy for the next two hours, get dressed, go to check on the progress of the venues, and then just do whatever in the hell we want?"

I perked up a bit, "You mean that? I know that this is a really busy time for us."

He quickly shook his head, "Nothing is more important than you. We have a great team behind us, the marketing is going well, and we're up to speed with staffing."

"I love that you're willing to do this for me. Let's finish this bottle of wine and continue to be bums for the next two hours," I said as I raised my glass for a toast.

"To being bums," he echoed as he tapped my glass with his.

Kyle and I went through the rest of the day flawlessly. When we arrived at the last venue I couldn't stop smiling. It was becoming the exact vision that we had in mind. We walked into the restaurant, and it was breathtaking. We'd taken the space of an old bar and grill and turned it into a refined high end steakhouse. It was two floors, right off the magnificent mile, and so the traffic was going to be phenomenal.

The modern black and white décor with amber lighting was everything that I could have hoped for. Modern décor was amongst my favorite, and maybe that's because I never grew a real appreciation for the other stuff. I didn't enjoy the big bulky furniture, huge heavy curtains, or deep reds that some of the other high end restaurants had. It was easy for me and Kyle to agree because he and I had similar taste. The restaurant looked like it could have been an extension of our loft.

"There are some finishing touches that need to be done, but we'll be finished within the next few days," the foreman assured us.

"You're ahead of schedule," Kyle said.

"Yes sir. So if you want to add or change anything we'll have plenty of time to get it done."

"We'll be back in a couple of days, and Jack will check in with you tomorrow," Kyle assured him.

"So what do you think?" Kyle asked me.

"I love it. It's exactly what we had in mind," I said with glee, "I can already envision the furniture and where it will go."

"I've been meaning to ask you. Do you think that any of your friends would be interested in working at either of the locations?"

I turned to him and hugged him tightly, "Thank you so much! I wanted to suggest that, but I wasn't sure how you feel about it."

"It's clear that they love you, and they're like family to you, so we're going to take care of them," he said.

"That's amazing. I think they'll appreciate it a lot."

"There is more where that came from. We need to get them out of that neighborhood. So you can take them apartment hunting, and we'll pay it up for a year. By that time they should make a wage that allows them to continue the payments on their own."

"That makes me feel so good, I don't care if I have to drag them out of there kicking and screaming. They're going to move," I laughed.

"You know that if you wanted me to do something for your mother then I would," he said seriously.

"I'm not ready to even think about that yet. I may change my mind later but right now I don't want to deal with her at all," I said.

"Okay, I'll leave it alone for now," he conceded.

"Thank you," I said before I lifted to my toes and kissed him on the lips.

We spent the rest of the day enjoying Millennium Park. It wasn't a huge place, but I loved watching the kids play in the fountain and the garden was beautiful. I was at peace, and I couldn't stop hugging and kissing Kyle. I was safe with him, and he was not only taking care of my basic needs but he was taking care of my emotional needs as well. I couldn't wait to become his wife.

That night he took me to *Ruth Chris Steak House*, and we spent a lot of time critiquing the food, décor, and service. We took notes on the things that we liked and on the things that we didn't care for.

"You're so intelligent and sexy," Kyle said out of the blue.

I blushed, "Where did that come from?"

"It's just something that I've been thinking for a while now. I always knew that you were a catch, but it was confirmed after I saw what you came from."

"Thank you," I said.

"I really mean it. I have a new level of respect for you. I just wish that you would have told me in the beginning."

Before he could speak anymore I cut him off, "I know, and I've been meaning to apologize to you for that. I just didn't know how to bring something like that up. I've never searched for handouts or sympathy about my past, and I also wasn't sure if you would want to be with me."

"Of course I would have still wanted to be with you. I actually feel closer to you now than I ever have. Things have been rough, but we've needed to battle and face these obstacles together."

His words were a symphony to my senses, and a huge weight that I didn't know I possessed was lifted off of my shoulders.

"You don't know how great it feels to hear you say that," I said.

"Now that we're finally over all of this bad news, I have something good to tell you."

"Well don't make me wait," I laughed.

"I have set a date. We're getting married on July 27th in Fiji."

"SHUT UP!" I shrieked loudly and quickly quieted down as people looked at us. That got a hearty laugh from him.

"I think that you like the idea?"

"That's just unreal. That's something that I never even imagined as a possibility. Hell I would have been happy with the Bahamas."

"We can still do it there," he said.

"Oh hell no, I want Fiji."

For the rest of the night we laughed and talked with an ease that we hadn't had in a long time. We'd gone from a clear hierarchy to becoming equals. My collar had been abandoned in the drawer, and neither one of us had mentioned it. I had now submitted to Kyle in more ways then one and he seemed like he was satisfied with my commitment to him. He wasn't my Dom anymore, he was my fiancé, and soon he was going to be my husband. Everything was beginning to feel a lot more real.

We got back to the loft, and I went straight to the kitchen to get another bottle of wine.

"What do you think you're doing?" Kyle said as he placed both hands on either side of me on the counter.

He rubbed against my ass and I put the bottle down, "I was going to open a bottle of wine."

"There's no need for that," he said as he placed a kiss on the back of my neck.

A soft moan slipped from my lips as I pressed back against him. I began to slowly sway my hips against his center.

"Damn, I need to be inside of you right now," he groaned.

I needed for him to be inside of me too. I wanted to feel him pushing into my body, claiming it as his own. He didn't have to make me wear a collar because he owned my heart, and that was more valuable than anything.

"What are you waiting for?" I challenged.

He responded to my goading by roughly pushing my skirt up around my waist and placing a firm smack on my ass. It stung like hell, and it sent pleasure straight to my center.

"Mmm I know you liked that," he whispered against my ear as his hand rubbed my sensitive flesh through my panties. "Show me how much you want it."

I bit my lip and pressed back and forth against his hand. My underwear was becoming wet with my juices, and he lightly tapped against my clit.

"Please," I begged as I bent over completely and pressed my face against the cool marble of the counter.

He gave a triumphant laugh, and I knew that I wasn't going to make it so easy for him next time. I'd come to the point where I was unashamed to beg him for what I wanted sexually. I loved the cat and mouse game, and so he would have to do a little more work in order to get me to purr. But for now, I just wanted to be fucked.

I could hear him unzipping his pants and my pulse raced. I couldn't wait for him to give me everything that he had. He pushed my panties to the side and rubbed the head of his cock against my clit before he slowly pushed into me. I tried to squirm, but his fingers dug into my flesh and held me in place.

"Don't move, just take it," he growled.

I was getting frustrated because I wanted him to fuck me hard, and he was moving at a snail's pace. It was clear that he was enjoying himself. I slapped the marble hard, "Fuck Kyle!"

He pulled until only the head of his cock was inside of me and then he impaled me deep and hard. My pelvis hit the unforgiving slab painfully, but I didn't care because he was inside of me to the hilt. I gasped as my orgasm waited to erupt, I was close already. He withdrew and slowly inched into me again. My body shook with need, and I whimpered. He took mercy on me and sped his pace up.

"Fuck me back Camille," he demanded.

I could have taken that opportunity to turn the tables, but I needed to cum. My body demanded its own release, and I pushed against him. His huge cock slammed into me over and again, and I imploded. My legs shook, but I continued to meet each of his pumps without stopping. I wanted him to feel just as great as I did. He pushed inside of me with the fury of the energizer bunny, and he coaxed another orgasm from my body before spilling his seed inside of me.

I smiled in contentment as I thought about what a great day it turned out to be. My life was finally falling into place.

Epilogue

I always loved watching Camille get dressed in the morning. Her clothing choices lately reminded me of a sexy pin-up girl. She looked classy and sexy as hell. Watching her pull her pencil skirts onto her thighs and ass got my dick hard. Her shapely legs were pronounced when she slid on her tall Mary Jane pumps.

"Are you going to watch me or are you going to get dressed?" She asked as she stood there with her hands on her hips.

"Watching you is much more interesting that getting dressed," I said as I fumbled with the buttons on my shirt.

"Well maybe I can help you with that," she said coyly as she walked seductively over to me, kissed the side of my neck, before planting a kiss on my chest at the tip of my v-neck t shirt. I pulled her closer against me so that she could feel my arousal. If we kept going we were going to have to push our day back by a half hour.

My hand slid over her ass and squeezed as I captured her mouth and ravished her. I then heard the annoying buzz of my phone on the nightstand. Camille groaned against my lips as she went to grab my phone and bring it to me. I slapped her on the ass on her way to get it.

It was the security desk calling me.

"Hello?"

"Sir, I'm so sorry to bother you and I tried to call your home phone first."

"We cut the ringer off," I said gruffly.

I didn't want to give Sarah any attitude, but I was a little upset about being bothered.

"There is a woman down here that wants to speak with you. She asked to come upstairs, but I wouldn't allow her up."

"Please send her away. I don't take random meetings and certainly not with someone that shows up to my home. Give her the number to my assistant and have her call him," I said in annoyance. I was willing to bet that it was a reporter. I didn't take the invasion of my privacy very well.

"Mr. Kane she says that her name is Jane Foster."

My body went rigid as I heard the name. I had not heard from her in years. What could she possibly want?

"Is everything okay?" Camille asked.

I gave her a slight nod as I walked to my window.

"Ask her what her visit is regarding," I said.

"I did Sir, she says that she wants to talk to you about your son."

"Sorry, my son? I don't have a son."

"That is what I said but she is insisting. I think you had better come down as she is not going to leave..."

I sighed and gathered my thoughts as I began to make my way downstairs. Just when things are looking up, something else pops up to bite me in the ass....

The End

THE WHITE BILLIONAIRE'S BABY

#Chapter1

"I want you to be a father to your son"
Jane

My entire body froze when I heard what Sarah told me through the phone. I hadn't heard from Jane in years, and now she had emerged with life changing news.

"I'm on my way down," I said quickly before I hung up.

"Babe is everything okay?" Camille asked with a concerned expression on her face.

"I don't know. A woman is downstairs saying that she wants me to meet my son," I said honestly.

Her eyebrow raised," What?"

"Just give me a minute please, I need to go downstairs and figure this out," I said as I quickly finished buttoning my shirt.

"I'm so confused right now."

"That makes two of us. Just give me a moment to figure this out. I'll be back in a few moments," I said as I left the room. I didn't give her time to respond because I knew that it wouldn't have been a good conversation.

I paced the elevator as it took me down to the lobby. I was unable to stand in one spot because my life was possibly about to change forever. I stepped off the elevator and entered the lobby. Jane was standing there with a child that looked to be about 3 years old. Jane looked just like I remembered her. She was a petite raven haired beauty and her son was beautiful. I slowly approached them both, and she shuffled her feet nervously.

"I'm sorry to bombard you like this, but you've never replied to any of my messages and so I felt it was best that I come here and speak to you in person," Jane said quickly.

"I changed my number about 3 years ago," I replied.

I couldn't stop looking at the kid that was holding on to his mother's leg. I searched his face for features that looked like me. He was a downright adorable kid, but I wasn't sure if he looked like me at all. However, I knew that looks weren't enough to go on in order to determine paternity. I also didn't want to upset her by making such an accusation.

Jane and I hooked up a few times about 4 years prior. Neither of us was looking for anything serious at the time, and so it was a perfect match. However our brief encounters fizzled out, and I moved on my life. We stopped calling each other and so I figured that it was a mutual decision. She never had a real idea of who I was. She was aware that I had a substantial amount of money, but she never realized that I was a billionaire.

"That would explain it," she said with a half-smile.

"I'm sorry but please forgive me. I'm at a loss for words, this is really unexpected. Why did you decide to reach out to me now?"

She took a deep breath, "I was trying to move on with my life with our son, and I was doing just fine. It was difficult raising your child, and you weren't even aware that you had a son. So when you popped up in the press, I took it as a sign to contact you."

I took a deep breath and scolded myself for being so mistrusting. She never struck me as the devious type when we were involved, but I knew that most people operated with ulterior motives.

"So because you saw me in the press you decided that it was time to tell me that I had a son?" I asked. Much to my dismay, I wasn't able to mask the anger in my voice.

"You vanished! I tried to call you, and that was the only way of contacting that I knew of. We met in hotels, and it was only after seeing you in the press that I knew how to track you down," she said in exasperation.

"So what do you want from me exactly?" I said as I tempered my voice. I didn't want to scare her child.

"I want you to be a father to your son," she said in a matter of fact tone.

I ran a hand down my face, and I swallowed hard when I saw Camille get off of the elevator.

#Chapter2

"I just need for you to stick through this with me."
Kyle

Kyle couldn't have thought that it was that easy. I know that trick, hell I've done that trick. I'll say something really quickly and leave before the person has a chance to say anything back. There's no way that I was going to stay upstairs like a "good girl" while he went to see his son. Usually I would mind my own business but this was definitely in the realm of my business. Kyle and I were about to get married, and this was something that could affect the rest of our life. After I gave it a few moments I headed to the elevators. I hoped that he wouldn't be upset, but my curiosity had gotten the best of me.

When I stepped off of the elevator I could hear Kyle and the woman talking.

"What do you want from me exactly?" He asked the woman in a strained voice.

She was pretty good looking. She was about 5'4, jet black hair, pale skin, and a great body. When I saw her I immediately thought of her as a vampire if that makes any sense. Her beauty was ethereal, and it annoyed me to no end because I just wanted her to go away. A twinge of jealousy struck me, and it was crazy because we were about to get married.

"I want you to be a father to your son," she replied. Ugh, even her voice was like liquid gold.

Kyle's eyes locked onto mine, and he looked guilty. "Now isn't a good time. We'll have to meet later during the week to discuss this further," He told her. She responded with a flustered look and she wasn't sure what to say. I looked down at the boy that was holding on to her leg. He looked just like his mother. I walked over before the both of them walked out.

"Hello," I interjected, "I'm Camille, Kyle's fiancée, and it's nice to meet you." I extended my hand, and she quickly took it.

"Hi, Camille I'm Jane, and this is Jason," she said as she motioned towards her son.

"Hi Jason," I said brightly to the little boy. He gave a shy smile and hid behind his mother.

"He's shy," she said.

"It's okay. He's a real cutie, and he looks just like you."

We all stood there in silence for a moment and everything felt awkward but I wasn't going to be the one to break the silence.

"Well, I guess that we'll get going," Jane said as she picked her son up and placed him on her hip, "I'll be in touch."

"One moment," Kyle said before he reached into his blazer jacket and pulled out one of his business cards, "Here's my card."

Jane looked at him with disdain and took the card from him before she walked out of the lobby. Kyle walked towards the elevator and I followed him. We got onto the elevator, and I watched him pace back and forth. His stress level was through the roof, and I couldn't remember a time when I'd ever seen him like that.

"You never told me that you had a child," I said as we stepped off of the elevator.

"This is all new to me too. She showed up today, and it's been at least 3 and half years since I've spoken to her."

I sighed heavily because this was something that I couldn't blame him for even though I wanted to. After all that I'd put him through I didn't have room to be judgmental about his past.

"Okay, now what?" I asked.

"I don't have a clue about what's going to happen with that. But I can promise you that this won't change anything with me and you," he said seriously before he grabbed my hand and kissed it.

I smiled nervously, "Do you promise?"

"Yes I promise. I will have to work something out, but I will make good on my promise. I just need for you to stick through this with me."

My heart felt like it dropped when I realized the vibe that I was giving off. It never entered into my mind to leave him over something like this. He'd been through hell and back with me, and this was the least that I could do for him.

"I'm not going anywhere Kyle," I said.

He gave a small sigh of relief, "I'm happy to hear it. Everything has just happened so fast and so it's hard to know what to expect."

"Nothing is going to keep me away from you, I'm here for the long haul," I said as I leaned in and kissed him.

I was telling him the truth, but my insides felt twisted as if I was about to jump off of a cliff. I kept seeing the little boy's cute cherub face in my head, and I felt a twinge of jealousy. It was my dream to be able to give Kyle his first child, and that wasn't a possibility for me anymore. My idea of perfection had just been shattered.

#Chapter3

"I planned on being more than a walking ATM for my son."
Kyle

The following few days were tough to get through.

Camille and I were focusing on opening up our new business ventures but my thoughts kept shifting to my son. I wondered how Jane managed to keep him away from me for so long. I'm not the kind of man that would be a deadbeat father. The Kane men always took care of our responsibilities, and I felt like I'd been robbed out of the beginning of his life.

Camille wasn't saying much about it, but I was worried that she wasn't happy with what had occurred. She'd entered our relationship and engagement under the assumption that I didn't have any children, and now we'd been sidelined with the news. I knew that I had to get everything under control as soon as I possibly could so I set up a meeting between me and Jane. She called me the day after I spoke to her, and we set up a meeting at my bar. It was a great way for me to check out the progress that had been made and a private spot for us to meet.

I was proud of Camille for allowing me to go alone. I gave her the option of tagging along, but she declined. It had to be really hard for her considering the circumstances and considering the fact that she's really nosy. It was something that I wanted to do alone, but I wasn't going to shut her out of that portion of my life. She was my fiancée, and I refused to withhold anything from her. That wasn't the way that I wanted us to begin our life together.

I was sitting at one of the tables in the bar having a glass of wine when Jane arrived. I was very happy with the way that everything was coming along, and I felt like a king in his castle. There were a few people buzzing around the bar and making preparations for the opening. I got up to open the door once I saw her arrive.

"Thanks for coming," I said as I held the door open for her.

"No problem, I'm just happy that you didn't blow me off."

"I wouldn't do anything like that," I said as I escorted her to the table.

"It's good to see that you still have manners," she laughed.

"My mom raised me well."

"That's what I'm trying to do with Jason."

"Would you like a glass of wine?" I asked as I poured her a glass.

"Umm sure."

We sat in silence for a few moments as we took small sips of the robust red wine. I hated being at a loss for words. I was used to being in complete command of situations, but this was something that I didn't have any control over. I had to tackle this the same way that I tackled everything else because it was the only way that I knew how.

"So what do you want?" I asked.

"So you've just cut right to the chase," she said with a nervous laugh.

"I don't want to waste your time and it's clear that we need to face this head on. Jason has been here for over 3 years, and I'm ready to get the ball rolling because I'm late," I said honestly.

"It hasn't been easy raising him all by myself. Actually, it's been a huge struggle doing it alone. I need money to help support our son, and that's really all that I want."

My lips pressed into a straight line because I planned on being more than a walking ATM for my son. I still regretted the way that I met and ignored him when I first met him. I was going to become an active part of his life, and I felt fortunate that he was still pretty young.

"That's not a problem but I refuse to be a deadbeat dad. I will be a part of his life from here on out."

"I'm glad to hear it and that's really what I hoped for. I didn't want to ask more of you than what you were willing to give; I understand that this is a shock. Maybe you can take him out this weekend?"

"That would be great, I'm ready to get to know him However, I do have to say that I'm engaged to be married, and nothing will change that," I explained.

She gave a wave of her hand, "I don't want to ruin your family. I just want to give Jason the opportunity to get to know the other part of his family."

"Good. I'll talk to my lawyer today, and we'll work out how the money situation will work. Don't worry about it; I'll make sure that the both of you are very well taken care of."

She smiled appreciatively, "I'm not worried about it. Thank you." She rose from the table, "I guess I'll be hearing from you soon?"

"Yes, very soon. Please allow me to escort you out."

**

I had to get out of the house to calm my nerves while Kyle was seeing Jane. I did my best to be a big girl when he asked me if I wanted to go with him. I wanted to say 'hell yes' but the rational portion of me wouldn't allow me to. It was something that he needed to do alone, and my presence would have only made things tense.

So I went to see my friend Cynthia because I knew that she would make me feel better. She was a beacon of light in a dark world. I know that's being overly dramatic, but the positive energy that she gave off on a consistent basis was baffling. I was happy because soon I wouldn't have to drive to the hood anymore to come and see her because Kyle agreed to move her and Sandy into a better apartment. The fact that he was willing to do that for my friend's only made me love him more. He treated them as if they were my family and at this point they were all that I had. My mother was a complete basket case and so I relied on my friends for love and support.

"Camille calm down," Cynthia said in a soothing tone.

I had just finished telling her about everything that had occurred with Kyle and his son. I was trying not to overreact, but I felt fortunate that I didn't have to hide my feelings with her. She never judged me for my tears, and she always made me feel better. That was a lot more than I could say for my friend Sandy. Sandy always gave you the raw and unadulterated truth even when it was unwarranted. It was also her version of the truth and her thinking could be pretty warped. However, she really loved me, and I loved her back. I'm sure that I had my qualities that she couldn't stand either.

"I'm trying to calm down but I'm freaking the hell out on the inside. It's tough trying to keep a calm exterior when I feel like breaking down whenever I think about it," I admitted.

"Have you ever considered telling him the truth about how you feel? He strikes me as the kind of man that can take the truth. You aren't doing your relationship any favors by with-holding your feelings," she said with an extreme amount of patience.

"You're right but that's easier said than done. This is pretty new for him too, and I don't want to add to his stress."

"You won't be adding to his stress. He will probably be happy that you're finally being honest with him. Trust me; he knows that something is wrong with you because you wear your heart on your sleeve. He loves you, and this is something that you can work though. This isn't the first time that something like this has happened in a relationship, and it won't be the last. He has a kid, so what?"

"But what if he wants to get back with her since they already have a child together? Kyle is an honorable man and it would be the 'right' thing to do," I said emphasizing my words with finger quotes.

"Girl, that's not the honorable thing to do. They've been out of contact for years for a reason. It sounds like he knocked her up and moved on. It doesn't seem like they had a relationship based on anything other than sex. He loves you, and you're who he wants to be with. He's been through hell with you and back, and he's not going to let that slip through his fingers."

"I hope you're right," I said as I leaned back on her couch, "Have you gone apartment hunting yet?"

I smiled when I saw excitement enter her eyes, "Yes I found an apartment in the Hyde Park area. I've always wanted to live there; do you think that it will be too pricey?"

"He didn't put a cap on how much your rent could be. So feel free to pick wherever you want."

"I know but I don't like to waste people's money. He really doesn't have to do this, is he sure?" She asked.

"He's absolutely positive so stop trippin'.

"Okay."

"So make the phone call and go check it out. If it's what you want just let us know and have them invoice Kyle for a year's worth of rent."

"Oh my god, I'm so excited. I swear I'm never moving back over here," she said.

"Good that's the plan. Also have you put in your two weeks' notice at the diner? Your training starts next week at the restaurant. It's my hope that you're manager in a few months. He's hired on someone temporarily to teach you the ropes."

"Yes yes yes I've put it in. This is all pretty damned surreal and I don't think I'll believe it until it all happens."

"It's happening and trust me I know the feeling. But it's time for me to get out of here. If you need me call me."

"Alright girly, I love you," she said as she rose to her feet to give me a huge hug.

"I love you too."

I walked out of Cynthia's house, and all I felt was disdain for the neighborhood that I'd grown up in. It chewed people up and spit them out with no remorse. When people from my neighborhood made it out of there it was in spite of it and not because of it. The area was downright evil and designed to eat you alive. My decision to move to the southern suburbs was the best that I could have ever made for myself. That move drastically changed my life forever.

"Hey Cam," I heard a voice say behind me.

I turned around to see Rico. He was one of Marcus' flunkies, and I wasn't in the mood to entertain his bullshit.

"Hi Rico," I said as I continued to walk to my car.

"You know it's pretty fucked up what you did to Marcus. He loved you and took care of you and your crack head ass momma for years. This is exactly why I don't trust females now," he said.

I wanted to ignore him, but something about what he said struck a horrible cord within me. Maybe it was because of the guilt that I still harbored for putting Marcus in jail. It was a hard pill to swallow but it was either him or me, and I made the tough decision. The truth was that I would have never did to him what he did to me. I watched him have a baby and move on with someone else, and I didn't cause him one fourth of the grief that he caused me.

I turned around, "Shut the hell up. You don't know anything about what happened between me him. Furthermore, me and Marcus took care of each other. If it wasn't for me your raggedy ass wouldn't have had a job. Do you really think it's smart to talk shit to me? Especially considering what happened to Marcus? Who is going to protect you now Rico?" I asked angrily.

He looked stunned, and I was satisfied by the dumb look on his face. I didn't wait for a response as I got into my car. It felt good to let out some of my frustration, and I didn't feel bad for unleashing a bit onto him. He didn't have any right to speak to me whatsoever. I never liked him because I've always thought that he was a sleaze ball. He had at least 4 children by 4 different women that I knew of, and only God knew the rest. I hated people that didn't take care of their children, and that's probably because of the way that I grew up.

I hoped that that Kyle was home when I got back to the loft because I'd worked myself into a tizzy, and I needed him to make me feel better. I also wanted to know about what happened and about the progress of the bar. I would have to make sure that I kept my feelings suppressed until I figured out what was going on with him and Jane. Cynthia's words flowed through my head, and I knew that she was right, but communication was something that I was going to have to work on.

When I came in I asked Sarah if Kyle had arrived yet and she assured me that he was upstairs. I smiled happily as I headed to the elevator. It's funny how a person can become your world in such a brief period of time. I knew that I could make it without him if I had to, but I just didn't want to. He was a beautiful surprise, and I was sure that I had built up some incredibly good karma in a past life in order to meet a man like him. It was about so much more than money although that was an amazing bonus.

I dropped my purse on living room sofa and went in search of Kyle. He was in his favorite spot of the house, upstairs on the balcony. I stepped out and took a seat on the opposite side of him at the table.

"Hey darling," he smiled.

"So how did it go?" I asked.

"And I thought that I was direct," he laughed.

I smacked my lips, "Whatever, just spill it."

"I had a really positive meeting with Jane. She expressed that she was having some financial problems."

"Oh really?" I said sarcastically.

"I know how it looks, but raising a child can be expensive. Luckily that's something that she won't have to worry about anymore. But she and I have a good understanding about what is going to happen from this point on."

"What do you mean by that?" I asked.

"I mean that I explained to her that you and I are going to get married, and nothing is going to change that. I won't abandon my son, but this isn't going to put a dampener on our plans either," he said with sincerity in his eyes.

"I've really needed to hear that again. I'm sorry if I'm coming across as needy, but for some reason I just feel so fragile right now. I think it may be because of everything that we've just been through," I said as tears began to form.

"No need to cry. We're stronger than all of this, and it will be okay," he said as he stood to his feet to come over and hug me.

"I know, it's really silly to cry to about but I'm just so afraid that something catastrophic is going to happen. I'm constantly waiting on the other shoe to drop."

"You can't think this way because it only brings more negativity. I need you to believe that we can make it through anything because we will."

I lay my head on his shoulder and tried to pull myself together. I heard someone clear their throat.

"I'm sorry to disturb you," Bill said.

I was startled and jumped slightly at the voice of Kyle's lawyer.

"It's okay Bill, I asked you to come over and so you're not disturbing us at all," Kyle told him. "I asked him to come over so that I we could draw up the paperwork for child support payments as well as setting up a trust fund."

"Oh, do you need me to leave?" I asked.

"Please stay, I want you to be a part of this," he said. "Bill please come have a seat and let's get started."

We all took a seat at the circular table. Bill immediately got down to business, "Before we begin Kyle, I just want to make sure that the child is actually yours. How certain do you feel?"

"It's kind of hard to tell because Jason looks so much like his mother," I interjected.

Kyle seemed set on believing that the child was his and I wasn't going to keep any child from having a father. I grew up without my father in my life, and if Kyle wanted to step up to the plate for Jason, then I would stand by and let it happen because every child deserves to be loved.

"I wouldn't be doing my job properly if I didn't bring this up," Bill said.

"That won't be necessary," Kyle said, "The time line matches up, and I believe her. I can't deny that I had my doubts, but that was just the douche-bag in me. After giving it some thought I'm ready to move forward and take care of my flesh and blood."

"OK Kyle but please consider this as an option. We can get a test done. It can be done very discreetly. We just need a swab from the child's mouth and one from yours to see if they match. It's so easy to do. Don't you want to be sure before you share your family's lineage and wealth?"

I watched Kyle fight a war within himself. I would have given anything to be able to hear the dialogue that was playing out in his head and heart.

He sighed, "I will meet him this weekend, and I can probably get it done then."

"I will get you the kit tomorrow. We won't be releasing any funds to her until we have the results," Bill said. "So you will have to delay that somehow, I am sure you will think of something."

***

Watching Kyle nervously get ready on Saturday was bittersweet. He dressed down for the occasion, but he'd put on 3 different outfits. I kept telling him that toddlers don't really care about fashion choices, but this didn't have any effect on him at all. He settled on one of his Superman T-Shirts and a great pair of jeans. He looked relaxed even if he didn't feel that way. I could tell this was a big moment for him and I felt sad it was not something we could share together.

"How do I look?" He asked.

"You look like you're ready to see your son," I said before I gave him a kiss on the cheek.

"Thanks," he grinned as he handed me an envelope.

"What's this?" I asked.

"It's cash. Go and treat yourself to something nice while I'm gone. I don't need you to sit here and be over-thinking everything while you're alone."

"You know me so well. But I have your cards, why would you give me cash?"

He shrugged, "Plastic is great, but nothing beats the feeling of crisp hundreds."

I laughed and shook my head, "You've grown up so sheltered, and it's cute."

"What?" he said in fake defense.

"Only the people that sold drugs in my old neighborhood would carry around this much cash. Shit, even they knew that they couldn't carry it around for long periods of time because they're already walking targets. I'm a plastic kind of girl for safety reasons," I said.

"Okay, enjoy the cash today and I'll keep that in mind for the future."

"Thank you and make sure that you enjoy your son today. Don't be nervous."

"I think that I'll be fine once I get him. I just hate the thought of having to swab him while we're out, it just seems so damned underhanded."

"It's not underhanded, it's being fiscally responsible. Besides, you need to know for your own peace of mind. You don't ever want to look at your son and wonder if he's yours. Get it out of the way now so that you can enjoy him without any doubts in the future," I suggested.

"That's a better way to look at it," he said, "I'll keep that in mind when that time arrives so that I don't wuss out. We're taking them to the lab today, and they're going to process them today."

"Wow," I said.

"What now?"

"I'm only used to results coming back that fast for people on the Maury Show," I laughed, "The things that money can buy a rich boy."

"Well you can't judge me anymore because you're a rich girl."

"You know what I mean," I said.

"I know and I can't wait until you get used to the idea of having money. Whatever you want just let me know, and I'll get it for you."

"I have you, and that's more than enough," I said.

"You're such a sap," he said as he tweaked my nose between his two fingers.

"You make it easy to be and don't make fun of me. Get out of here before you're late."

"Okay I'm about to leave. You need to be out of here within the hour, and I mean it. I know how you are."

"Yes sir," I responded with a roll of my eyes.

"Someone is in desperate need of a spanking I see."

"Well I have been a very bad girl."

"It's only funny until you can't sit," he warned playfully.

"You wouldn't!" I squealed.

"Oh, but I would and you'd like it."

"We'll just have to see about that," I challenged.

***

I loved shopping, but it's something that's done better with friends. I felt lonely out on Michigan Avenue alone, and I wished that I had Sandy with me. She wouldn't have had any problem with dragging me from store to store to buy stuff. When I'm alone I get bored easily, and I can be really indecisive. I mull purchases over in my head for what feels like hours before I commit to spending my money. Although I could have spent anything that I wanted, I just couldn't bring myself to pay exorbitant prices for certain items. I found that to be pretty amusing because I swore to myself that if I'd ever gotten rich that I would buy whatever I wanted carelessly. My past self was severely disappointed in me.

I exited the Burberry store, and I was really unimpressed. If they thought that I was going to pay them that amount of money for the same pattern that they'd been making for years, they had lost their damned minds. A part of my frustration could be chalked up to my incessant thoughts about Kyle and Jason. I wondered if they were having a good time and I also wondered how and when Kyle was going to swab him. I looked up from my phone and saw Chastity. It was as if we spotted each other at the exact same time. She was the girl that Marcus cheated on me with, got pregnant, and left me for. I didn't want to have a huge argument with her in such a public arena, and I played around with the idea of ignoring her but she was headed straight for me.

"Look I'm not in the mood for any bull-"

"No, I'm not going to start any shit with you. How are you doing?" She said with genuine concern.

Her expression and tone completely knocked me off of my square. For as long as I'd known her she'd been a selfish bitch that only cared about herself. She didn't have one decent bone in her body that I knew of but then again it's hard to see good qualities in the woman that stole your man.

"I'm okay," I said cautiously, "How are you?"

"I'm making it. Everything that's been going on with you and Marcus has been crazy. He must have done something really horrible for you to do him like that," she said.

"Actually he did."

"I believe it. He's a poor excuse for a man and a father. He was avoiding me for a while before he got shipped off to jail. He treated me like shit and then abandoned his son," she shook her head.

I fought the urge to tell her that karma was a bitch. A man isn't going to respect you if you're cheating with him. She was an easy trick, and he only chose her because I had become too much work. She was lucky that I didn't feel like rubbing salt in her festering wounds.

"Oh I'm sorry to hear that," I said.

"Girl don't be. You're the last person that I would expect to feel sorry for me."

"What are you doing down here anyway?" I asked.

"I've been putting in some applications at some different retail stores. I can't afford any of this shit, but I can sell it. I've been selling the knockoffs for years and so this stuff will be easy as hell to move," she laughed.

"Going legit huh?"

"Right now that's the only way to be. I have a little boy to look after, and I can't do that if I'm behind bars."

I raised my eyebrows in surprise because I couldn't ever remember a time where she sounded so rational before.

"It's really cool to hear you say that. Good luck on your job search," I said.

"Thanks girl. Enjoy your new man and I'm happy that you didn't let Marcus make you miss out on that fine ass white boy."

I shook my head and laughed, "Bye girl."

"See you later chic," she said as she walked off.

All of a sudden the money was burning a hole in my purse, "Chastity!" I called after her.

"Wassup?" She said as she turned around.

"I want you to have this. Hopefully it will help."

"Wow, are you serious? Why would you do something like this for me?"

"I just felt the need to do it and so I won't second guess it."

She gave me a huge hug and her entire body was shaking, "You don't have any idea about how much I've been struggling. This is going to keep us from being put out on the streets. We were going to get evicted in three days.

"Exactly, you need it more then I do. That should be enough to cover your back rent and pay it up for a few months."

"I don't even know what to say. So I'll just leave it at thank you."

"The pleasure is all mine, take care of yourself," I said as I walked off.

I left feeling 50 pounds lighter. One of the huge chips on my shoulder had been lifted, and I'd made amends with someone that I hated with a passion. I was even able to bless her and her son. My life had been put into perspective when I realized that I had a man that was loyal to a child that may not even be his. If I had stayed with Marcus I would have probably ended up with the a man who was not loyal to a child that was his.

I felt quietly impressed with myself. A year or so ago I would have probably ended that conversation with Chastity with violence but now I had grown as a person and I could realize that we are often victims of our own circumstances more then anything.

When I looked at Chastity I saw how I would have probably ended up if I was not strong enough to make changes in my life. I just hope I have made a positive change in her life and she does not end up back where she came from.

As I had all these thoughts I realized I was turning into Kyle and in a good way. He really has been the most amazing positive influence on my life.

#Chapter4

"I always leave room for dessert,"
Kyle

I arrived home in a much better mood than when I left. I couldn't
wait to tell Kyle about what had just happened to me. Although I
couldn't imagine that he would be thrilled about me giving the
money away. I'd learned my lesson about that. The last time I hid
something from him regarding money it blew up in my face. Some
mistakes I just wasn't going to repeat. I wanted to ask him if he
would consider giving Chastity a job, but I wasn't going to press
my luck with him that day.

Kyle was home when I arrived, and I went to the kitchen to find
him at sitting at the table and looking over some paperwork.

"Are those the results?" I blurted out.

He turned around and smiled, "I didn't even hear you come in, but
these aren't the results. Bill is taking them to the lab right now."

"Oh okay," I said in disappointment. I was ready to get the results
so that we could move on with our life either way.

"I know how much you hate waiting," he laughed, "I'm not fond of
it myself but even I can't rush some things."

"How was your day with him?"

"It went well but I'm not great with kids just yet. It felt a little
uncomfortable because we don't know one another, but he warmed
up to me in the end. With more time, we'll be better."

"I have no doubt about that because you're hard not to love," I
smiled.

"I have an idea," he said.

"Oh yeah? What is it?"

"How about we work like maniacs for the next four hours and then
unplug from the matrix and have a nice quiet evening here."

I warred with myself because he and I had done quite a bit of
'unplugging' already, and we had a lot of things to get
accomplished before our businesses opened.

"I don't know babe. We have a lot to get done," I said.

"Believe me, I know. But today I just want to not think about anything. I don't get the results until tomorrow. I just want to enjoy my time with you," he pleaded.

There wasn't any way that I could turn down such a heartfelt request from him. I tried to calm down my inner panic and go with the flow.

"Okay, let's get to work so that we can enjoy our evening."

His face lit up, "That's great. I have a wonderful evening planned for us."

"Just surprise me later. I'm going to get out of here and swing by the restaurant to make sure that everything is on task. The bathrooms still weren't quite right when I swung by yesterday. The wood wasn't the right color. I haven't spoken to Stacy at all today either."

He shifted into work mode with me, "Wasn't she supposed to call you?"

"Yes she was," I said.

Stacy was our business publicist, and she was supposed to update me on the response to our press release that we'd sent out the week before. It wasn't my job to have to track down the people that worked for us. It was her responsibility to do what she said that she was going to do. She was getting paid a huge chunk of change to be on top of things.

He groaned, "I'm going to call the agency today. We should have only dealt with Spencer, and she's just not working out. We can't afford to deal with someone that isn't getting back to us in a timely manner."

"You're right but don't worry about it. I'll call and get it all sorted out, I'm sure that Spencer won't have a problem picking up our account. He wants to keep us with the agency and so he'll have to oversee our project personally."

"Alright then," he sighed, "I'll let you handle it. I'm going to call Andrew back because he's at the club now."

"You really have to delegate more task to him," I said, "He's your personal assistant for a reason, use him. He's practically begging for you to give him more work, and I think that he can handle it."

"I know. I'm not used to having a male assistant and so it's a huge adjustment. How do I even talk to him?"

"You tell him what you need him to do and you keep your eyes off of his ass."

Kyle snorted, "I don't think that's going to be a problem."

"Good, let's get to work."

***

For the next four hours me and Kyle worked diligently as promised. I loved being in the thick of things and helping him bring his ideas into fruition. It's hard to believe that they're 'our businesses'. Kyle constantly tells me that I'm not his assistant, and that I'm his partner. I'm still working on wrapping my mind around that concept. Just to ensure that he's drilled it in, he's given me a huge stake of the company, and it's written into our prenuptial agreement. He's not the kind of man that holds on to his money with a tight fist and he's acknowledging that I'm working just as hard as he is to get everything off of the ground.

I was looking forward to getting home and seeing what he had in store for the both of us. I wanted to take the time to be in the moment and not think about everything that was surrounding us. He made the right call by deciding to wait until the following day to find about the paternity. It would be great to spend some time with him without being sad or worried about the future. It didn't matter what was coming our way because we would go through it together.

Kyle greeted me as soon as I stepped off of the elevator.

"Good evening, happy to have you back," he smiled with a boyish grin. He was wearing pajama pants and no shirt. My throat went dry as my eyes hungrily took in his entire body. I would never tire of seeing him without a shirt on.

"It's good to be back. I feel severely overdressed," I responded.

"Don't worry, we'll remedy that soon," he winked as he took my hand and walked me further into our loft. All of the lights were out, and everything was lit by candlelight.

"This is wonderful," I exclaimed. We stepped into the living area, and there were two massage tables side by side and the sound of rain was playing lightly from the surround sound speakers. His hands wrapped about my waist as he pressed against my back.

"Go and get prepared for our couples massage and I'll let the masseurs know that you're here."

"Now you're just spoiling me rotten. I've needed a massage for weeks," I said before I gave him a passionate kiss.

"Then I'm doing my job."

We spend the next few hours getting our massages, having a delicious dinner, and dancing half clothed. It was without a doubt one of the best dates that I ever had. As the night was winding down I was tipsy and looking forward to getting to the bedroom. Connecting with Kyle sexually is something that I obviously enjoy, and I needed the stress relief. We made our way to the bedroom after a few too many drinks.

"I've needed this all day," Kyle said with a slight slur.

"That makes two of us," I giggled as he lifted my oversized t-shirt over my head exposing my body. I quickly pushed his pajama pants down to the floor, crawled into bed, and laid on my back. I opened my legs enticingly.

"Are you offering?" He asked with a lick of his lips.

"Yes, although I'm not sure if you're still hungry," I said.

"I always leave room for dessert," he joked as he crawled between my legs.

His tongue circled around my belly button before he dipped his tongue inside. I giggled uncontrollably because it tickled me to my core.

"That isn't a very sexy feeling baby," I laughed.

"Well I love to hear your laugh and so it's sexy for me," he said before he ran his tongue from my knee and down the inside of my thigh. My legs quivered as his velvety tongue had its way with me. My pussy tingled in anticipation, but he continued his sweet torture until I was writhing against the bed and tempted to grab his head to place it where I wanted it, where I needed it.

His tongue finally flicked against my small bundle of nerves, and it added gasoline to the fire that was burning within me. Before I had time to recover from the first lick his mouth was all over me again. His probing tongue dipped inside of me, and I instinctively moved away from him. His hands wrapped around my legs, pulled me closer to his face, and prevented me from moving. I whimpered slightly at his mouth's relentless assault to my center. His tongue flicked faster and faster against my clit until I released.

I lay against the bed panting, limp, and tired. I could have gone to sleep right there, but he needed his release as well, so I happily welcomed his weight on top of me. He pressed his lips against my own and ran my tongue across them. I've always enjoyed tasting myself on his lips. I reached between us and stroked his long thick rod. He was already hard and pulsating for me.

He let out a slight hiss, "I need to be inside of you."

"I'm more than ready," I groaned.

I rubbed the bulbous head of his cock against my slick folds and he pushed deep inside of me without warning. His thrusts were erratic. He took long slow strokes and then harder and faster ones. I couldn't predict what he was going to do next. Each push inside of me brought me closer to another orgasm. My muscles contracted around him and tried to milk him for the nectar that I loved so much. I placed my hands on his ass and pushed him deeper inside of me. He was filling me completely and creating space where there wasn't any.
I opened my eyes, and he was staring directly at me. My heart sped up because all over again I remembered where I was. I was with the man that was going to love me forever. I was overwhelmed with love and lust at the same time. I placed my arms around his neck and brought him closer to me.

"I love you so much," I panted as he pushed deep inside of me causing me to erupt.

He didn't slow down; he fucked me through my orgasm and joined me. He made noises that would have embarrassed him at any other point in his life. His body went lax, and we laid there in a comfortable silence.

"I love you too," he replied.

#Chapter5

"Maybe in about 8 years,"
Kyle

"I deeply apologize for the inconvenience but I am more than happy to take over your account. I shouldn't have delegated it, and so it was my error. Stacy was a bit out of her league on this one," Spencer assured me.

"I appreciate your time and attention. I thought that Stacy was wonderful but she just wasn't able to deliver what we needed," I said.

He nodded quickly, "I completely understand. I emailed you and Mr. Kane the schedule of interviews that you all have coming up. Your press release has been received very well by the media, and I think this is a great chance to get some of the heat off of your relationship."
I shifted uncomfortably in my seat at the mention of the past. He was right about the amount of negative press. I was still considered the urban Cinderella amongst the Chicago elite. I had made a conscious decision to ignore it all because it didn't serve any positive purpose. It only made me feel like crap, because I was still suffering from feeling a bit inferior and undeserving of all of the good that was happening in my life. Every day, even the bad ones were better than my life before I met Kyle.

"You have a point; we could use the great press. I'm happy that they're eating it up. It's time for Kyle to be in the forefront of the media for something positive."
Spencer's brow furrowed, "What do you mean by that?"
"You know what I mean, you even said it yourself."
"I think we mean it for two very different things," he said, "Kyle doesn't look bad because he's marrying you. We're living in the 21st century and yes we have some that are bigoted, but they're in

the minority. Screw whoever tried to hold your past over your head. It's obvious that you've left that behind, and you'll only get past it when you stop feeling guilty about it."

"Well then what are you talking about?"

"I'm referring to the fact that Kyle has left his father's company. Many people think that he is going to fall flat on his face. In fact, many are HOPING he falls flat on his face. He has a great business plan, and I know that his chains are going to go national. When people take a look at the places that the both of you have created, they'll be singing your praises. The media has a very short term memory, and we can use that to our advantage," he said confidently.

"Wow, thank you for that. I think that I really needed to hear it. I see why Kyle wanted you in the first place."

"I am the best," he said with a cocky grin.

"I think that you may be right. Do you have a hard copy of the itinerary?"

"Yes, my assistant will give it to you in binders on your way out. That's all for now, and I'll be in contact with you a little later today. You're my direct contact right?"

"Yes that's right," I responded as I rose to my feet and gave him a firm handshake.

I left his office with my head a little higher than it had been before I entered. I never expected a pep talk from our publicist. That just proved that you could get inspiration from anywhere and that people were a lot nicer than we really think that they are. I took his words to heart, and I was determined to stop allowing my guilt to eat me alive. I was punishing myself worse than anyone else ever could have. I was a good person that deserved love, and I was blessed that Kyle loved me.

My phone rang before I got to my car, I picked up quickly because it was Kyle.

"Hello?"

"Are you finished with your meeting?"

"Yes, I've wrapped it up," I responded.

"Come home as soon as possible, I have the test results," he said.

"You're not going to tell me over the phone?" I said.

"Nope, just get here please," he said before he hung up.

My heart dropped because I couldn't peg his tone. It was rare that I couldn't read him and so I didn't know how to feel as I drove home. I didn't know if I was going to have to console him, listen to him rant, or celebrate with him. He knew how much I hated waiting, but he still did it to me anyway. I nervously drove back to the loft and hoped for the best. Whatever the outcome, I was going to support him in whatever way that he needed me to.

When I arrived at the loft I searched for Kyle. He wasn't on the first floor so I went upstairs to search for him on the balcony. I resolved to start looking for him there first in the future because it was where he usually was, and the weather just didn't matter to him. I saw him through the glass panels laughing with Bill. I was a little confused as I stepped out onto the balcony.

"Hey what's going on?"

"It's good news! The baby is 100% not mine…well 99.9%."

I was stunned, especially since Kyle was in such great spirits about it.

"Are you sure it's not yours?"

"We're absolutely sure. Hell, I had them run it twice," Bill laughed, "I wanted to tell the both of you yesterday, but I had to respect your wishes."

"Please tell her the rest of the news," Kyle said when he came over and kissed me on the cheek.

"There's more?" I asked.

"Yes there's a lot more. I spoke to my contacts at the police department and offered them cash to find out if there was a DNA match. We got a match, and we found the kid's father. His father is a junkie that was convicted of robbery and he's been in jail for the last year," he said with a widespread grin.

I know that I was supposed to be overjoyed in that moment, but I kept seeing that cute angelic face in my head. He deserved two parents that loved and cared about him. I was a little saddened that he wouldn't get that opportunity with Kyle.

"Do you think that she knew all of this beforehand?" I asked.

"It's hard to say," Kyle said, "but she did know that she was sleeping with someone else around the same time. I'm thinking that's probably why she didn't come forward sooner. She was hoping like hell that it was mine, and it just didn't turn out that way."

"I think that she was pulling an all-out scam," Bill interjected. "Kyle this may not be the last time that a face from your past pops up wanting money. You're in the media now more than ever and so we're going to have to be a lot more careful. There are a lot of leeches out there."

"I just want to say thank you to the both of you for convincing me to do it. I would have hated to find out that he wasn't my son later down the road after I got attached to him," Kyle said.

"I'm sorry that things turned out this way. It's never fun being lied to or betrayed, but everything turned out the way that it's supposed to," I said.

"You're right. I had a feeling that she was lying to me, but I didn't want to believe that about her. Bill, you can contact her tomorrow regarding our findings and let her know to never contact me again," he said coldly.

"That's a task that I'll gladly take."

"Let's all go out to celebrate our averted close call," Kyle suggested.

"Unfortunately, I have to decline," Bill said, "I have somewhere that I have to be. But I will catch up with the both of you later."

I tried to temper my annoyance because we didn't have the time to go out and celebrate. I almost wondered if there was any truth to what the media was saying about my future husband. If we went out to celebrate, we would be out for hours and it wasn't something that we could afford at the moment. I decided to give him an alternative.

"How about we have a glass of champagne here and then get back work," I said with a tight smile.

Kyle picked up on my cue, "Umm okay, that's cool too. We'll see you later Bill."

"I'll let myself out. Have a wonderful day."

"Bye Bill," I said as I walked over to the mini bar and got a bottle of champagne and brought over two champagne flutes.

We sat on the balcony and enjoyed a glass of champagne in silence for a few moments. I needed to let it calm my nerves because I felt on edge, but I couldn't put my finger on why. The alcohol had gotten into my system, and I poured the both of us another glass.

"I feel sorry for the boy for having to grow up with a mother like that," I said.

Granted his mother didn't seem as trifling as my own. I hoped that Jane would get her life together so that she could raise a healthy son because that's what children deserved.

"I feel bad for him too; he's a pretty great kid. But I'm relieved because I'm not ready to be a father right now. I'm happy that I don't have to just yet."

"Oh yeah?" I asked, "Are you interested in ever being a father?"

I couldn't believe that he and I hadn't discussed something so crucial yet. Children were a huge sticking point in most relationships, and we completely glossed over it.

"Maybe in about 8 years," he responded.

I damned near choked on my champagne when he said it. That was such a long time away, and I never saw myself as being an old mother. I didn't want to start having children in my mid 30's because that would put me in the high risk category. I had to remind myself that he and I grew up in entirely different cultures. Where I was from most people had their children when they were in their late teens and the pregnancies weren't planned. I was considered an old maid already and people always wanted to know what was wrong with me and my friends because we hadn't 'popped any kids out' yet. He grew up in an environment where kids were almost always planned, and everyone had them later in life. However, I wanted kids within our first year of marriage or at least in our first few years.

I drowned my disappointment with another glass of champagne.

"Are you okay?" He asked.

"Yes, why?"

"I don't know, you just feel a little different. If there's something that you need to talk about just tell me and we can talk about it."

"No I'm fine. I just have a lot to get done. Next week is it for us," I said in mock excitement.

"Yes it is. I'm looking forward to celebrating that accomplishment."

"Oh, I bet you are."

#Chapter6

"I'll happily smack your ass anytime,"
Kyle

What a difference a few months make.

Our businesses were going really well, and I've been so amazed at watching Camille grow into an amazing business woman. In many aspects she's put me to complete shame in this arena. She's taken to it like a fish to water, and it's definitely her element. The first month put a huge strain on our relationship because it always seemed that she was upset with me about something. I wasn't sure what I was doing wrong and so I had to eventually just put my food down and demand that she speak to me about what was peeving her.

She revealed to me that she was frustrated with my lack of work ethic. Initially, I wanted to bite her head off because I've been working since I was 15 years old, and hard work is something that I'm very used to. But she pointed out that I'm used to having to answer to someone and that maybe I'd gotten too comfortable because I didn't have an official "boss" anymore. After I got finished nursing my bruised ego for about a week I realized that she was correct. I was spending way too much time celebrating and not enough time working and learning. It's true that I can delegate a lot of my tasks but in the beginning phases of my projects I need to be a lot more hands on with what's happening in my businesses. I had a lot riding on their success, and I was leaving it in the hands of others, and that was unacceptable. Not many people would have told me the truth that way. Actually only my father would have told me that and it wouldn't have been as nice. She was swallowing a lot of frustration, and I felt lucky to have a woman like her. She was 100% invested in making our businesses worked and not just on spending money, and that says a lot about her as a woman. Technically neither of us has to work again, and my children would never have to work either but I want to build them a legacy that they can be proud of. I knew that I'd chosen the right woman for me; she was my partner in every sense of the word. It was amazing to see how much she had grown from that shy and awkward girl who walked into my office for an interview all that time ago.

I'd gotten some bad news, and I wasn't sure how to break it to Camille because of her excitement about the wedding but I knew it had to be done and neither of us was going to like what would happen next.

"Hey so what did you want to talk about?" Camille asked as she took a bite out of the apple she grabbed from the kitchen table. "The date for the trial has been set, and it's the week before the wedding," I told her.

"Oh no," she said as a look of sadness crept across her face, "Does he have to ruin everything? I'll be so happy when I don't have to think about Marcus ever again. What do you suggest that we do?"

"I think that we should push the wedding back because it could completely ruin our plans. I want you to be stress free, and we don't know how this is going to play out," I said.

She gave a labored sigh, "You're right, I just want the trial to be over so that this chapter can be closed. I want to start another book," she laughed.

"We're already in another book; we just have some loose strings to tie up. It doesn't matter what happens because we're going to be together and we did the right thing," I said.

"Yeah," she said dispassionately. "I just hope our next book does not have quite so much drama."

***

The next 3 months went by faster than the previous 3 months.

The businesses were booming, and we were already thinking about opening another restaurant just like it the southern suburbs within the next year. People were interested in franchising the bar, and we were seriously entertaining the thought. I sat in my new office and looked out at the lake. I was proud of myself for building something new and separate from my father. I was also back on speaking terms with my family and my sisters were coming around a lot more.

Camille stormed into my office, and she looked pretty shaken up. "Kyle," she said with a quiver in her voice.

I was immediately alarmed, and I stood to my feet. She rushed to me and wrapped her arms around my neck and started crying. I instinctively pulled her closed to me and kissed the top of her head. "Tell me what's going on sweetie," I said.

She continued to sob for a few more seconds before she started pulling herself together. I waited patiently as I rocked her back and forth. I hoped that she was just frustrated about something petty instead of it being a major issue. But she rarely got that upset about something minor, which meant that it was a huge deal.

"I got a horrible email," she said as she sniffled. I pulled myself away from her and went to my bathroom to get her some tissue.

"What did it say?" I asked as I handed her the tissue.

"It was an anonymous email saying that I wasn't to testify against Marcus, or I was going to die," she said.

My blood began to boil at the thought of someone threatening her. No one was going to do any harm to her as long as I had something to do with it. I considered calling the police, but I knew that may have delayed the trial further if we went that route and she was ready to get it over with. I didn't want to take that choice away from her either.

"So what do you want to do?" I asked.

"I just want to get through this. I can't live my life in fear, and I can't let Marcus get away with everything that he did to me. He probably had someone send me threats as well. If he goes free, then I'm never going to get from under his thumb."

My chest swelled with pride because she was able to push through her fear and be rational even when she was emotional. Camille didn't need me to tell her what to do or to save her from anything because she was strong enough to do it herself, but she was going to get my help anyway.

"We're not going to let them get away with this bullshit," I said, "I'll have the IT guys come in and we'll trace down the IP addresses and figure out exactly where that email came from. Everything is traceable, so that won't be a problem."

"That would make me feel a lot better. I need to know where it's coming from, and that would give me a better idea of what I'm dealing with," she said.

"I'm also going to up your security in the meantime until the trial is over."

She nodded her head in agreement, "I think that's a good idea even though I don't like the idea of being followed around all the time. But if that will keep me safe, then I'll do it."

"We may also need to seriously consider moving after this blows over. I personally wouldn't mind getting a fresh start."

"What about everything that we're building here," she said quickly.

"We have a very capable staff and it will free us to start building in another city. We can come back whenever we want to check on things, but we may be better being away from all of this."

"I'm going to need some more time to think about that. I don't know if I would want to be that far away from Cynthia or Sandy."

"We don't have to make a decision now, it's just something to think about," I said.

I honestly had forgotten how close she was to her two friends. She rarely went a week without seeing either of them. They were her family, and she took family very seriously. I don't know what she would do if she couldn't randomly drive to one of their houses to go for a chat. Sometimes I think that's the only thing that keeps her sane. I was probably going to have to find another solution for us. I guess if we were going to leave I would have to bring her friends along with us.

**

I rushed over to Cynthia's place after I'd spoken to Kyle, and I was happy to find out that Sandy that was there as well. They still worked odd schedules even though they worked at our businesses.

I guess that's the nature of the industry, and I was grateful that they were available to me because I was still a little shaken up.

I still couldn't get over how great it felt to drive to Hyde Park to see Cynthia. It fits her personality so much better than the west side of Chicago did. She adored her new neighborhood and couldn't get over how friendly everyone was and how she could walk down the street at 2 in the morning and feel relatively safe. Sandy chose an apartment not too far from her and they were in walking distance from one another.

I walked up the steps to the huge brownstone 2 flat that she lived in. It was huge, and it had been renovated. I fell in love with it from the first moment that I saw it, and I could see why she was so set on having that particular one.

"Hey girly," she said as she greeted me at the door, "Oh no, what's wrong?"

"Do I look that bad?" I asked.

"You don't look bad; you look frazzled as if you've seen a ghost."

"I need to talk," I said.

"That's what we're here for. Sandy's psycho ass is in the kitchen eating up all of my food," she said.

"Well, you're about to have two psychos eating up all of your food because I'm hungry."

Soon we were all sitting around her kitchen table eating pita chips and hummus. I wished that I had some wine to go along with it, but I was trying to stop using alcohol to deal with my anxiety. My mom used to use substances to deal with her problems, and that's how she became a junkie. I didn't want that to be my reality, and so I vowed to try to deal with my stress better.

"I got a death threat today," I said.

"From who?" Sandy asked immediately.

"I'm not sure who it's from but Kyle is going to trace it. We should have a good idea of who it is within the next couple of days. I don't know why, but I really wasn't expecting something like that."

"Not to be harsh or anything," Cynthia said softly, "But Marcus has proven that you can't put anything past him. He's already done things that we never thought he would do. Now that he thinks you've betrayed him, the gloves are off."

"The gloves were already off when he started blackmailing her," Sandy interjected.

I shook my head, "I don't care what started this shit, and I just want it to be over."

"So what's going to happen from here?" Sandy asked.

I gave them the rundown of what Kyle and I had planned. I also let them know that a security detail was sitting outside of the house. It was a necessary evil for the time being.

"It's going to be okay. They're just thugs, and they're not used to dealing with anyone outside of their tiny little box. They will get a lot more than they bargained for if they try to mess with you. Kyle doesn't strike me as the kind of person to take these things lightly," Cynthia said.

"He was pretty upset when he found out about the threats. I don't think that he'll do anything stupid, but I know that he won't allow anything to happen to me either. I'm just so mad that I've brought that hood drama to his doorstep. He shouldn't have to deal with this shit," I said.

"No one should have to deal with this shit," Sandy said, "But it's the hand that you've been dealt. You're worth the trouble, so stop worrying about what he has to deal with."

"She's right. Kyle is a very intelligent man and he isn't going to do anything that he doesn't want to. So calm the hell down and allow him to be there for you," Cynthia said.

"I'm trying to let him. But I haven't told him about how terrified I am."

"What's scaring you?" Cynthia asked.

"I really don't want to testify against Marcus. We've been through so much together and for it to end like this…it's tearing me apart on the inside," I admitted.

"This situation isn't your fault. He's the one that put you in this predicament, and you had to do what was best for you. He didn't care about betraying your trust. Don't feel guilty that you're the one that came out on top. You won and so you need to enjoy your victory," Sandy said cold heartedly.

She was absolutely right but that didn't make it any easier to process. I loved Marcus with all of my heart and I thought that he was going to be the man that I grew old with. I didn't want to be the reason that he was locked away for a long time, even with the threats. But it was clear that I had to choose between him and Kyle. That wasn't a tough decision at all because Kyle held my heart. I had to do whatever it took to make sure that Marcus couldn't harm my future. I just wish he had never done all this in the first place.

***

Talking to friends was great but it didn't do much to calm my nerves. I was just ready to get the whole ordeal over with. My hands were still shaking, my heart was still pounding, and my stomach was still in knots. Wine was a temporary savior, but the effects were quickly wearing off and I was left alone with my over reactive body. My thoughts were racing as I lay across our huge bed. Emotional exhaustion was something that I was learning the meaning of. I groaned as I thought about all of the cameras that were going to be in my face in the morning. The new security guards had managed to thwart the few that had approached me as I got out of my car in our parking lot.

I was enveloped in darkness, and our thick down white comforter had become my source of comfort. I wished that Kyle was home with me so that I could cuddle with him. We only had one last huge hurdle before we could get married, and it seemed like a mountain. I'd been prepped so much by our lawyer and his assistants. They told me that the defense was going to try to discredit me and destroy me on the stand. I just had to be strong and tell the truth. That seemed so much easier said than done, especially since I hated talking about my past. I've justified it by saying that I didn't have any other choice, but I couldn't help but think about the lives that I helped destroy.

I hated what my neighborhood had done to my mother, and I helped to perpetuate the same cycle. I didn't feel like I was any better than Marcus even though I'd never literally sold the drugs. However, I helped facilitate the distribution of narcotics in my own neighborhood. I helped create the very thing that I hated. I felt like

I deserved to be in prison right along with Marcus. That level of guilt alone was enough to make me want to crawl under a rock and never show my face again.

Kyle showed up while I was in the middle of my pity party.

"Camille?" He asked before he cut on the bed lamp, "Are you sleeping?"

I played around with the idea of pretending to be asleep. I wasn't in the mood to have a full conversation about my feelings. I just wanted him to crawl into bed and hold me.

"No," I responded, my voice was muffled from beneath the bed sheets.

"Are you okay? Did something happen? I've been calling you for the last couple of hours."

"I'm sorry," I said as I emerged from the comforter, "I forgot to take my phone off silent."

He looked visibly relieved, but his face was still full of concern, "I'm worried about you. I hope you know that I'm not going to let anything happen to you."

I wanted to tell him that there are certain things that money can't protect you from. If someone wanted you bad enough, they could get you, and it didn't matter who you tried to use as a shield. However, that wasn't a reality that I wanted to share with him because I didn't want to sound negative, and I didn't want to shatter his world. I just hoped that the threats were idle and that they didn't see me as worth it. I didn't know how long it would take them to pinpoint where the person sent the message from. It was probably just one of Marcus' idiotic friends.

"I'm really nervous about tomorrow," I said.

"Yeah, Bill and the prosecutor said that they've been trying to call you too."

I shrugged, "I don't want to prepare anymore. I'm freaked out enough already, and he will only make it worse. I will see him bright and early in the morning, and we can go over things then."

"Okay, I'll let him know to back off."

I appreciated how he didn't question me any further about it. I didn't want to argue, and I definitely didn't want to be forced to do it. I didn't have it in me to be nice about it anymore. If Bill asked me one more question I was going to bite his head off, figuratively of course. No one deserved my nervous wrath because it would be one of cataclysmic proportions. My temper can be very short when I'm nervous, and I would potentially ruin Kyle's working relationship with Bill if he pushed me any further.

"Thank you," I said in relief.

"You know what will help you?" Kyle said with a mischievous glint in his eye.

"What?" I asked warily.

"A spanking."

"Are you kidding me? How in the hell is a spanking going to help me at a time like this? That seems like something that would be more for you and not myself. I'm not in the mood for that kinky shit tonight," I snapped.

My attitude didn't deter him, "Tsk tsk tsk Camille. I've warned you about that little snarky attitude, but I am very serious about what I've offered. Have you ever heard of spanking therapy?"

I scoffed. The only spanking therapy that I knew of was the ass whippings that I received from my mother when I was younger. Black parents used that kind of therapy all the time, and I wasn't about to allow him to whip me like I was an unruly kid. He was really annoying me with his suggestion.

"No, I've never heard of the shit. It sounds crazy, and I don't see how something like that could even help me."

He raised an eyebrow, and I realized that I'd maybe gone too far, "It's very real and I think it that it will help refocus you and relieve some of your stress, at least for tonight."

"I don't know," I said hesitantly.

"Do you trust me?"

"Of course I trust you," I responded immediately.

"Okay, then let me help you," he said as he took off his shoes.

My pulse raced as I thought about really allowing him to spank me. It was something that we'd done during sex or as a precursor to sex. But this time felt different, it was a completely different kind of surrender.

"Am I going to have to lay over your lap?" I asked.

"Yes," he laughed, "You are going to have to lay over my lap. This can be a very therapeutic and intimate experience if you'll just give in. Will you try it once? If you hate it then we'll never do it again but I think it's worth an honest try."

"How many other women have you done this 'therapy' with?" I asked.

"One," he said honestly.

My face scrunched because I hated the thought of him being with another woman even if it was just spanking. I scolded myself for asking the question that I wasn't ready to know the answer to. But now that I think about it, I realize that it would have nagged me for days and so it's good to just rip the band aid off from time to time. It's okay to be upset with an answer that you asked for as long as you don't punish the person for telling the truth.

I sighed, "Alright, I don't really have anything to lose but my self-respect so I guess I'll do it."

"Someone is being a little dramatic," he said in amusement.

I pouted, "I know I'm being a big baby right now but cut me a little slack. I did have my life threatened."

"I know, and I'll do everything within my power to keep you safe. But for now, it's just you and me so let's enjoy it," he said as he walked over to the bed and sat on the edge.

I sat up and pulled my legs to my chest, "Are you sure that this is going to help?"

"I'm not absolutely sure because it's really up to you. I wouldn't have suggested it if I thought that it wouldn't. So come on, lay over my lap with your butt in the center."

My eyes widened, and I took a few deep breaths to gather myself. I felt like such an idiot in that moment. What grown ass woman willingly submits to a non-sexual spanking? But then again, Kyle and I had done a lot of things that the average couple probably didn't do. It seemed kind of ridiculous to draw my line there. I pushed the comforter down to my feet and looked at him as he waited patiently. I hated when he got quiet because that meant that he wasn't going to entertain my bullshit anymore. I'm used to talking my way out of everything, and that's hard to do when the person won't give you an opening. .

I got on all fours and crawled over to him and laid across his lap as he requested. My cheek pressed against the sheets, and his hand slowly ran over my panty clad bottom and down my legs. I didn't realize how on edge I was until his hand slowly explored my body and brought attention to all of the areas that I was tight in.

"As much as I love these skimpy lace panties, I'm going to have to take them off," he said. He tugged at the edges, and I lifted to make it easier for him to slide them off of my hips and down my legs.

He slowly rubbed my ass in a circular motion. His huge hand started at the top and worked it's way around both cheeks, "We're going to start off with some light slaps, and they're going to slowly get more intense. I want you to tell me if something is too soft or too hard. Focus on your breathing and I want you to be here in the moment with me."

"Yes sir," I said instinctively, I bit my lip to suppress a moan. He wasn't trying to ignite a desire within me, but it was hard not to get turned on. It all felt pretty erotic even though that wasn't it's purpose. It was going to be difficult not to try to arouse him while I was laid across his lap. I figured that we could forgo the spanking and get straight to the good stuff. We both knew that it was inevitable anyway. But he seemed set on spanking me, and I was now mildly curious about it.

"Very good girl," he said and it touched me to my core. He had the ability to turn me into a warm puddle even when I didn't want to. I wanted to be way too liberated to beam at those words, but I reveled in them. I needed to hear them and in that moment I was okay with being dependent on him for support. I needed him, and I wanted whatever he had to give.

He placed a firm smack to my backside that sounded worse than it felt, "Harder," I said.

He did as I asked and landed another one to the fleshy portion of my behind, and it still wasn't hard enough. I could handle a lot more than what he was giving me, and I wiggled in frustration. It just seemed like a tease. He'd slapped my ass way harder, and that was when we were fucking. I knew that he had more in him, and I didn't need him to treat me like a porcelain doll. I didn't break easily, and he knew that.

"Okay, I see that it's still too light for you," he laughed lightly and then smacked my ass with enough force to make me yelp.

"Shit!" I exclaimed loudly.

"Too hard?" He asked quickly.

I got quiet for a moment and really took the time to think about how I felt in that moment. My ass stung but oddly enough I felt good, and I wanted more. I definitely didn't want to get hit that hard again, at least not so soon.

"Do it a little bit lighter and then maybe we can work our way up to that?" I said.

"That sounds good," he said.

For the next 15 minutes he delivered slap after slap to my ass. He would soothe me with rubs and then get started again. I saw the merit in his method. I was forced to be present and in the moment. The tension in my body released and my ass felt like it could glow in the dark. I absolutely loved it, and I was hard pressed to think of a time that felt more intimate than that moment. His erection pressed against my lower belly, but he didn't make mention of it until I had enough.

"We have to do this again at some point," I said as I rested my head against the bed, and he rubbed the back of my legs. I wanted to fall asleep, but I knew that his hard on was going to require some attention.

"You just say the word, and I'll happily smack your ass anytime," he said. He bent over and placed a big kiss to my left cheek and then the right.

"Keep doing that, and you're going to get a lot more than you bargained for," I teased.

"I'm more than ready to receive whatever you have. Give me what you've got Mrs. Kane."

"I'm not Mrs, Kane yet," I said as I got up and rested on my knees on the bed.

"We're going to do it as soon as we can. We're going to get through this and then I'm dragging you down the aisle."

I smiled at the thought of that because we both knew that he wouldn't have to drag me anywhere. I would willingly follow him anywhere, and I wouldn't need any coaxing or convincing. He would be lucky if I wasn't at the front of the church waiting on him to walk to me. I couldn't wait to become his wife because I wanted him in every way possible. It was time for us to take the plunge, but he was right about waiting. I couldn't help him run the business, plan the wedding, and prep for the trial at the same time. I could have gotten a planner to handle every single detail, but I liked being more hands on and I couldn't just let someone do all of it for me. That was never my dream as I was growing up. I always saw myself taking care of a lot of the details myself.

"Tonight I want to go for a ride," I flirted.

It didn't take him any time to rise from his seated position and rid himself of this clothing, "What do ya know? I think I have a ride that's just your size."

"Your ride is bigger than what I require but I'm sure that I can make some adjustments. I'm pretty flexible.

He laid on his back and placed his hands behind his head. He was clearly ready for me to take over. The sooner I got us both off the quicker I could get to bed. I know that makes me sound a little evil but hey, if I could have gone to sleep and skipped the sex I would have. I love my fiancé, but it had been a long ass day. That being said, men have their needs, and it wouldn't hurt me to give 10 minutes of my time.

I climbed on top of him and placed myself above his massive erection. My body hadn't gotten the memo that I was tired because it was buzzing with anticipation. I wanted him inside of me, and I wanted to see the look on his face as I rode him. He made the best faces. I think I liked them because they were ugly faces. I always knew that he was enjoying himself when his attractive features contorted into ones that resembled a beast. I always had a few more notches added to my self-esteem. I took pride in knowing that I was tight and wet down there. I randomly did kegals throughout the day out of habit. It was probably due to my irrational fear of being stretched out.

That was always a hot topic of discussion as I was growing up. It was a way for men to reverse the shame of their small dick. If a girl complained about a boy's dick being too small, he would counter with saying that she was stretched out, and then she would be labeled a hoe. Both of these situations are pretty fucked up. It's not like the man picked out his dick, he was born that way. Also, I doubted if a 17 year old girl had seen more action than a Madison and Cicero prostitute.

His hands moved to my hips and pulled me down on top of him. His engorged cock head parted my lips and pushed inside of my tight cavern. I wasn't sure if my pussy would ever get over the shock that he sent to my senses when he entered me. He always felt so big inside of me, and I have to try to completely relax so that it won't hurt.

"You okay?" He asked.

"Yes, I'm alright. I just need a minute," I laughed lightly.

I looked into his eyes as I rocked back and forth gently on his erection. The juices from my arousal created a delicious friction within me, and my implosion wasn't going to take long. I lifted and placed my feet flat onto bed, leaning back and using my hands for support. My legs were spread open, and he took full advantage of the view. One of his hands stayed on my hip, and he gripped it for dear life. He licked his thumb and rubbed my clit as I created a steady rhythm of taking him in and out of me.

"Fucccck baby, that feels so good," he groaned through his clenched teeth. His face was beginning to contort into the look that I loved and knew so well.

I slowly teased him by rotating my hips in circular motions; his steel rod wrapped in velvet filled me to the brim. His cock head pressed against my g spot and then at the top of my womb. His thumb increased in pressure, and I came immediately. My body shook and trembled as my muscles contracted around him. He grabbed my hip with his other hand and fucked me with piston like force. His hips lifted from the bed, and he delivered thrust after thrust. He pushed against my resistance and created space where there wasn't any originally. His erratic breathing matched my own and with one last thrust he unloaded his seed.

In that moment my brain stopped functioning. He saved me from my thoughts and feelings, and I was grateful to him for that. I knew that they would come rushing back in the morning, but I was determined to enjoy the temporary reprieve and bask in the bliss that he provided.

#Chapter7

"That's my girl,"
Kyle

I had the feeling of walking the plank when I walked into the courtroom with Kyle at my side.

I looked like perfection on the outside, but I felt like I was going to experience a nuclear meltdown. The reporters stormed us as soon as we stepped out of the limo and I didn't see why what we were doing was that big of a deal. People were currently on trial for murder, and yet they were all in my damned face. I absolutely hated it because it freaked me out. They were all asking me questions and some of them were extremely loud and rude. The rage that flowed through my veins was palpable in that moment, and I probably would have been arrested for assault if the guards and Kyle weren't with me.

I second guessed my decision to wear heels because my equilibrium felt off. I made a mental note to never wear 5 inch heels when I feel like my world is about to tilt off if it's axis again. I was worried that there wouldn't be enough evidence to convict Marcus and that he would get off. My life would probably be absolute hell if he went free because his thirst for revenge is unparalleled by most of the people that I know. After he's decided that you've crossed him, there aren't any lengths that he won't go through to get back at you. He can be a very irrational person, and now all of that anger was directed towards me. I had to be living in an alternate universe because I never saw that coming to me in a million years.

"Are you okay?" Kyle asked with concern after we took our seats.

I gave a slight nod of my head and then my mouth began to water. A wave of heat washed over my body, I felt faint, and I had the sudden urge to release the content of my breakfast all over the floor. I quickly stood to my feet and rushed out of the courtroom without warning. Everyone looked at me, and my security was on my heels. I frantically searched for the bathroom and found it just in time. I pushed the door open and ran to the nearest stall. My omelet and orange juice made its way into the porcelain bowl. The thought of having to regurgitate into a public toilet made me heave all over again. I was sick and disgusted at the same time. I just wanted to go home, but I couldn't be afforded that luxury in that moment and it sucked.

I wanted to cry, but my makeup already needed to be touched up, and I had to focus on getting it together so that I wouldn't look a hot ass mess on the stand.

"Camille?" Kyle said hesitantly through the cracked door.

"I'm okay, I just felt a little sick. I'm better now, just give me a few moments to freshen up." I said.

"I've brought your purse," he said as he poked his arm through the opening.

I walked over and grabbed it, "Thanks so much."

"This is going to be over soon," he said in an effort to ease my stress.

"That's what I keep telling myself," I said with a weak smile as I walked over to the mirror.

"We're going to be out here waiting," he said.

"Okay."

I took about 5 minutes to freshen up my make-up and pop some breath mints. I still felt queasy, but I was determined to ignore the feeling. When we returned to the courtroom, Marcus was in his seat and wearing his beige uniform. He looked my way with a blank stare, and it was as if he was staring through me. I tried to maintain my composure and return his look, and I'm not sure if I succeeded. Shortly after the judge arrived, and court was in session. I didn't look at anyone because I was surrounded by people that I knew. Sandy and Cynthia were in the back, and the rest were there to support Marcus. I could feel all of their eyes boring into me. They saw me as a traitor, and I couldn't blame them, especially when they didn't know the full story. But even if they did, they wouldn't have cared because there is a strict "no snitching" policy in my community. Even if Marcus had tried to kill me it was still wrong to snitch according to them.

But nothing made me feel as bad as seeing Marcus's mother looking at me. She looked like I betrayed her trust. I wanted to walk over and apologize to her. She didn't deserve any of the grief that she was being put through. She loved her son very much, she hadn't been the best mother, but she was way better than the one that I grew up with. She genuinely loved her son and all of this had to be ripping her apart. She probably hated me, and I couldn't say that I blamed her. If I was here I would have hated me too.

To keep my mind off of the people that I was surrounded by, I paid close attention as the prosecutor and the defense made their opening arguments. I clenched Kyle's hand each time my name was brought up, and I wanted to disappear. Witnesses began to hit the stand, and most of them seemed useless because they couldn't provide any real information regarding the case. Eventually I was called, and I could hear my stomach gurgle. I stood to my feet and made my way to the hot seat. I focused on my breathing, put one foot in front of the other, and hoped like hell that I didn't fall and embarrass myself in front of everyone.

After I was sworn in, the prosecution asked me the questions that we rehearsed. I talked about how me and Marcus met, what he meant to me in my life, and how we worked together in the drug trade. I then spoke about why we parted ways, and about his blackmail. When I talked about how much I loved him, I could see Marcus's jaw clench. As if he thought that I was full of shit or if he knew he fucked up with me. I rattled off my answers from pure memory and all of my coaching came into play. I then understood why I'd been drilled over and over again. If I hadn't practiced beforehand, my mind would have went blank, and I would have looked like a driveling idiot on the stand.

It was a pity we could not practice the questions from the defense as this was to prove much trickier.

Marcus's lawyer began to question me, and he didn't pull any punches. Everything about him was intimidating. He was small in stature, but he had the most menacing look that I'd ever seen. He was a Caucasian man who looked to be in his 50's and it was clear why Marcus chose him as his lawyer. They had similar dispositions, and I knew off of instinct that he wasn't just unpleasant in the courtroom. I felt sorry for whoever had the misfortune of having him in their life on the daily basis.

"So you're saying that you weren't seeing Marcus anymore after you met Kyle?" He asked.

I frowned, "No I wasn't romantically involved with Marcus during that time. I stopped seeing him months before I ever applied for the position."

"I find that really hard to believe," he said slowly. He looked at me as if he was scolding a child. I held my head high and returned his disapproving gaze.

I didn't appreciate what he was trying to imply, and I hoped that he really didn't take it there.

"I'm sorry that you find it hard to believe but that doesn't make it any less true," I responded.

"What attracted you to Mr. Kane?" The lawyer asked quickly.

"Well I find him to be incredibly attractive, and I fell in love with him once I got to know him," I said.

"I'm sure the money didn't hurt either," he said.

"Of course not, it never does," I said truthfully.

"So you were using Mr. Kane for the money? He basically took you from rags to riches within a couple of weeks of knowing you. I won't even speculate about what was happening behind those closed doors, but we all know that everything comes at a price," he said with a hint of amusement in his voice.

I wanted to hop off of the stand and punch him in the face. How dare he try to insinuate that I was trying to use Kyle for his money. I had no intention on disclosing the nature of how our relationship began because that wasn't anyone's business. Our relationship started out as mutually beneficial and turned into something more, but I was attracted to him the entire time. I looked at Kyle as all of the thoughts raced through my head. He looked at me with a peculiar expression, and I realized that it was because I hadn't answered the question. I was having an entire conversation in my head in front of everyone. I pulled myself from my thoughts so that I could answer his question.

"No I wasn't using him for his money. I wouldn't do something like that," I said.

Who in the hell did he think that he was? I'd always prided myself on not being a gold digger. I worked hard for everything that I owned and my tenacity and fighter spirit had served me well. I didn't need Kyle in order to make it. I would have been just fine keeping my apartment in South Holland. I was with Kyle because I loved him, and that was it.

"But yet you gave the defendant $5,000 of Mr. Kane's hard earned money," He replied.

I shook my head quickly, "I was blackmailed into giving him the money."

"Then why didn't you go to the police. According to my client, you gave him the money to treat himself with."

"That's just not true. I didn't give him that money freely. I didn't go to the police because it was pretty effective blackmail. I didn't want him to go public with the information that he had about me. I thought that it would have ruined me," I pleaded.

"And we're supposed to believe that? The jury is supposed to believe that the man that you grew up with and loved turned on you? This is the same man that made sure you were taken care of as a teenager and was your lover, correct?"

"Yes but—,"

"So I'm led to believe that you sold out the man that loved you because your meal ticket realized what was going on. You lied about the blackmail so that you wouldn't look bad," he said cutting me off.

"Objection!" the prosecution lawyer called out.

"Sustained," the judge replied, "Jurors disregard that last statement. Watch it counselor," the judge said to the defense lawyer.

"Yes your honor," he digressed. "Camille, is it true that you used to participate in robberies with Marcus?"

My heart beat out of my chest because I didn't think that it would come up. That was something that Marcus and I did together a long time before we ever go into drugs. Just like with the drugs, I hadn't stolen anything but I did help distract people, case their houses, and facilitate the process. I felt like complete shit on the stand, and I did my best to hide my shocked expression. I never told Kyle about that part of my life and all of it was playing out in front of his eyes. I wondered if he thought less of me because of my past. I couldn't perjure myself and so I had to tell the truth.

"I didn't steal—,"

"It's a yes or no question Camille," he interjected sternly.

I took a deep breath, "Yes."

I fought back the tears that were threatening to pour out of my eyes. I felt like I'd completely ruined the case because I wasn't prepared. I never told the prosecution about my participation in stealing. I knew that they were going to be pissed about that. If Marcus got released because of me I would never forgive myself. The familiar mouthwatering began again, and it was only a matter of time before I had to make my way to the rest room again.

The lawyer wore a cocky expression throughout the rest of my questioning, and I tried not to rush my answers. I answered clear and concisely to each one in the same manner that I did with the prosecution. His case was that since Marcus and I had conspired to rob people before this showed that we were conspiring to rob Kyle also as some sort of "long con". It is amazing how these lawyers can twist things like this.

I'd mentally checked out. Once I was freed from the stand I went straight to the restroom. My dry heaves were painful because there wasn't anything in my stomach to release. I didn't want to return to the courtroom. I was way too stressed but I was finally off the stand and my portion in the entire mess was done. I didn't want to see Kyle because I was ashamed. But once again he was outside of the bathroom when I emerged.

"Are you okay?"

"I'm fine," I said.

"Maybe you should go home for the rest of the trial. This is just too hard for you and your part is finished."

I thought that I would have welcomed the opportunity to go home, but my resolved strengthened. Kyle still had to take the stand, and I wanted to be there to support him in the same way that he supported me. I couldn't let him down.

"No, the worst part is over and I'm going to see this through to the end. I don't want to have to wait for a phone call or the media to figure out what happened."

"That's my girl," he said before he kissed my forehead and escorted me back into the courtroom.

Shortly after we returned Kyle took the stand, and he was cool, calm, and collected. He was everything that I wasn't on the stand and my faith in the case was restored. He had an eloquent and honest answer for every question. When he discussed our relationship my heart swelled with pride and love, and I knew that the jurors couldn't deny that we genuinely loved one another. What we had wasn't superficial, and I didn't appreciate the defense trying to pervert it.

*

The trial was one of the most mentally exhausting times of my life but it was now close to over. Waiting for the jurors to return for the sentencing was long. It took them over 2 hours to reach a verdict. I know that in the grand scheme of things it wasn't a long time, but it felt like forever. I kept going over all of the mistakes that I made on the stand and cringed. Kyle kept stroking my hand and kissing my temple. He didn't kiss me on the lips, and I understood why. I mean I had thrown up twice that day and breath mints and gum could only cure so much. I couldn't wait to get out of there so that I could brush my teeth.

When it was announced that the jury had reached a decision, I could feel my heart pounding in my throat, and my entire body began to shake. I sure could have used another one of those spankings. Maybe he should have taken me to the limo to give me one while we were waiting. I giggled at the absurdity of it all. Kyle gave me a puzzled look, and I clamped my mouth shut.

When the verdict was being read, I was having one of those experiences from the movies. Everything was background noise, and I could only read lips. There was only one word that I wanted to hear, and I was granted my wish.

As they read the charges, the juror said, "Guilty."

Kyle gave my hand a huge squeeze, and I went numb. I watched as Marcus was taken into custody again. I listened to the sobs throughout the courtroom, and I couldn't muster up a reaction. Marcus was placed back into handcuffs and escorted out of the room. It was most likely the last time that I would ever see him again. I was sure that he was going to look back at me and give me a sinister glare, but he never looked in my direction.

#Chapter8

There is only so much that you can do for a person in a difficult situation.

You can support them to the best of your ability, but you can't shield them from it all. Not being able to take away Camille's stress and pain was one of the toughest feelings that I've ever experienced.

Shortly after we took our seat I saw that she had a pained look on her face. She didn't look well at all. I asked her how she was doing.

"Are you okay?" I asked.

She gave a small nod of her head, but I never took my eyes off of her. She was far from okay, and she confirmed my thoughts when she rushed out of the courtroom. Our security detail quickly rushed after her, and I followed behind them. She went to the bathroom to throw up. That was when I knew just how badly all of it was affecting her. Taking her home away from it all was a huge option in my mind but if she didn't suggest it then I wasn't going to say anything. We needed to see the case through to the end. But I was willing to sacrifice it all if that's what she needed from me.

She walked out of the bathroom with her game face on. I saw past the façade that she put up, but I allowed her to display her strength. We returned and took our seats. We were all there for Marcus, but most of the eyes were on her. She was getting horrible stares from those seated around us, but she seemed to be oblivious to it all. She was engrossed in what was being said by the attorneys. I couldn't help but return a few of those icy glares that were focused on her. She didn't deserve to be under so much scrutiny. She was a woman with a heart of gold that made a few mistakes. It wasn't her fault that we were there, it was Marcus's fault.

I couldn't deny that I felt a little guilty about all of it. It was because of me that she turned him in. We could have gone to the police over the blackmail and ended it there. But I didn't like the fact that he was trying to steal my money, and I wanted him ruined. I've mulled it over in my head quite a few times, and I've wondered if I did the right thing by putting Camille in that predicament. I'm still not entirely sure if that's what was best for her, but we were on that path now, and it was now an issue between Marcus and the state.

Camille did great in the beginning when she took the stand. She answered the questions that the prosecutor asked perfectly. She looked poised and confident. The jury seemed to like her, and that was a good thing. They nodded sympathetically as she talked about her past and the things that she'd done. She was winning them over, and that was easy to see. Once the defense questioned her, it boggled her a bit. She got upset at a few of the questions, but that didn't really hurt her. It really just made her look human and in this case that was fine.

She looked downright embarrassed when she admitted that she helped steal. I didn't care about her past, and I'd told her that a million times over. I respected her even more for turning her life around. Most people would have gotten sucked into that lifestyle, but she clawed her way out. I didn't know many people that had gone to the dark side and then quit cold turkey, but she managed to do it and to make it look easy. This is what the defense was trying to harp on. It seemed a little too good to be true to believe that she was 'good,'". But I knew from personal experience that Camille wasn't the average woman, she was everything good, and more.

After she left the stand she went straight to the bathroom, and I met her there when she came out. That was when I decided to give her the option of going home. The body isn't built to take that kind of stress, and she'd dealt with more than her share for the day. She refused to go home, and I respected her decision. We returned to the courtroom, and I took the stand. Everything went very smoothly with the prosecution and I was ready for the defense. That little prick couldn't intimidate me. I'd dealt with worse than him in my lifetime. Hell, I'd grown up with my dad and so a mean look, and a shitty attitude wasn't enough to make me cower. I could buy and sell his simple ass a million times over.

Him and I went back a forth a few times and then he asked the question that I was waiting for.

"How do you know that she isn't just using you, especially considering her sordid past?"

I gave a slight chuckle, "I'm a very intelligent man that has not only a high IQ, but high emotional intelligence as well. I've met more than my share of users and manipulators. I can spot them a mile away, and I assure you that Camille is 100% genuine. It's impossible not to fall in love with her, and I'm extremely lucky that we crossed paths."

I stared at Camille as I was saying how I felt. I wanted my words to sink into her soul. She could do no wrong in my book, and I needed her to know that I wasn't ever going to forsake her. I wanted her to be in my life forever, and I was in it for the long haul. So many people in her life deserted and betrayed her, and she deserved to have someone that loved her unconditionally. I planned on being that person in her life.

When we heard the guilty verdict I was overjoyed because it all had been a long time coming, and we had the payoff that we were looking for. I kept my delight discreet because I was surrounded by sadness, and I didn't want to disrespect the feelings of those in the courtroom. Marcus was a piece of shit, but there were people there that loved him, and it would have been rude to express joy in that moment. Camille looked stunned, and I didn't know what she feeling, maybe she was nauseous again.

**

Kyle and I went to one of my favorite restaurants to celebrate the end of such a stressful time.

I was able to go home for a minute and freshen up. I couldn't get to my toothbrush fast enough. I was happy to have a glass of wine in my hand. I was ecstatic to have filet mignon and lobster on my plate. I thought that I would have focused on the wine a lot more, but my glass remained untouched as I tore into the contents of my plate. I was practically starving, and my stomach thanked me.

"You made it," Kyle said happily.

"I did!" I laughed, "Although I was beginning to doubt that I would for a minute there."

"That thought never crossed my mind. You're one of the strongest people that I know."

I blushed as I ate a piece of broccoli. I was still adjusting to all of the praise that he doted on me continually. I had a hard time believing what he was saying, but I was working on it. Kyle wasn't the kind of man that lied to get what he wanted. He was a straight shooter and so if he said something then he meant it. The key was to allow myself to believe it.

"I spoke to Bill when you were in the bathroom freshening up at home," he said.

"Oh yeah?"

"Yeah, he said that the prosecutors are pretty certain that Marcus is going to get the maximum sentence. The judge is a hard ass, and his track record shows that he isn't going to take it easy on Marcus by any means."

"What's the maximum sentence?" I asked as I put my fork down on my plate.

"4 years," Kyle said slowly and emphasized each word.

That familiar gurgling in my stomach took place again. I didn't realize that he would get so long for blackmail. He was also up for a murder charge and so things weren't looking good for him at all. I didn't want to think about him behind bars and about the life that he was going to experience. I'd watched way too many episodes of OZ, and I was scarred by them. Marcus was tough, but he wasn't as tough as a lot of the men there. His life was over, and it was partially my fault. He was about to be someone's bitch, and I had something to do with it. I pushed away from the table and ran to the bathroom again so that I could relieve myself of my steak and lobster. 'I should have known better than to eat seafood,' I thought to myself. My stomach had been shaky all day, and so it wasn't a good idea at all.

When I returned to the table Kyle started to talk about our life together, "After we get married, I want to go traveling. We need to see the world, and we can open up restaurants all over."

"That sounds amazing," I said. I couldn't wait to get married and go traveling He was also talking about working vacations and that was something that I could get with. I wanted to continue our business and enjoy our lives, and that seemed like the best of both worlds.

"Since we won't have to worry about kids for a long while, we'll have a lot of time," he said as he pulled out his phone looked at his calendar. "How about exactly one month from today?"

"Whoa, you're not wasting any time are you?"

"We've waited long enough and one month seems like forever. I want to steal you away and do it now, but I know that you want a real wedding."

He was right, I did want a wedding. If we didn't have one, I would regret it for a long time. I only wanted to get married once and so it had to be right because it was a moment that I would never get to experience again.

"I do want a wedding."

"Okay, the date is set, and *nothing* is going to stop us this time," he said matter of factly.

I was excited for the first time in days. I was more than ready to be Mrs. Kane. He was everything that I wanted in a mate and so much more. Once again I felt like I was in a fairy tale, and we'd finally gotten to the good part. We went through all of the adversity and emerged relatively unscathed. Things would be tense for a while, but I wasn't going to let anything steal my joy. I had my man, a career, and my wonderful friends. They were all that I needed to get by. I was rich in so many other ways than money. Once I put things into real perspective, I perked up and pushed all thoughts of Marcus to the back of my mind. He made his choices, and I made my own. I just happened to make a lot better choices, and I deserved every ounce of happiness that was coming my way.

***

A few days later I went to hang out with Sandy. She couldn't wait to catch up on all of the good news. I had been noticeably absent from my friends since the trial, but it was because I still wasn't feeling well. My nerves were still on edge, and it was effecting my day. I cared way more about Marcus going to jail than I originally thought because it was taking a toll on me physically.

"You know how much I hate it when you disappear," Sandy said.

"I know, but I've felt like crap for the last few days," I admitted.

"Believe me, I noticed. Your trips to the bathroom were hard to ignore in the courtroom."

"It seems to be getting worse. It's been this way all day too."

"If I didn't know any better I would think that you're pregnant," Sandy said with a raised eyebrow.

I rolled my eyes at her and was about to combat what she was saying. I then thought about my lack of a period. I contributed that to my stress as well because I'm known for skipping it when I'm being a high strung mess.

"I don't know about that. I'm on the pill," I said.

"Girl please, we know how the pill can be. They're not 100% especially if you aren't taking it at the same time every day."

"I guess I'll grab a test on my way home. I really hope that's not the case for me," I said in a low voice."

"You don't have to worry about that," Sandy said as she jumped up from her couch and headed towards her bathroom, "I have one here already."

"Who just has a pregnancy test lying around?" I asked.

"Don't judge me Camille," Sandy yelled from the bathroom, "You should be thanking me."

I slowly rose from the couch and met her in the bathroom. She pulled it from her medicine cabinet and placed it in my hand, "They work pretty fast and so we'll know in a few minutes."

"I'm getting sick just thinking about it," I said.

Sandy walked to the door and peeked her head in before closing it, "Get it done so that you can know for sure and not obsess over it."

I sat on the toilet for a few seconds and thought about it first. I was afraid to take the test because I knew that there could be a real possibility of me being pregnant. I wasn't ready for such a huge step yet.

Sandy knocked on the door, "I don't hear any peeing in there!"

"Get away from the door girl. I'm about to do it now creep." I said.

A few moments later the digital stick was sitting on the edge of her sink and I was pacing. I didn't want to wait alone so I stepped outside of the bathroom.

"Don't worry," Sandy said, "Either way you'll be okay."

I shook my head, "I'm on the pill for a reason. I'm not ready for this to be a possibility in my life."

"You're probably not even pregnant. That's why it's important that we find out for sure. We both know how you can over think some shit," she said.

"I wasn't even thinking about this until you brought it up. I'm stressed enough as it is without you fucking with my head," I countered.

"No need to snap at me for stating the obvious. You are having sex regularly, and pregnancy happens. You are having sex regularly right?" She said.

I giggled, "Hush up. You know that we get it in all the time. He can't lay next to all of this every night and not want a piece."

"Just freaky," she laughed.

"Alright I think it's time to go look," I said.

Our eyes locked and her look mirrored my own. It was one of uncertainty. I walked into the bathroom and looked at what it said. I stood there staring because I was unsure of what to say. So many mixed feelings were running through my body.

#Chapter9

"I see him a little differently now."
Camille

"What does it say?" Sandy asked.

I handed it over to her, and she squealed, "I'm going to be an Auntie!!!!!"

Hearing her say those words out of her mouth jarred me and my reality came crashing down.

"Yeah that's what the test says," I said.

"I always thought that you would be the first one to have kids out of the three of us. Oh my god, wait until Cynthia finds out. She's going to freak out, and she'll probably start buying baby stuff 5 minutes after she finds out."

"Cynthia will find any excuse to shop and we both know that," I responded flatly as I walked back to the couch and sat down.

"You're pregnant now baby girl. You have every reason to be happy. It's something that you can't take back, and you're about to get married in less than a month. It's not the end of the world, but the beginning to a new one," she assured me.

"I know but Kyle would have wanted to plan this and discuss it beforehand. He didn't want a kid for at least 8 more years," I admitted.

"8 years! He's crazy as hell. You don't want to start popping out babies in 8 years, that's some white people shit," she said.

"You're so ignorant but I thought the same thing when he told me that. I've never wanted to be an old parent," I admitted.

"Now you won't be. I think that once you tell him, he will get with the program. He loves you, and he really doesn't have a choice at this point."

The more Sandy spoke the more excited I became. I didn't want to admit to myself that I was overjoyed about having Kyle's baby. I was nervous about telling him the news, and it wasn't something that I'd done on purpose. I hoped that he would be happy once I told him because it would crush me if he wasn't. He'd been very clear about what he wanted, and this was going to throw a huge wrench in our future plans. Timing was everything in this situation, and so I was going to have to wait to break the news to him.

"You're right but I'm going to need you to keep quiet about this. I'll tell Cynthia the next time I speak to her, but only the two of you can know until I break the news to Kyle."

Sandy mimed as if she was zipping her lips closed, "Not a peep from me."

"Thank you."

**

I really hated the fact that Kyle set up an appointment for me to go wedding dress shopping with his little sister. But it seemed to be pretty important to him and so I caved in. I would have preferred to go with my friends, but his family wanted to be involved in the process, and he thought that it would be a great opportunity for us to bond. I was just grateful that only one of them was coming because I wasn't sure if I could take them both at the same time. Twins could be overwhelming, and they were both really opinionated.

It turned out not to be as bad as I thought that it would. She took me to some great wedding dress boutiques that I never knew existed, and we got the VIP treatment. A glass of champagne was in our hand from the time that we entered each place. I couldn't drink any of it because I was pregnant. So I had to constantly make excuses as to why I couldn't partake. I chose to go with the 'I want to have a clear head while I make my choice,' route.

I'd tried on over 15 dresses, and I was starting to get pretty tired. I also kept envisioning myself with a baby bump in the dresses. I knew that I was tripping because my wedding was a little over 2 weeks away, and I wouldn't experience that kind of rapid growth in such a short period of time. Then I tried on a simple mermaid dress with beautiful beading underneath the bust. It fit to perfection, felt wonderful against my skin and accentuated all of my curves. It fit me perfectly which was a surprise because I was about 2 sizes larger than the tradition sample sizes. When I looked in the mirrors I knew that it was my dress.

"This is the one isn't it?" I asked in excitement.

"Yeah, I think it is."

"You're glowing in this dress! Pose for the camera," she said as she took a picture of me with her phone. "I've gotta send this to my sister."

"Have you thought about accessories?" The beautiful blonde attendant asked.

"No, I'm really starting from ground zero."

"So do I have permission to jack you up?" She asked.

"Absolutely and don't hold back," I grinned.

The attendant clapped excitedly and quickly sauntered off to find the overpriced accessories in the store. As she went off the rest of the attendants oohed and ahhed over me and told me how beautiful I looked. I welcomed the adoration because I could use all of the positive energy that was coming my way. Shortly after, I had on a veil, a bracelet, a beautiful necklace, and earrings.

"This is beautiful," I said, "You don't think that it's too much?"

"Absolutely not!" The attendant exclaimed.

"You're supposed to be too much, it's your wedding day," Ashton chimed in.

Tears started to fall down my face as I continued to look in the mirror. My wedding was right about the corner, and I was about to really be Mrs. Kane. It had been such a long journey that felt endless, and now it was coming to a close. Marriage wasn't going to be a cakewalk, but a lot of our drama would come to a close. I was going to stick with him forever, and I believed that he was going to do the same for me. We were about to be an official team, and nothing was going to tear us apart.

"I can't believe that this is really happening. Kyle is about to really go through with it," she said.

I scrunched my face, "What do you mean?"

She looked as if she said something she shouldn't have, "I just mean that I couldn't believe that this is happening."

"No that's not what you meant at all. Tell me please."

"No it is nothing Camille. The champagne just got to me a bit."

"I don't think it did. Is there something I should know?" I knew something was up, she was not a very good liar.

"If I tell you then you have to promise not to tell Kyle that I said anything," she said.

I thought about it for a moment. Some things were better left unsaid and some things you just don't need to know about your partner. However, all of my past had been exposed to Kyle, and he still was with me anyway. He also claimed that it made him love me more. He felt closer to me because he knew what I'd been through. I was too curious to let this moment slip through my fingers, and I hoped that I wouldn't regret digging into his past.

"I promise that I won't say anything."

"We'll take it all," Ashton said to the attendants. "I'll help you out of all of this while I fill you in."

We walked back to the huge dressing room, and she started by taking my veil off, "Kyle has been engaged once before a while ago."

"How long ago," I asked quickly.

"He was 21 then," she said.

"So what happened?" I asked.

"Well during the engagement she got pregnant and it all went downhill from there. They couldn't stop arguing. Kyle was pretty adamant about the fact that he didn't want children, and he felt like she was trying to trap him," she said.

"That's one of the craziest things that I've ever heard. He was about to marry her so why would she feel the need to trap him?" My head was spinning because he'd never shared that information with me before, "So where is the child?"

"He arranged for her to have an abortion and after she had it they broke up," she said.

"He forced her to get rid of it?" I asked in disbelief.

"Not technically but he made it pretty clear that he wasn't happy about it and that he preferred for her not to have. I really think that he's afraid of having children."

"Wow," was all that I could muster.

"I'm sorry. I shouldn't have told you that. Besides it was a long time ago, and I'm sure that he's grown and matured since then. Besides it's not like you're preggers. There's no way that you would look so fabulous in this dress if you had a baby bump," she laughed.

My word. I was really not expecting to hear this.

***

"You need to let it go," Sandy scolded.

"But I can't. It's really bothering me," I responded.

"I'm sorry, but that was a long time ago, and you shouldn't have promised her to keep it from him. Now it's bothering you and you can't even say anything. Is this how you want to start off your marriage?" Sandy asked.

I looked at Cynthia for support, but she looked away and took a sip of her water.

"So you're not going to back me up?"

"I'm sorry but she has a point. He was 21 then, and 21 year olds make messed up decisions. That was over ten years ago for him and so I really don't understand why you're holding it against him," Cynthia said.

I regretted telling him about the conversation that I had with Ashton. It had been over a week since I'd picked my dress and the information was eating me alive inside. I needed to confide in my friends, but they weren't telling me what I wanted to hear.

"I see him a little differently now. What if he treats me the way that he treated her?" I asked.

"He's not going to do that. He's been through the ringer with you, and he's not going to let you go over a baby. He'll probably even be happy and see it as a second chance to get it right," Sandy said.

"Just tell him about the baby and see what happens. He loves you and I don't think you'll be disappointed,"

I rested my head against the table and thought about it. My biggest fear was that he would ask me to get an abortion. I knew that was something that I just wasn't willing to do, even if that meant that I had to lose him. I wanted my baby even if it was unplanned. My wedding was around the corner, and my fiancé didn't even know that he had a baby on the way. It was time for me to spill the beans, or I would regret it.

#Chapter10

"Some things school just can't teach,"
Kyle

My plan to tell Kyle was an absolute bust.

I kept trying to find the perfect moment but the time never seemed right. I would try at night but once his hands were all over me, I didn't want to ruin the morning. I couldn't tell him in the morning because I didn't want to ruin his day either. We were in a state of perfect bliss, and I wasn't ready for it all to be over even if it was a lie.

So there I was, on the private jet and on my way to get married in Fiji, and I was still holding a secret. It was hard trying to cover up why I wasn't drinking. Kyle was getting suspicious, but he chalked it up to me not wanting to be like my mother and I let him go with that idea because it was partially true.

"Are you okay babe?" Kyle asked.

"I'm fine," I said as I sipped my ginger ale.

"You're not thinking about backing out on me are you?" He asked in amusement.

"I wouldn't ever do that! You belong to me," I grinned.

"Now that's what I like to hear," he said before his attention returned back to his laptop.

It felt like we were always working, and I wasn't mad at that because it was what I preferred. But now that I was pregnant, my thoughts and priorities were changing. I wanted to be an active parent in my baby's life, and I refused to have a nanny raise my kid. I didn't mind some help, but I wanted me and Kyle to be the main people in it's life. Those were the kinds of things that we hadn't discussed at length. But then again, maybe we hadn't because Kyle thought that he had at least 8 years before that kind of conversation had to be taken seriously.

We arrived at our resort, and I was still taken aback by the beauty of the places that Kyle took me to. I probably should have been used to exotic locations, but I didn't think that I would ever get over it. Living in a metropolitan city will make you forget that there is life outside of modern furniture and steel buildings.

"When is everyone else arriving?" I asked Kyle as I lay in the bed.

"They're arriving later on tonight but we won't see them until the morning." His face nuzzled my neck. We weren't going to be leaving our room for a few hours because we had other things to do and a huge nap to take. Our morning was going to be beyond hectic because we were getting married pretty early in the morning, and the jet lag was already beginning to settle in with me. I was usually a bit more resilient, but I think that the baby may have been making me more tired, then again it could have just been in my head.

"Are you nervous?" I asked.

"No, I'm not nervous. I'm anxious because tomorrow can't come fast enough. I've never been so sure of a decision in my entire life," he said honestly.

I could see the truth in his eyes. He really meant every word that he said to me, and I was worried that I wouldn't see that glint in his eyes after I told him the truth about what was about to occur. I didn't think that I could handle him thinking that I was trying to trap him.

"Are you okay?" He asked.

"Yes, I'm fine. I'm a little nervous about tomorrow but in a good way. I can't believe that the time is finally here."

"Before tomorrow I wanted to run an idea by you," he said.

"Okay, what's up?" I said as I rolled over onto my side to face him.

"The businesses in Chicago are really taking off and we've been really hands on. I think we're ready to focus on other things. Your friends have been phenomenal while managing the businesses. I think that they need a raise and promotion," he said.

"Oh wow, do you really think that they're ready for something like that?" I asked.

"I really think that they are. They're great managers, and I think that taking on the club will be a bit difficult for them at first but they can manage the three of them together. Of course it will be a process because we'll need a new management team beneath them," he said.

"This has been our baby for so long. I don't know if I can just relinquish power like that," I admitted.

"Well the business isn't a baby anymore. We now have to focus on doing it again. It's time for some serious growth and now is the time."

"You're right. It's time for us to take our hands off of the wheel. They'll be overjoyed at the news because this is going to really change their lives forever. I don't even know how to begin to thank you for everything that you've done for my friends," I said.

"We just gave them a chance. They did the rest. When people find out that they don't have a degree, they're flabbergasted because those women are savvy. They remind me so much of you with their keen eye for detail and business. Some things school just can't teach," he said.

"Actually they're going back to school," I said.

"They didn't tell me that," he said.

"They didn't want you to think that they couldn't handle the workload. Both of them are taking classes at Northwestern part time."

"I had no clue. If I'd known then I would have paid for it."

"It's okay. They seem to be able to handle it, and I think it's making them happy to be able to afford it on their own."

"I'm proud of them. I feel like they're my family now," he said.

"That makes sense because they're pretty much like my sisters. I'm just happy that you've taken to them so well. Because they love you," I playfully rolled my eyes.

"Oooh, is someone a little jealous?" He lightly tickled me.

"It's not jealousy. It's just that I don't have anyone to complain to anymore. If I say anything bad about you, they put on their capes and come to your defense."

He laughed, "I knew I was doing something right by wanting to give them raises and just what do you complain about?"

"Well you have this annoying habit of leaving the toilet seat up, you're one of the messiest eaters that I know, you're a know it all, and that's just the bottom of my list," I grinned.

He playfully grabbed his chest, "You're hurting my heart."

"No I'm not. You know that I love you."

He smiled mischievously, "I'm not sure about that. Maybe you'll have to have to show me just how much you love me."

That was something that I was more than willing to do. I put aside my thoughts about the baby and made love to the man that I was going to marry in the morning.

#Chapter11

I'd completely ruined my wedding day.

That morning was supposed to be the happiest moment in my life. Yet I felt sick to my stomach, and I refused to answer the door for any of my friends. I knew that I had to tell Kyle the truth before we got married. If I waited until afterward I would never forgive myself. He deserved to know what he was getting into before he made such a huge decision.

"At least let the makeup artist and the hair stylist in," Sandy yelled through the door.

I sat at the table in my room and cried when I looked into the mirror. I looked an absolute mess, and unless that makeup artist was a miracle worker, she wasn't going to be able to hide my puffy eyes. How in the world was the team going to make me look good if I wouldn't even let them in. I was struck with fear because there was a possibility that there wouldn't be a wedding once he found out the news.

"Let me in Camille, or I'm going to Kyle's suite and you'll have to answer to him," Cynthia warned loudly.

I ran to my door and cracked it, "You better not do that and keep it down. I just need a few more minutes."

Sandy put her hand on the door and pushed it open forcefully, "We don't have time for this foolishness."

"One moment please," Cynthia said to the glam squad before she and Sandy stepped inside of my room and closed the door.

"Don't start with me," I warned.

"Somebody has too," Cynthia scolded, "You have a man who plans on marrying you today, and you're in here sulking like a child!"

I looked at Cynthia in disbelief because she was never harsh with me. She was always the one that coddled me and told me that things were going to be okay.

"I don't want to hear it. I'm emotional, I'm pregnant, and I'm scared."

"There's no reason for you to be scared and shame on you for not telling him that he has a child on the way. Don't you think that he deserves to know? Now you're here crying on the morning of your wedding because you haven't handled your fucking business. Get it together," she reiterated.

"Well," Sandy said, "I guess she said it all. I don't really have anything to add." She walked over to the fridge and grabbed a bottle of champagne.

"Really, you're about to start drinking?" I snapped.

"Oh no ma'am. Do not start snapping at me because you are upset. Go do what you need to do and then get your ass back in here so that we can get started on time," Sandy said before she popped the bottle open and poured herself a glass.

"Whatever," I retorted.

"Goodbye Camille and we don't want to see your face until you'll let that man know the truth," Cynthia said as she walked over to get herself a glass of champagne.

I was more jealous about their ability to drink. I could have used a drink in that moment but for the very same reason I couldn't have one. I opened my mouth to say something else.

Cynthia put her hand up, "We don't want to hear your voice either. Just go and get it done."

I knew in that moment that we could trust Cynthia to run our businesses. I didn't know where her no non-sense attitude came from, but it was very effective. I shut my mouth and put on my slippers and headed out the door.

"Well damn you sure told her," I heard Sandy say. I would have said a smart remark back, but I was afraid of what Cynthia would do.

"You all can go in and get started on the girls," I mumbled to the glam squad that was patiently waiting outside the door.

I tried to find the words that I was going to use when I told him the truth, but all of the good ideas escaped me. All I could see in my head was him blowing a gasket and telling me that he wasn't ready for children. I got to his suite door and knocked lightly. My hands were shaky, and I was sure that I was going to throw up again soon.

He opened it without asking who it was, "Oh no!" He exclaimed before shutting his eyes tightly, "I'm not supposed to see you until you're coming down the aisle"

"I need to see you now." I pushed the door open and began to pace around his living area.

"Camille? Is something wrong?" He asked. "Have you been crying? What's going on?"

"I have something that I need to tell but I'm afraid at how you're going to react. I should have told you a while ago but I kept it to myself," I admitted quickly.

He rushed to me and placed my face between his hands, "Hey, we've been through everything together. Just spit it out so that we can work through it. I can deal with pretty much anything except if you used to be a man."

I gave a slight giggle, "I just don't know how I'll handle it if you don't want to be with me anymore."

"Give me a chance to show you," he pleaded.

I blinked back my tears, and I inwardly prayed for the best, "I'm pregnant."

He gave a slight frown, and my stomach dropped. He then backed away from me, and I stood frozen in place. I wasn't prepared for my nightmares to become a reality.

"Why didn't you tell me?" He chuckled and then his face completely lit up. He walked back over to me and put his hand on my stomach. "How far along are we?"

"I'm guessing that I'm only a few months along," I responded.

"That would explain how sick you've been," he said with clarity in his eyes. "How long have you been keeping this from me?"

"I found out about a month ago," revealed.

"What am I going to do with you?" He sighed, "Why didn't you tell me as soon as you found out?"

"I was afraid. I was scared that you were going to leave me."

"Why would I do something as ridiculous as that?" He asked.

"I talked to you sister and she told me about what happened in your past."

"I'm going to kill her when I see her, but I'll wait until the reception. That was a long time ago, and I wasn't ready for a child that young."

"But you were pretty clear regarding how you felt," I said.

"Right but that was before I knew that you were pregnant! I'm excited that we're having a baby. Some adjustments will have to be made, but I'm more than willing to do that. The main reason that I wanted her to have an abortion is because she cheated on me. I wasn't going to father her child after that abortion, and I wasn't even sure if the baby was mine. I'm not saying that my decision was the right one to make, but it's done and I've moved on," he said.

I gave a sigh of relief and tears of joy streamed down my face, "I thought that you were going to leave me." I leaned my head against his shoulder, and he embraced me.

"I don't want to ruin our moment Camille, but you have to go get ready," he said.

"I know," I responded and pulled away from him. Before I could get too far away he pulled me back and gave me a passionate kiss.

"That's the last kiss that you're getting from me until we're married. I'm not going to let you use me for those anymore."

I rolled my eyes, "You're so damned silly."

"And you love it."

"And I love you."

I was flooded with love and relief as I walked back to my room. I also felt downright ridiculous because I'd doubted him. He'd been doing everything within his power to prove to me that he could be trusted. I had to stop doubting the man that was about to make me his wife in a few short hours. He was everything to me, and I didn't want to ruin it with my own insecurities. I had to stop keeping my feelings and thoughts away from him because he was more than equipped to handle it.

I opened the door to my suite, and Sandy and Camille were getting their hair and makeup done. Little did I know what was waiting for me on the other side of that door.

#Chapter12

"It's great to know what's happening in that big ass head of yours,"
Camille

There were two stylists that were sitting on the couch and waiting for me. Next to them was my mother.

My word.

My entire body tensed, and I closed the door behind me. 'What the hell is she doing here?' I thought to myself. I was happy to see her on my wedding day, but I hoped that she wasn't going to start any drama. I didn't invite her for that very reason.

I looked at both of my friends, but they strategically looked everywhere else but me.
"Ummm hi," I said as she rose to her feet to meet me in the middle of the room.

"Hey Cam, can we go and talk privately?" She asked.

I gave her a once over and I noticed that she looked pretty healthy. She was looking a lot better than the last time that I saw her. She'd gained about 10 pounds, her hair was beautiful, and her skin was returning to its beautiful shade. I was a little impressed, but I wasn't going to tell her that just yet. I motioned for her to follow me, and we went back to my room.
She closed the door behind us, and I looked at her expectantly.

"First let me just say that I'm here to support you. I'm not here to cause you anymore hurt or pain," she said.

"That's good to know. Have a seat." I pointed her towards the chase lounge, and I sat across from her on the bed.

Her hands clasped one another as if they were holding on for dear life. She sat on the edge of her seat and stared at me intently. She was waiting on a reaction from me, but I really didn't know what to say. I was at the point where I was finally coming to terms with the fact that I may never see my mother again. I thought that the next time that I saw her, she would be dead. The reality of it hurt like hell, but I couldn't live for her. She was in control of her own life, and I didn't want to sit around waiting on her to care about herself. She was dealing with a lot of demons, and I had to release her for my own sanity.

"So what do you want to talk about?" I asked impatiently. All I could think about was the fact that the make-up and hair stylist had a lot of work to do on me. "How did you even get out here?"

"Kyle contacted me and had me flown out here," she said.

She inhaled deeply, "Camille, I'm so sorry for everything that I did to you and for everything that I didn't do for you. I made a lot of bad decisions in my life, and I always blamed you for them. The truth is that you were the only reason that I've survived this long."

I was stunned because my mother has never given me an apology in my entire life. She's always justified her mistakes and projected her shortcomings on to me. She would blame me every time a man left her. When our lights or heat got cut off she would say it was my fault, and she blamed me for us living in the shelter as well. I'd internalized all of that which is why I felt obligated to take care of her. I felt guilty for being born and ruining her dreams of a better life. It was Marcus who taught me that she should have been taking care of me. But he also taught me to be loyal.

"I don't really know what to say mom," I admitted.

"No need to say anything Camille. I'm so proud of you. You're 100 times the woman that I ever was, and I really wish that things could have been different," she said.

I rolled my eyes and thought to myself, 'I bet you do wish that, especially now that I'm marrying Kyle.' I didn't want to be closed off to her, but it's hard to trust people's intentions when money is involved. She was one of the meanest and selfish people that I'd ever met, so the change of heart was a little suspicious.

"You grew to be successful in spite of me and not because of me," she continued, "I should have been a better mother to you, and I don't blame you if you never want to see me again after today. I don't want anything from you or your husband, I just wanted to be able to share this day with you. That is all Camille." she said.

I fought back my tears and said the only thing that I could think of, "You look really good."

She smiled, "Thank you. I went into rehab 4 months ago, and Kyle helped me get permission to come here."

"How did he know where you were?" I asked.

"He didn't tell you? He came and found me at my friend's house and offered me a chance to turn my life around. He was tough on me, but everything he said was true. He gave me the option right there and then to come with him, and I did. He flew me out to a rehab in California, and it's been a rough process but a much needed one. I won't ever be returning to Chicago, and I want a better life for myself. I just hope that you can be a part of it, I want the chance to really get to know you," she said.

"So when did Kyle tell you about the wedding?" I asked.

"He told me about 2 weeks ago and he invited me last week. There's nothing I would love more than to be able to give you away today. Will you allow me to do that?"

I almost slid off of my bed at her request. My chest heaved with a little bit of anxiety and I tried to cram some real self-reflection in about 20 seconds. I was impressed that Kyle had reached out to my mother and helped her clean herself up. It was something that she'd always refused when I suggested it. I didn't have to ask how she was doing in the program because she looked great, so it was obvious that she was doing well. I was experiencing a lot of emotions at one time. Kyle really is full of surprises, good ones at that.

She was telling me all of the things that I longed to hear from her since I was a child. She was my mother and I used to crave her approval. She'd finally seemed to come around, and I didn't want to miss the opportunity to love her while she was displaying sanity. Her change of heart may have originated from my huge lifestyle change but did that make it any less real? I had to give her a chance. She was pretty much the only biological family that I had left. Her parents had passed away when she was younger, and she was the only child. We had extended family, and they were at the wedding but I didn't know them very well. They all lived in Virginia, and me and my mother never went to our family reunions.

I was going to cry, and I fought back my tears because I'd cried enough and I didn't need to torture the make-up artist any further, "Yes, I would like that a lot."

"Can I hug you now?" She asked timidly.

I laughed, "I would like that too." I stood to my feet and closed the space between us. She rose to her feet, and we embraced. I couldn't remember the last time that I hugged my mother. So much was communicated between us in that one hug, and I had the feeling that my life had finally come full circle.

"Okay, let's get you back out there so that you can start getting ready. You also need some champagne in your hand."

"I can't," I said, "I'm expecting."

Her eyes grew big and the tears that she'd been holding on to spilled down her face, "I'm about to be a grandma?"

I nodded shyly, "Yes you are."

"When are you due? Not for another 6 months and so we have some time," I said.

"I will be more than happy to be there if you'll let me," she said.

"If you keep on the path that you're on, I won't have any problem with that."

Her face expressed gratitude, "I am, I promise."

In that moment I believed her. Some people had a problem with their parents breaking promises. Their parents will give them an endless stream of promises that they never intend to keep. My mother never promised me anything ever. She always told me what she wasn't going to do, and she made no apologies for it. The person that I was seeing before me was a stranger that I couldn't wait to get to know. Her past had been filled with hurt and pain. She was trying to work through it, and maybe she would finally let me in.

We walked back out into the common area, and Sandy and Cynthia's eyes bored into me. They didn't have to ask the questions verbally because I knew them already.

"You both were right about Kyle," I admitted, "He's excited about the baby and he's a little upset that it took me so long to tell him."

"Told ya," Cynthia said.

"When in the hell did you get to be so damned mouthy?" I asked her.

She took a few moments to think, "I think it happened when I became a manager. I had to learn how to speak up because they were trying to run all over me. I don't play around with my paper and anyone standing in between me and my money has to get dealt with. Now it's spilling over into other parts of my life. Sorry girl, I'll simmer down."

"No need for that, I actually like it. It's great to know what's happening in that big ass head of yours," I grinned.

Sandy laughed obnoxiously loud, "Her head is big."

"Shut up," Cynthia responded and rolled her eyes.

"I think the opposite is happening to me. I'm learning how to motivate people by using different forms of communication," Sandy said, "I had to tone my personality down a bit because I've made a few of those bar tenders cry."

I laughed, "Yeah I heard about that but you were right about what you said so I didn't say anything. But your team seems a lot happier now, and they're happy to be on your good side."

"I came in guns blazing so they're all afraid of me now. I put that fear in them early and now I don't have to worry about em'," she responded.

"I may as well tell the both of you now. Kyle wants you two to take over the complete management of all three of the Chicago properties. We'll be discussing salary within the next two weeks," I said offhandedly.

"What!" They both shrieked simultaneously.

"You heard me. So congratulations on your promotions, they're well deserved."

I looked at both of the stylists, "I'm so sorry for the hold up and the drama this morning. I'm ready to get started."

"It's your world," the hairstylist said brightly.

"Don't worry. We have enough time to get the job done," the other attendant stated.

"Wait, so everything is okay with you and her?" Cynthia said as she gestured towards my mom.

"Yes we're good, and she's giving me away today," I smiled as I hugged my mom to my side.

"In that case, welcome back mom!" Sandy squealed as she clapped her hands together.

"Okay, now I'm ready to get married!"

"Well sit down then and let them work," Cynthia scolded.

I began to rethink my thoughts about her new bossy attitude.

*

I could only smile as I watched Camille leave my suite.

There were some things about her that I just couldn't get enough of. I was about to marry that over analyzing woman, and I'd never felt luckier. We were about to become a family and the baby was the icing on the cake. I thought that I wasn't going to be ready for children for at least another 8 years but once she told me that she was pregnant I was filled with anticipation.

I was inundated with thoughts of our future. In a couple of short months Camille would begin to swell, and I couldn't wait to place my hand on her stomach and feel our baby kick. I was going to be able to be a part of the process without wondering if the child was mine, or missing the few years of its life. Everything had come together perfectly, and I could only shake my head at the universe in awe. Soon I would see my child, it would take its first steps, and Camille would be its mother. I didn't know what I'd done to have gotten so lucky, but I wasn't going to question it.

All of my reservations went out of the window. I felt like I didn't deserve children because of my past. I'd gotten my previous fiancé to abort what could have possibly been my child, and I never forgave myself for that. She wasn't the person that I was meant to spend the rest of my life with but I wonder every now and then if that child was my own. My brash thinking and my hurt feelings made me lash out at her. That's partially why I was a little excited about the possibility of Jacob being my own son. When I found out that he wasn't I had a mix of relief and sadness.

I just hoped that I could be a better father to my child than my father had been to me. My father was the typical over achiever who spent more time working than he did with his family. I understand that businesses take a lot of work to maintain, but he was only interested in talking to me when we were talking about school and future plans. He never got the chance to get to know me outside of my accomplishments and work ethic. My dad was so set in his ways that I doubted he would ever change, and I'd come to accept that as being a part of him.

When my child was born it would know just how much I love him or her. I planned on not just being present financially. I had a chance to get it right, and I was going to make the most of it. It was a little surprising that Camille had kept the news from me for so long. But I didn't have the best track record when she delivered me bad news. She probably immediately thought about the time when I asked her to leave, and my sister telling that story certainly didn't help. I should have told her about that part of my past, but I didn't want her to look at me differently. I'd grown a lot since that time in my life, and I was over that kind of behavior. Everyone makes mistakes.

I thought that when Camille came to the door, she was coming to chew me out about her mother. But she hadn't mentioned it and so I knew that she hadn't seen her mother yet. I hoped that she would receive her mother well. I'd learned to appreciate my family a lot more by looking at Camille and her small family. The things that I hated and complained about seemed trivial when I put them all into perspective. At the end of the day I knew that my family loved me. Camille didn't have that luxury. Even though they weren't as present as I would have liked them to be I was always taken care of. I had no clue what it was like to come from absolutely nothing, and I don't think that I would have made it if I had to be my parent's caretaker.

Camille had taken the initiative and created her own family. That was a true testament to her resilience and her will to thrive. I'd learned so much from her since I met her, she made me a better person and I would love her forever. I never thought that I would have so much to learn from a person like her, but she proved me wrong time and time again.

That's why I knew that going to find her mother and giving her an ultimatum was the right thing to do. Although Camille would never speak about it anymore, it hurt her to her core to not have her mother present in her life. If her mother could get on the straight and narrow path she would be able to forgive her. I didn't know what to expect when I approached her mom, but I knew that it was something that I had to do. I was pleasantly surprised when her mother came with me. I sent my personal assistant with her to California, and he set her up in a rehab facility the exact same day. I didn't tell Camille because I didn't want to get her hopes up. There was a very real possibility of her mother dropping out of rehab, and that would have crushed Camille. I decided to give her mother a chance to get it right without the pressure. I maintained contact by calling her every week and checking on her progress. She had a few rough patches, and that was to be expected but she'd done very well considering the circumstances. Detoxing is a very difficult thing to get through from what I hear and so she was on the right track. She was determined to get her life together not just for herself but for her daughter as well. She knew that she wasn't a very good mother, and that contributed to her drug and alcohol use. Not to mention that she had a pretty fucked up childhood herself. Family is important, and she doesn't have much of it, so it delighted me to help bring hers back together. Her mom would possibly walk her down the aisle, we had a baby on the way, and my judgmental family was present. It was going to be a great day indeed. Some things may never change, but I had all that I needed to be happy. I counted my blessings every day, and I couldn't wait to see her walking down the aisle towards me.

I wanted our wedding day to be perfect, not just for me but for my bride to be. She had a rough morning, but she'd gotten through it with flying colors. Now we could enter into our marriage without old baggage hanging over our heads. We deserved each other, and we deserved to be happy. Our happy ending was long overdue, and I was going to do my best to make sure that Camille lived her happily ever after. I'm far from a prince, but I would be willing to give it a try for her and our new family to be.

The best part of my life was about to begin.

#TheFinalChapter

I couldn't have imagined a more emotional ceremony. I can be a crybaby, but my hormones really had their way. The beauty of getting married on the island, seeing my friends go out before me, having my mom walk me down the aisle, and Kyle at the end waiting for me was just too much to take. It all went by in a huge beautiful blur, and before I knew it, I was kissing Kyle. Being his wife felt different. I thought that it would feel the same. People always ask you if you feel a year older on your birthday, and the answer is no. But I felt completely different after I kissed Kyle. We were official, and we belonged to each other.

We'd been through hell and back. Something good finally happened to me, and there were times when I didn't think that I would make it. I definitely didn't think that I would be on speaking terms with my mother again. I was willing to put the past firmly behind us if she was willing to change. I knew that it was going to be a process, and there were times where she may be difficult, but I'd gotten a wonderful glimmer of hope that I was holding on to.

"There's no turning back now. You belong to me forever," he said in my ear.

I inwardly laughed because to anyone else he would have sounded completely insane, but it was endearing. I was perfectly happy belonging to him because he belonged to me too.

"Why would I ever want to turn back?" I asked.

"I'll make sure to never give you a reason too," he replied before he kissed me again.

The small crowed before us cheered, we looked out on our friends and family and smiled.

We walked down the beach with our group in tow and our dinner and drinks were served to us there. I swear that food tastes better with ward wind blowing on your face as you look out on the water. I was happy to be able to share the moment with those that I loved, but I couldn't help but focus on Kyle. We were in our own world as we slowly danced along the shore to the live music. However, I was really entertained by seeing Cynthia and Sandy's shenanigans.

They'd each found themselves a date from the resort and it looked as if they were going to be more than okay in my absence. On my way to the restroom I told two of our security detail to stay behind and keep an eye on them.

When I returned Kyle was standing outside of the bathroom, "Are you ready?"

"Ready for what?" I asked.

"To go on our honeymoon," he said.

"You mean we aren't staying here? I mean this is Fiji, and we just got here yesterday."

"Oh, so you're saying that you don't want to go with me?" He asked with a pout, "And here I was thinking that my wife loved me."

"Of course I'll go with you. I'm just surprised," I laughed, "I can't believe there's more to this dream."

"There is a load more." He grabbed my hand and walked me to the elevator of the hotel. I was confused.

"We're not going back out with our guests?"

"Our guests are where we're going. They made their way up as soon as you headed to the bathroom. Don't worry, just trust me."

"Okay, I trust you," I said before I rose on my toes to plant a kiss on his soft lips. I was sure that I was never going to get tired of that feeling. "Now I can have as many kisses as I want because I married you."

"It's a shame that I had to threaten to take them away just to get you to show up," he teased as he got onto the elevator.

I stared at our clasped together hands, and we both had on our wedding rings, "Is this even real? I think that I'm going to wake up at any moment."

"I know how you feel, but yes this is real. I've pinched myself a few times just to make sure."

We went to the very top of the building, and he walked me out to the roof. Everyone was out there and so was a helicopter. My hands flew to my face in surprise. We walked through the crowd and hugged everyone goodbye. I embraced my mom and fought back tears. I hugged Cynthia last, and she said, "Don't worry about us. I've handled all of the travel details. Have a great time."

"I love you," I said.

"I know," she grinned.

Kyle helped hoist me into the helicopter. We got strapped in and soon we were taking off as we waved goodbye to everyone. Once we were too far away to see them anymore I leaned against Kyle, and he kissed the top of my head. I lifted my chin to get the kiss that I loved so much; my husband's kiss.

"Where are we going?" I asked.

He winked, "Some place where we can start a new book."

I rested against him once again and took in the beautiful scenery. I was content with no worries and it was a luxury that I hadn't experienced in a long time. That was absolutely priceless.

It had been a long journey but I had finally got the happy ending I had longed for.

Everything had finally fallen into place.

One Year Later....

Mr & Mrs. Kane went from being semi-famous to being considered as Chicago royalty. The fallout from the trial, the success of Kyle's business, the coverage of their wedding, and the announcement of the pregnancy put them in a brand new light. The press loved how Camille showed the world that you can stand up to bullies like Marcus. Her resilience was admired, and she'd did a ton of interviews to share her story.

Camille used her influence positively and started a "Love is Love" campaign that encouraged couples from all walks of life to love one another and not be afraid of the interracial taboo. She gained the support of many Black woman across America who were inspired by her. Suddenly, a black woman dating a white man never got a second glance in most parts of the country and Camille was proud she had used her profile to help this happen.

Camille's relationship with her mother vastly improved and her mother was still sober ever since the wedding. The longest she has ever been in he adult life. She is now studying culinary arts with Kyle promising to fund her bakery once she completes the course.

The Kane franchises of restaurants did incredibly well. With Camille's help, Kyle doubled his inheritance within a year, and they branched out all over Europe and Asia. Kyle's father's business took a slight hit due to him no longer being the CEO. His father offered him a chance to come back, and Kyle said, "no way."

Kyle and Camille own multiple properties all over the world, but Chicago is still considered their home and after a year of jet setting they finally returned back on a full time basis. It's important to them that their child "Kyle Kane Jr." gets a huge taste of the windy city.

It was a long journey and it was not without it's challenges but in the end true love found a way. Some people are just meant to be.

The End

Note From Publisher:

Lena would like to thank everyone who has supported the "White Billionaire" Series which includes YOU. She has plans for a one-off full length novel entitled "*Mr & Mrs. Kane*" set a few years later and which will be a touch more on the erotic side ;-)

If you would like to see this happen then please give a positive rating to the _white billionaire complete series box set_ on the Amazon store. If we see enough interest we will get her to write it.

FREE BOOKS & NEW RELEASES

Heyy,

Really hope you enjoyed my story and you have not heard the last of Kyle and Camille that is for sure!

If you have enjoyed reading my book and you are interested in hearing news of forthcoming multicultural romance stories then please go to my website and submit your email so I can keep you all posted.

www.LenaSkye.com

Otherwise turn the page to view some of my other popular titles...

Peace, Love and High Heels

Lena xxx